A Specter of Truth

BEST WISHES!

Kathleen McKee

Kathleen McKee

Cover design by Robin Ludwig Design Inc.
www.gobookcoverdesign.com

ISBN-10: 1976417287
ISBN-13: 978-1976417283

“Emmor Kimber's arrival in the unnamed village in 1817 proved significant. The Quaker entrepreneur acquired three of the crossroads properties, including the 1787 stone house with its later (before 1812) lateral addition. He added to it the next year, in 1818, a three-bay, thirty-foot-wide northern extension, and opened the twenty-room building as the French Creek Boarding School for Girls..."

“Although a Quaker by faith, Kimber opened his school to children of all denominations, and orphans or students from distant parts were admitted at any time without previous application. The curriculum evolved over the years to include reading, writing, English grammar, history, geography, arithmetic, astronomy, botany, chemistry, and sewing. He also offered, for an extra five-dollar fee, courses in drawing, oil and watercolor painting, French, Greek, and Latin.”

“Unlike many schools of that era, Kimber's school had no petty rules of discipline or dress restrictions. Most schools at the time emphasized rote memory and strict discipline, often enforced with corporal punishment, but at Kimber's school, the Golden Rule governed behavior; hours were regular; methods were systematic, and within those limits personal freedom and curiosity were encouraged. Students were free to enjoy the gardens and groves surrounding the school, and botanical classes gathered rare plants near French Creek...”

Kimberton Village. (1997-2017). Retrieved from http://www.livingplaces.com/PA/Chester_County/East_Pikeland_Township/Kimberton_Village.html

Chapter One

Yellow Springs, Pennsylvania
June 1818

There was a chill in the early morning air when I tugged on my shoes, wrapped my shawl around my shoulders, and headed to the outhouse in my chemise. Pa and the older boys were already dressed and out, feeding the animals and milking the cows.

Ma, too, was ready to face the day. She had stirred up the embers in the kitchen hearth, and added a log before putting the coffee pot on the trivet over the open flame. As for me, there'd be time enough to help with the young'uns before everyone would be clamoring for breakfast.

"You'd best be wearing your Sunday frock today," Ma said as I carried in the pail of fresh water I pumped from the well. "I want you to go with Will when he takes the grain to the grist mill. He can drop you off at the general store. Can't do much baking without more sugar and molasses."

I nodded as I added water and rolled oats to the cast iron pot, then lifted it up to the crane over the fire.

"You need anything else?" I asked.

"Might be. I'll think on it."

Will's the oldest boy in our family. He turned 15 last month. His given name is William John Mitchell, same as Pa, though he resembles Ma's likeness more so. His straight hair is light brown, flecked with golden highlights, and his wide-set eyes are hazel. He's grown taller by a few inches just this past year, with peach fuzz sprouting above his upper lip. Won't be long, Pa says, before the girls take a liking to him.

I'm the firstborn, Elizabeth Jane Mitchell, but folks call me Lizzie. My grandmother would probably cringe in her grave if she knew I go by a variation of her fancy name. Nonetheless, she's the one who called my mother Jane, and that's somewhat plain. Her name, that is. Ma, herself, is rather pretty. She usually braids her long chestnut hair, which she pins up under her day cap. Her sparkling eyes are sultry, with dark lashes that enhance their beauty.

Ma's slender and petite, while I'm built somewhat sturdy and tall. My toffee colored hair is unruly and my ordinary blue eyes do nothing for my appearance. Pa says I shouldn't fret about my looks, probably because I resemble him. That's not such a terrible thing, as Pa is strong and fine-looking in his own way.

Ma gave birth to nine of us, though two boys died at an early age. I'm 16, a fact that Will's not happy about. He'd rather be the oldest child, but I don't see how that would matter much.

Will's lucky to have Benjamin, close in age at 13. They get along good, and they're similar in appearance, but completely different in their likes and dislikes. Seems to me that Ben takes after Pa, finding enjoyment in planting and harvesting crops.

There are two more boys in my family. They're too small to do much around the farm, except get into trouble. Matthew Joseph is 6 years old, and George Alan is 4. Matt's chore is to feed the chickens and rooster, then collect eggs from the hens every morning. George attempts to help though, more often than not, some calamity occurs.

Just the other day, George tripped over the feed bucket and fell into Matt, knocking the basket of eggs to the ground. All but three of them broke. Ma was upset enough about that, but angrier that Matt took retaliation by pushing George into the slop by the pig's trough. They both got punished; George for being clumsy, and Matt for being mean. Don't know yet if they learned their lesson.

Pa talks about his girls being at the top, middle, and bottom of the heap. In addition to me, Ella Sophie is 12, and baby Julia Anne will be 2 come August.

Ellie's very different from me, which is probably a good thing, at least from Ma's point of view. I'm more headstrong, liking to find my own way in life. Ellie prefers learning the skills that will one day make her a good wife. Already she can sew and cook, and she's now learning to spin wool.

Not sure yet whether Julie will follow in Ellie's footsteps, though I have a feeling she's going to have my "can do it myself" personality. She can be feisty when she wants to be.

We don't talk much anymore about Daniel or Ezra. I was only about 7 years old when Dan died of the measles. Will, Ben, and I got them, too, but not as bad as the baby. Ezra, on the other hand, was a puny little thing. Ma said he came too soon. Didn't have much of a chance at all.

Dan and Ezra are both buried out past the clothes line, under the big oak tree by Mammy and Pappy's grave. Sometimes when Ma's had enough of our shenanigans, I see her sitting out there on the grass, just resting in the shade. Maybe she talks to all of them. Leastwise, it seems like it to me.

While the oat porridge was cooking, I hurried upstairs to the room I share with Ellie and Julie. Ellie was already dressed, busy changing Julie's diaper.

The baby was doing everything she could to exasperate Ellie, twisting and turning every which way. It was only when I began to chant *Hickory, dickory, dock* that Julie settled down. Of course, by then, she was trying to move her fingers as if a mouse ran down the clock. Ellie and I both laughed at her attempt.

"This child's got a mind of her own," Ellie said, shaking her head. "I'll bring her downstairs, if you'll get Matt and George moving. The day's going to be half done by the time those slug-a-bugs get out of bed."

"Just call 'em. Ma's going to be waiting for her eggs."

"Done that about five times already. Don't seem to make much difference."

"Tough times call for action," I said as I picked up the chamber pot and stomped into the boys' room. "Which one of you hooligans wants to be the first to get pissed on?"

Don't know which of the two was faster, but I handed the pot to Matt as he barreled out of the room in his chemise. "Best you empty this in the yard before you visit the chickens. And don't you be giving me that look." George followed him down the steps, rubbing the sleep out of his eyes.

Now alone upstairs, I could get dressed in peace. After slipping on my stockings, I tied the garters just below my knees. On top of my chemise, I donned my stays and kerchief, and secured my pockets. Then came my two petticoats, my Sunday dress, and best apron. As I slipped into my shoes again, I thought it would be so much easier if women could wear pants.

It gave Pa such dismay when I told him my opinion that I've since kept quiet about it. If he was alarmed, just imagine how Ma and Ellie would react.

Chapter Two

It didn't take too long for me to move from room to room, straightening bed sheets and comforters. Pa was smart to design four bedrooms, two on each side of the second-floor center hall, when he hired out to build the big stone house. He instructed the craftsmen to add on from the one-room log cabin that was Mammy and Pappy's house. That now serves as our kitchen off the back.

I don't remember much about Mammy at all. Just what folks told me about her. She was Pa's mother, strong willed 'til the day she died, they say. Guess she'd have to be, raising five boys practically on her own while Pappy served as a patriot in the Continental Army.

Pa was her youngest. Wouldn't have thought he'd get the farm, but his brothers longed for adventure. Once they were old enough to take off on their own, they each headed west. Last I heard, they had scattered pretty much all over the country.

Pappy was a funny old coot, drinking his whiskey and cussing up a storm. At night, he slept in the loft of his cabin, even after the big house was finished. By day, he'd sit in his rocking chair by the fire or out on his porch. Watching the birds, he'd tell me, when he got that far off look in his eyes.

Then he'd start on his stories. How he thought Mammy was the prettiest girl in Chester County, and how she nursed him back to health after he got his leg near shot off.

He didn't talk much about the war at all, except about the British drummers. His belly still curdled every time he heard a drum beat, he told me.

I thought about Ma's family as I picked up the clothes laying on the floor in the younger boys' room. Scot's Irish she is, coming from Belfast to Philadelphia with her family as a young girl. Sad part of it is, they all got the pox on the ship. Ma was an orphan by the time they landed, her parents and two brothers buried at sea.

Ma was taken in by a kindhearted Quaker couple whose daughter also died in the same outbreak, and they sent Ma to be educated at a Quaker school in Philadelphia. She was just a little bit more than my age when she met Pa delivering goods to the farmers' market in the big city. Her adoptive parents didn't approve of Pa, given he's Presbyterian and didn't have much schooling. They disowned her when she ran off with him.

Taking Matt and George's work clothes with me, I trudged downstairs and stirred up the embers in the front parlor fireplace. Both younger boys have had breeching, but George still needs some help with the buttons of his trousers.

Guess by now they brought in Ma's eggs, and she'd want the boys dressed before breakfast. Sure enough, I had barely added a log to the fire before they both arrived, picking fault with each other all the way.

"You won't be having lessons today," I said, handing each of them their stockings, garters, and pants. "Ma wants me to go with Will when he delivers the grain to the mill. Guess you'll be weeding the garden."

"Probably you mean that I'll be weeding," Matt groused as he tucked his chemise inside his pants. "George will end up looking for frogs or worms, leaving all the work for me."

"Will not," George retorted as I fussed with his buttons. "'Sides, we'll be needing some worms if we go fishing after our chores."

"If you don't eat 'em all before we get to the pond."

"I don't eat no worms."

"You did once, a long time back."

"Probably you forced me, or told me they was good or something."

"Did not."

"Did, too."

"Enough, you two. Go on and get your porridge before it gets cold. No doubt, Pa's got old Nellie hitched to the wagon, and she's chomping at the bit for me and Will to get out there."

"You gonna buy me something at the market?" Matt asked, looking at me with great anticipation.

"You got any money?"

"Not a penny. But I got something I can barter."

"Like what?"

"Like one of them eggs I hid in the barn."

"Ma's going to give you a switching, if she finds out," I said as I prodded the boys towards the kitchen. "You'd better get out there and bring that egg to her right quick."

George found his place at the table, between Pa and the older boys. Matt continued out to the barn.

"What's that boy doing now?" Pa said after taking a sip of his hot coffee.

"He thinks he might have missed an egg this morning," I said with a wink. George giggled, though he readily took the bowl of porridge Ma put in front of him.

"You boys up to no good?" Pa asked in his sternest voice.

George shook his head, gave Pa one of the angelic looks he's known for, and continued eating his oat porridge. None of us glanced at Matt as he sat in his appointed spot between Ellie and Benjamin, though we all noticed that he had unobtrusively added another egg to the basket on the counter. Ma put his bowl of oatmeal on the table, then continued feeding pap to Julie.

"Best you'd also be getting me two pounds of coffee and a pound of fine salt at the mercantile," Ma said. "The jug for the molasses is already in the wagon."

"How much sugar you want?"

"Better get five pounds. Take a gander at the muslin and get a couple of yards if it's got a fair price. There's some money in the tin cup, and you can bring the basket of eggs to barter. You got any change left over, get some suckers for the young'uns." Guess we all saw Matt's grin from ear to ear.

"You drive careful, Will," Pa said. "Back of the wagon is filled with baskets of grain from our winter wheat. Avoid the ruts so you don't lose any of it. Take it to Chrisman's mill over on Hares Hill Road. Can't get used to calling it Kimber's mill, but I heard the new owner has the best toll rates for grinding. Kimber also converted the Sign of the Bear tavern across the street to a general store. Will can drop you off there, Lizzie."

"I could sit in the back of the wagon, making sure the grain don't fall out," Benjamin said as he handed me the cherry jam for my bread.

"You're needed here, boy. We got more threshing to do, and I want you to bale the chaff. You can help me carry it up to the hayloft in the barn."

I knew Benjamin would have enjoyed an outing, but he didn't argue about it. Besides, he likes working side by side with Pa.

"You need any tools sharpened while I'm waiting for the flour, Pa?" Will asked.

"Couldn't hurt to take the axe. Offer the blacksmith a cup of flour for his services. Now, you'd best be on your way, or you'll be waiting in line all day. We've got plenty to do around here."

Chapter Three

Will wasn't much for talking as he directed Nellie down the hill from our house to the road. He gets a funny furrow in his brow when he's concentrating on anything important. Sure enough, he knows Pa would be really upset if anything happened to the wagon or our hard-earned cargo. Not to mention Nellie. She's our best work horse, pulling the plow or the wagon, even the sleigh in winter.

Once we got down the steep incline, Will relaxed a bit, but there are plenty more around here. We've got hills all over Pikeland. Hills and creeks. Good thing most of the better roads have a crossing over the streams nowadays, though some folks will often just ford them at the shallowest spot if they're looking to get someplace faster. Will seems content to stay on the main roads.

We passed by Emery's farmhouse, and I waved to Mrs. Emery hanging wash on the line. Like us, Jacob and their boys plant corn, wheat, and soybeans, though they have a few more cows and pigs than we do. They must do pretty good, because their house and barn are bigger than ours.

Can't say we're doing poorly, though. Pa says we're lucky we got a roof over our heads, and food in our bellies. He was smart to also put sheep on our land because Ma, and now Ellie, spin enough wool to provide for our needs and barter the rest.

"Don't be calling attention to everyone when we pass by their homesteads," Will said. "They'll be wanting us to stop and talk, and we ain't got the time today."

"You don't want to be sociable? Don't know why you're in such a hurry. You don't even like farming. And that's what you'll be doing as soon as we get home."

"I'll be plenty amiable when we get to the crossroads. I figure I'll be talking to the folks waiting for their flour. Besides, there's a lot going on what with the blacksmith and tannery right on the premises. I sure would like to apprentice with one of them tradesmen. Mark my words. One of these days, I'll find me an opportunity to be a businessman and get rich. I'm not going to spend my life breaking my back, fighting with Mother Nature to eke out a living."

"What's Pa say about it?" I asked as Will made a turn that led us through the deeply wooded Phillips' land.

The road is barely a wide enough path, with tree limbs that reach across above our heads to form an intertwining green canopy, leaves only rustling as the birds returned to feed their young. Smaller branches brushed the wagon as we slowly made our way up one curvy hill, and down the next.

"He wouldn't hear none of it. Said I was talking crazy, like his brothers used to do."

"Don't think any of them got wealthy. Leastways, not as much as we know."

"Might be. Might not. Maybe I'm smarter than they were." Will looked sideways at me, with a grin for good measure.

"What about you?" he asked. "It doesn't seem to me like you're planning to be a farm wife. That is, if you ever had any callers except maybe pimply Henry Harris."

I'd have laughed if I hadn't felt a cringe of disgust at the thought of chicken chested, stringy haired Henry taking a liking to me. "He never called on me, and you know it!"

"He asks for you every time his ma sends him over to barter for butter or wool."

"That doesn't count. He's just being neighborly. I'll find me a man who's strong and masculine, but gentle as a lamb. One who'll treat me as an equal partner in marriage."

Will laughed out loud as he maneuvered Nellie around a fallen branch. "Sounds like one of them fairy tales that Ma tells the young'uns. You'll be a spinster for sure if you're waiting around for some figment of your imagination. Kind of like the ghost in these woods."

"William Mitchell, you sure know how to get my dander up! Now you're trying to scare me. What ghost are you talking about?"

"Just listen," Will said, almost in a whisper. "If you listen real careful, you can hear crying way off in the distance."

I couldn't hear much except the clip clop of Nellie's hooves making their way over the packed trail. Still, I tried to focus my ears to pick up sounds deep in the woods. Will seemed to enjoy my sudden silence.

"Legend has it," he continued, "one of the early white settlers built a cabin on Pickering Creek. I'm talking about a time even before William Penn took ownership of this land. Mostly Indians lived around here. Anyway, he had a wife and a passel of kids, but don't know how many exactly. He lived peacefully among the Lenape, fishing and hunting, trading pelts for his livelihood. Then one day, a different tribe tried to take over this whole area. Killed the settler and his boys, and took the wife and girls as their bounty. If you listen good, you can hear them girls crying."

I looked intently at Will, trying to see if he was teasing me, as he often does. He was staring straight ahead, serious as all get out. Suddenly I heard the sound, soft as a whimper at first, building almost to a low keening.

"It's animals," I said, trying to reassure myself. "Probably foxes or coyotes."

"Might be. Might not. Just telling you what Pa told me, and he knows because Pappy told him."

I figured that Will's story might be true, especially if it came from Pappy. Pappy knew all about this county, and he never told a lie, leastwise as much as I could tell. Still, the tale brought a chill to my heart, thinking about what might have happened to the settler's girl-folk.

As the trees thinned and the road widened, we passed several log cabins and a few stone houses so I knew we were nearing our destination. I thought about how nice it would be to live closer to neighbors, able to walk there, and not have to spend an entire day to visit. Ma had experienced that as a girl in Ireland, and then in Philadelphia. I wondered if she ever gets lonely, or if she regrets the decision to run off with Pa.

As we approached the main intersection in the village, Will pulled up to the side of the general store on the northwest corner of the crossroads. The frontage has a large covered wooden porch with about nine steps leading down to the road. I counted five windows across the front on the second floor, with four windows and a door under the eaves on the main level. The less prominent side entrance is obviously used only for deliveries.

Directly across the street is a larger tenement, perhaps serving overnight visitors arriving on the stagecoach. I noticed a buckboard ahead of us, and recognized old man McClure and his son, David, just sitting there chewing the fat.

David's not bad looking, though he's a bit scrawny. Guess he's about my age, and it looks like he shot up another couple of inches since I last saw him. Once he fills out, he might even be considered handsome, not that I'm interested.

Will nudged me, and whispered that I should act like a girl so David notices me. I poked him in the ribs and rolled my eyes as I maneuvered my petticoats to modestly disembark from the wagon. Once my feet touched the ground, Will handed me the jug for molasses and the basket of eggs, and told me I should wait on the front porch of the store when I finished shopping. He'd meet me here as soon as he was done with his business.

"'Morning, Mr. McClure. 'Morning, David," I said, nodding politely to them as I passed by to take the front steps up to the store. David seemed to blush, but his pa responded that I should have a pleasant day. They were obviously waiting for someone, probably busy-body Mrs. McClure getting her dry goods.

I braced myself for our impending encounter, dreading the thought of making conversation with the judgmental woman. Luckily, she was busy gossiping with several other ladies in the far corner by the crockery and dishes when I entered the store. She barely took notice of me, though I detected a sideward glance from her dark, beady eyes indicating that she saw I was wearing my Sunday finest.

Chapter Four

Gazing around the dimly lit store, I was impressed with the variety of available goods. Several chairs were placed in front of the large hearth on the distant side wall, not far from a counter that might have served as the bar in the old tavern. They made the pace look inviting. Numerous barrels located throughout the mercantile contain sugar, salt, crackers, pickles, flour, potatoes, jerky, and other commodities.

Every wall is lined with wooden floor to ceiling shelves, bins, and drawers. Horse bridles, halters, and harnesses, as well as other farm paraphernalia are hung from the rafters. Buckets and lanterns surround hardware items such as axes, hammers, and nails. A large table with bolts of fabric has a prominent place next to the sewing notions and household goods.

I put my basket of eggs and the jug for molasses on the cashier's counter, while I waited until the customer ahead of me completed his transaction. Never laid eyes on the heavyset man, so I figured he was recently arrived in these parts.

When they were finished, I introduced myself to the tall, spectacled clerk, newly hired by Emmor Kimber. Mr. Kimber's the Quaker who took ownership last year of two hundred acres of land, gaining three businesses at the crossroads that were already in operation.

"I'm Lizzie Mitchell, daughter of William Mitchell of Yellow Springs. Ma gave me these eggs to barter, and some money to buy sugar, molasses, coffee, and fine salt."

"Pleased to meet you, Lizzie. I'm Joseph Price, manager of Kimber's general store. How much of each is your mother wanting?"

I gave Mr. Price the order, thinking all the while what a perfect name for a store clerk. Not that it's so unusual around here, but most Price's I know are farmers.

"Ma also wants me to see if you have any muslin, if it's a fair cost."

"The Price's have good prices," he said with a chuckle. We both laughed at his play on words. "You'll want to talk to my wife over by the fabric table. Emily, you've got another customer."

Emily Price greeted me warmly as I made my way to the clothing section. I liked her instantly, a slender young woman with a big smile, dimples in her cheeks, and dazzling blue eyes. Looked to me that she's not more than two or three years older than I am, still in her prime.

I asked to see the muslin, and she showed me three bolts. The finest choice was bleached, but the others were unbleached of lower quality. I felt a swatch of each, my gaze lingering on the beauty of the bleached muslin. In the end, I chose the better of the unbleached at $.36 a yard. Emily gave me three yards for just a dollar.

"We have some nice gingham," Emily noted. "Only $.48 a yard. Don't you just love this shade of pink? Makes a real pretty underskirt."

Out of the corner of my eye, I noticed busy-body McClure looking shocked that I would consider such blatant disregard for established social standards. She pursed her thin lips, then returned to her chatter about what this world is coming to.

"The gingham's quite wonderful," I said. "But I'll have to talk to Ma about it."

"Of course. I can cut a swatch for you to take home. You can tell your mother we have all colors of the rainbow."

I nodded as she took her scissors from the shelf, then gave me a piece of fabric. "Thank you for your kindness. Have you and Mr. Price been here very long?"

"Only a month," Emily said. "Mr. Kimber gives us some of the second floor as our living quarters. He taught Joe at the Westtown Quaker School a few years back. Joe's always been good with numbers, and he's an honest man, so I suppose Mr. Kimber thought he'd be fine to manage his general store. He doesn't mind that I help. It's a good thing, because I'd go crazy if I had to sit upstairs by myself day in and day out."

"You don't have any children?"

"Not yet. We've just been wed for a couple of months. My family lives in West Chester. That's not so far as the crow flies, but it takes a long time to travel by wagon or stagecoach. I must admit that I'm a little homesick. Joe promised me we'd go home for a visit over the 4th of July."

"I can't imagine what it'd be like without my family," I said. "Of course, sometimes I'd like to be on my own without all the hootin' and hollerin' of the young'uns, but kin is kin."

"You live close by the crossroads?"

"We've got a farm in Yellow Springs, a couple miles away. It's been in Pa's family for a long time."

"That's not too far from here. Maybe next time you come, we'll just sit in the back room and have a cup of tea. I think we could be friends."

"I'd like that," I said as I noticed several new people enter the store. That must have been the signal for busy-body McClure and her gossiping friends to take their leave. I waved discretely, and she nodded her pinched nose in my direction. I was relieved not to have to make small talk with her.

"Looks like the stagecoach just arrived," Emily said as she wrapped my muslin. "Passengers like to browse and get a cup of coffee while they stretch their legs. I'd best be seeing what I can do to assist Joe."

"I'll pay for my wares and sit on one of the rocking chairs you've got out front. My brother will be coming for me as soon as he finishes his business."

Mr. Price tallied my order, and lugged it to the porch for me. I had enough money left over to buy six suckers. Matt was going to be a happy boy when Will and I returned home.

I called out my farewell to Emily, and nearly bumped into an older bearded man coming in the front door. A disgusting odor of stale sweat and cigar smoke engulfed me, as he cussed for his wife to hurry it up.

The woman looked somewhat sickly, pale in the face and lips, and skinnier than I've ever seen. She was struggling with an apparently heavy traveling bag, and didn't seem to have much strength to even make it up the steps to the porch.

I hurried to her, offering to carry her satchel. She looked grateful for my assistance, and motioned to her husband that she'd be setting a while outside while he took care of business. He went inside, shaking his head and calling her some foul name I never heard before.

It was none of my concern, but I offered to get the lady some water since Nellie and our wagon were still parked at the grist mill, and Will wasn't in sight. She looked at me with blank staring eyes, sunk deep in their sockets, then nodded that she could do with something to drink.

"I'll be right back," I said. "If you don't mind, please keep an eye on my purchases."

I was asking Emily for a glass of water when I overheard the fetid man ask Mr. Price how he might get transportation to the Mitchell farm in Yellow Springs. The look on my face must have betrayed my sudden apprehension.

Emily and I locked eyes, as Mr. Price said, "You're in luck. This here's the Mitchell girl. She's waiting for her brother to come get her."

"Let me take a look-see at you, girl," the foul man said as his gaze travelled from my head to my toes. He rubbed his thick, dirty fingers through his beard, wiping some snot dripping from his nose.

Emily immediately came to stand beside me, handing me the glass of water, as if the two of us could present a formidable force to be reckoned with.

"What business do you have at the Mitchell farm?" I asked warily.

The man emitted a chesty laugh, then cleared his throat and coughed a wad into the spittoon on the floor by the counter. "I'm coming home. You must be my brother's girl. Can't deny you resembling my ma in her younger days."

Chapter Five

I wasn't sure to believe this bear of a man with his dirty, shoulder length gray hair and matted beard. He didn't look like Pa, nor would his face remind me of Pappy. Not wanting him to think I was intimidated, I stood right up to him, staring him in the eye.

"What's your brother's name? And what's yours?" I asked, showing him my feisty attitude.

"We called him Willy, short for William. Reckon he was still a baby when I left home. I'm named after my pa, George Mitchell."

I knew Pappy's name was George, so I figured this was his oldest boy. I nodded to Emily that everything was all right, and she went back to waiting on customers with her husband.

"Why are you coming back after all these years?"

"Don't see how it's any of your concern, little missy," the old man said. "But me and the missus are mighty tired. When's that brother of yours going to be here?"

"When he's done," I said, about as rudely as he was with me. "I'll be bringing this water to your wife, and we'll be waiting on the porch."

"Her name's Mary, in case you be talking to her."

I nodded my acknowledgment while pushing open the door. The breath of fresh air was a relief from his stench.

Mary's eyes were closed when I sat in the rocker next to her. She startled awake, but looked at me as if for the first time. She reached to take the glass of water, then guzzled just about all of it down.

Mary returned the glass to me when she was finished, all the while staring blankly across the street. I followed her gaze, relieved when I saw William approaching with the wagon. He appeared surprised that I bounded down the stairs to the road, seeming to forget ma's purchases.

"Guess you want me to carry all the goods you bought," Will said with a chuckle. "You just going to sit and look pretty while I go get the stuff?"

I stood there, looking up at him, shaking my head for wont of what to say. I no more fancied taking smelly old George and strange Mary back to our home than visit the man in the moon.

"We've got guests," I finally uttered.

With that, Pa's brother started down the steps, towing Mary by the hand. I noticed that Will caught a whiff of old George when he got close enough, and the breeze came our way. Will handed me Nellie's reins and hopped to the ground.

"This here's Pa's brother, George, and his wife, Mary," I said to Will. "They just arrived by stagecoach."

George stuck out his grimy, pudgy hand to Will saying, "Didn't know how we was going to get to the homestead. Glad you're going to take us. I'll sit in the front with you, and the women-folk can ride in the back with the goods."

Will shook George's hand as if he were handling a cold fish. "Don't think Pa's expecting you," he said.

The disgusting man guffawed, then spat on the ground.

"Can't say that he is," George scoffed. "Go get our stuff, boy. We don't got all day."

I pointed out Mary's satchel, next to Ma's purchases on the porch. I'd have helped, but I wasn't about to let go of Nellie in case old George and Mary decided to run off with our wagon. I reckoned that Mary wouldn't be running anywhere with that strange look in her eye, but it wasn't worth taking a chance.

It would have taken Will two trips, if not more, to lug all the items, but Mr. Price stuck his head out the door, just in time. Guess he was checking on me, making sure I was all right, which I thought was real nice of him.

Mr. Price and Will loaded all the merchandise into the back of the wagon, then helped Mary get settled in. She flat out laid down, resting her head on a sack of flour.

I gave Will the reins, but was reluctant to ride in the back. There was obviously no other choice since the nauseating man already had settled himself up front.

"Don't mind the missus if she does anything strange," old man George said. "She's tetched in the head."

Mr. Price was kind enough to give me a boost up, then he whispered to me, "If you bend down low, you might not get a nose full of his stink."

Out loud he added, "Come on back soon and visit with Emily. She'd be liking a friend."

"I will. I promise."

Will clicked for Nellie to head home, and I sat cross-legged facing the road behind us. Mary was still flat on her back, staring up at the wisps of clouds in the sky. Didn't look like she was seeing anything there, which I thought was rather sad.

Will took another way home, more out in the open, so as not to go through the Phillips' haunted woods. That was just fine with me, though it extended our ride.

I couldn't imagine what Pa was going to think when he sees we've brought his oldest brother with us. Surely, he'll be happy to welcome him after all these years. If not, I don't rightly know what else we could have done. You don't leave kin stranded. Leastwise, that's what Ma would tell us.

The old codger was doing a heap of talking in between his hacking and spitting off the side of the wagon. I hoped he had good aim, since I didn't want any wind blowing it back to land on me. Will didn't have much to say, though I heard him ask about the man's travels.

Near as I could tell, Pa's brother has been mostly a drifter, though he obviously picked up a wife somewhere out west. I checked on Mary again, but she was still just staring at the clouds in the sky.

"You feel all right?" I asked her. She nodded that she was fine, though I figured her bony back side was probably going to be hurting by tomorrow.

Mrs. Emery's wash was taken down from the line when we passed their homestead. Must be she's in fixing supper, since the sun's in the west sky now. Ma's going to be surprised to have company, but it won't be too much of a problem for her to throw a couple more potatoes into the pot. Still, the closer we got to home, the more I had butterflies in my belly.

Will took the final incline real slow, just like Pa showed him. Pa says that Nellie's no spring chicken. In fact, she's pretty tuckered out by the time she gets home after a jaunt. As we rounded the bend at the top of the hill, old George let out a whistle.

"Well, lookee there," he said. "It's a mighty fine-looking house. That little brother of mine must be doing pretty good."

Nellie knew exactly where she was going. She headed over to the barn and stopped right next to her stall. Will jumped down and helped Mary disembark. He and I gave each other one of those looks that says a mouthful. Then he went to unhitch Nellie and get her some fresh water.

I straightened the woman's petticoats, and reached for her bag, all the while watching the old man grunt his way off the front seat, using the buckboard as a pivot. He landed hard on his feet before clearing his throat and spitting on the ground. Then he looked around, approval lighting his deeply rutted face.

I was about to walk Mary to the house, when Pa came out of the barn with the wheelbarrow. He stopped short when he saw we had visitors.

It was obvious he didn't recognize the guests, so I said in my most polite voice, "Pa, we brought home your brother and his missus. This here's George and Mary."

Chapter Six

Pa squinted as the late afternoon sun caught his eye. The two men walked toward each other, both about the same height, although at least sixteen years separated them. One clean-shaven with long sideburns; one with a scruffy, bushy, dirty beard. One sturdy and muscular; one fleshy and wizened. As much as I scrutinized, I couldn't say there was any likeness between them.

George put out his meaty hand, saying "You growed up real good, little brother. Last time I seen you, you was sucking on Ma's tit."

"Where you been?" Pa asked as he shook George's hand.

"Like I told your boy, I been all over. Had me a place in Ohio for a while. That's where I met the missus. Moved in with her after her husband passed. We sold her farm later when we lost all our crops, and kept going west. Ended up in some hell-hole on the plains with a bunch of Indians and not many white folks. That suited me fine, but it got Mary sickly."

"You're welcome to stay," Pa said. "Leastways until you get settled in the county, if that's what you're planning to do. You and the missus can sleep in the loft above the kitchen."

The brother gave a hoarse laugh, and cleared his throat. I wanted to warn Pa to stand clear if he didn't want spittle on his boots.

"Seems to me," he said with disdain, "I'm the firstborn. This place is mine."

"You up and left," Pa said firmly. "I got the land fair and square. Fact is, I paid off the mortgage and back taxes. The deed's in my name."

I looked at Will, wondering if this was going to turn out like that story about Cain and Abel in Ma's bible. Will just shook his head and started to carry the bags of flour to the pantry bin.

I took Mary by the arm to lead her to the house, lugging her satchel with my other hand. She pulled at me some, saying she had to pee first. We both made a stop at the outhouse, and I watched Pa and his brother disagreeing while waiting for her to be done.

Will must've told Ma about our guests, because she came on out to welcome them. "This here's Missus Mary," I said. "She's feeling poorly."

"I'm pleased to meet you," Ma said as she kissed her on the cheek. "My name is Jane. You can set awhile on the porch while Lizzie gets you some water. I'll go meet your husband."

Ma walked across the yard, and went to stand by Pa. She put her arm around his waist, the top of her head just coming to his shoulder. Despite their differences in height, they fit like a glove, and gave a united front.

I heard Pa say, "This is my brother, George. He's come to stay awhile." Ma shook George's hand, greeting him warmly.

They stood there talking while I went to get a cup of water for the missus. When I returned from the pump, Ma called over for me to send Matt and little George out of the house, and to get a bar of soap.

Ellie was peeling potatoes in the kitchen when I went looking for the boys. "They're being punished," Ellie said. "They got into a fight about noon-time, each one blaming the other."

"Well, Ma wants them outside right now. And she wants them to bring the soap. No doubt she'll have them take the man to the pond for a bath. He stinks like a polecat."

"Will said it's Pa's brother and missus out there. Where'd you find them?"

"They came on the stagecoach, looking for how to get to our farm. Didn't know what else to do but bring them here."

The boys came bounding into the kitchen from their respective corners in the parlor, both asking at the same time if I had bought them a sucker.

"I did, but you can't have it until Ma says you've earned it. Take this soap out to her, and go meet Pa's brother."

I told Ellie that I should take off my Sunday dress and change my apron, and suggested that she might carry Julie out to sit on the porch with Mary. I sweetened the offer by saying I'd peel the rest of the potatoes.

"The missus won't be talking none," I added. "She's real quiet."

By the time Ma returned to the kitchen, I had put on my short dress and working apron, and was finishing up the spuds. Ma sat at the table with me, just the two of us, like it must have been long ago.

"I didn't know what to do, Ma. That man doesn't look like kin, but he said he is. He's rude and ornery, and has a crazy lady for a wife. And he stinks!"

"You did right. Wasn't anything else you could have done. Your Pa will figure out if the man is who he says he is. We just have to be hospitable."

"I don't like him."

"It's no matter. You just be kind. It's what the Good Book says. Now tell me about your trip."

"Oh, Ma. It was wonderful. The crossroads are bustling with all kinds of people. It's got the feel of a real village now."

"Did you see anyone we know?"

"Busy-body… I mean, Mrs. McClure was there, but she was talking with some other ladies I didn't recognize. The clerk running the general store is real nice. His name is Mr. Price. Isn't that a funny name for a storekeeper? Anyway, he's recently married to Emily, who's not much older than me, and she's so pretty. She takes care of the fabric, and she gave me this piece of gingham to show you."

I reached into my pocket and pulled out the swatch. Ma fingered the fine-woven fabric lovingly, agreeing that it's quite fetching.

"Mrs. McClure appeared scandalized that I'd be eyeing something so fancy," I continued. "But I paid her no heed."

"That's good," Ma said with a far-off look in her eye. "Did you get any muslin?"

"Three yards for a dollar. The Price's have good prices. Get it?"

"Got it," Ma said with a chuckle.

"Do you ever miss it, Ma?"

"Miss what?"

"Living in town, close to people. You're not like Pa, hankering to live up on the hill so he doesn't have to bother with neighbors."

"I love your pa, and want to be with him. Wouldn't matter if it's here or there. Besides, I'm surrounded with my children. I've got all I need."

I thought about her words for a few moments. Then I said, "We're so different, aren't we, Ma?"

"In some ways we are. I worry about you sometimes, Lizzie. You've got a big heart, like me, but you've got a stubborn streak like your father. You got Mitchell blood running through you, making you want something else in life. I don't know if you're ever going to find what you're looking for."

"Your parents were out to find something different, else why would they have risked their lives to come to America? Maybe I've got their blood, not the Mitchell's."

"Might be. I was only a child when I lost them so I don't remember much about what they were like. I recall my father was serious, but very enterprising. My mother was kind and loving, from a well-to-do family. Still, I don't think I ever saw her having fun. Guess they stuck to their Presbyterian roots. No, I don't think you take after them."

"Is that why you wanted to marry a Presbyterian? Because that's how you were brought up before they died?"

"By the time I met your pa, I was pretty much raised as a Quaker. I fell in love with William Mitchell the minute I saw him. Didn't matter to me what his religion was."

"Pa's not very pious. I don't ever remember us going to church."

"Closest Presbyterian church is way over in Paoli. Your father says he's not going to waste a day of work getting to and from. He talks to the good Lord whenever he wants when he's out in the fields."

"It doesn't bother me none," I said. "But you'd probably like meeting up with the other women-folk."

"Seems to me it's nothing you need to be concerned about. You'd better get those potatoes on the fire or we won't be having any supper."

Ma helped me carry the kettle over and set it on the crane. I stirred up the embers and added a log, then said, "I'd like to go to the general store again next time we need something.

Emily and I are going to have tea in her back room and become friends."

"Depends what your father has to say about it. Go check the garden to see if we have any string beans worth picking. You can snap them on the porch, and take Ellie's place sitting with the missus Mary."

"I don't like her. She's tetched."

"Don't matter if she is or she isn't," Ma said as she handed me a bowl for the beans. "She needs watching, leastwise until your uncle comes back from his bath."

Ellie looked relieved that I was giving her a reprieve. She even offered to pick the beans if I would also keep an eye on the baby. Little Julie was busy bringing one pebble at a time to the porch from the path, already making a small pile of her precious stones at Mary's feet. The old woman followed Julie with her eyes, seeming for the first time to focus on her surroundings.

Worried that Missus Mary could trip over the stones if she decided to stand up, I tried redirecting Julie to create a new pile by my chair. Stubbornly, Julie continued to add to Mary's pile, totally ignoring what I was telling her.

I tugged on Julie's hand, attempting to show her where I wanted her to place the pebbles. Julie resisted, struggling to free herself.

Suddenly, a piercing shriek emitted from Mary's mouth. She stood and shoved me to the ground, screaming at the top of her lungs.

"Don't touch my child! Get your filthy hands off my baby! DON'T TOUCH MY CHILD!"

Chapter Seven

Everyone came running at the sound of Mary's blood-curdling screams. Ma was the first to reach her, folding Mary into the warmth of her embrace, crooning "You're OK. I'm here," as she held her tightly, just as she does when Matt has a bad dream.

Ellie dashed to grab Julie, who was also crying with the fearful scene. Getting up, I brushed the dirt off my petticoats and examined my scraped knee. By the time Pa, Will, and Benjamin sprinted to the porch, Ma had Mary settled back in the rocking chair, gently rubbing the woeful woman's shoulders.

"Damnation! What's going on here?"

"I don't know, Pa," I said. "I was just trying to get Julie to move her stones away from the lady's feet. Next thing you know, the missus went crazy screaming and hollering about touching her baby. What's she talking about?"

"Go on, all of you," Ma said quietly. "Leave us in peace. Ellie, take Julie in the house and give her one of them suckers. Lizzie, you can snap the beans. You men go back to finishing up your work. This woman's hurting real bad. I'll just sit here with her for a while."

"What got her hurtin'?" Will asked.

"Don't rightly know," Ma said. "But, if you ask me, seems like someone must have took her baby."

Will and I locked eyes, both of us pondering the haunting of the woods. I shuddered to think how a mother would feel to have her babies taken from her. How Ma must've felt when Dan and Ezra passed. Must be why the woman is so empty inside, just staring and seeing nothing.

Pa looked at Ma, and shook his head like he didn't know how we could deal with the intrusion of his brother and the wife. "How much longer we got before supper?"

"About another hour," Ma said. "Potatoes just went on the fire."

"Ben, you go on down to the pond," Pa said. "See what's taking my brother so long with his bath. If them young'uns ran off, he might not remember his way home. Will, you can help me finish up in the barn."

As they took their leave, I picked up the bowl Ellie left on the porch and went out to the garden to find more beans. All the while, Ma sat next to Mary, comforting her. The woman just rocked in her chair, eyes wide open, seeing nothing.

Ellie was setting the table when I joined her in the kitchen. Julie was perfectly content in her high chair, licking her sucker, stickiness all over her face. Already she seemed to have forgotten her fright.

I snapped the beans at the counter, then transferred them to a kettle. The stem ends went into the slop bucket we'd use to feed the pigs. "Don't rightly know how we can handle all this," Ellie said. "Why'd you have to bring them here?"

"Didn't have much choice in the matter. What's done is done. We've just got to accept it, leastways 'til Pa decides what's best."

Ellie shrugged as she went to the pantry to find two more plates and some additional knives and forks. I added water to the green beans, then lifted the kettle up to the other crane in the hearth. The two of us worked in tandem, one stirring the venison that had been roasting on the embers all afternoon, the other slicing the bread that Ma had made this morning.

Julie seemed to be tiring of her sucker, and wanted to get down from her chair. I got her settled with a piece of bread and butter, quickly putting the sweet on a towel out of sight. Ellie took a washrag to Julie's face, just as Matt and little George came tromping in, filthy dirty and soaking wet.

"You'd better get out there and dry off," I said. "Looks like the two of you took a bath in the mud."

"Ma said to come in and get changed," Matt said. "We're s'posed to put on a clean chemise, fresh from the laundry basket she left in the parlor."

"Well, take them clothes off first, and go get washed up at the pump."

"I ain't going out there nekked," Matt said.

"No one's going to be paying any heed."

"The old man might. 'Sides, we seen his pecker when he got undressed at the pond. A lot bigger than Pa's, that's for sure. Don't want him making fun of me." Little George nodded in agreement.

"All right. Put on your chemise in here, then go on out and wash up. You can throw your wet clothes on the line while you're at it."

That seemed to satisfy the boys, and I surely didn't want to encourage them to continue the discussion. I helped George undo the buttons on his breeches, then returned to the kitchen, lugging two straight-backed chairs from the parlor.

While Ellie was cutting the meat, I put the potatoes into a bowl and began smashing them with butter and milk. Before ladling out the beans, I went out to the porch, tugging on the cord for the bell to signal that supper was ready.

Ma was still holding the old lady's hand, both of them rocking, both seeming to be asleep. Ma opened her eyes, and attempted to cajole the missus to come in to eat. The woman just shook her head, muttering something about not being hungry.

Ma asked me to make up a plate with mashed potatoes and pan drippings. She'd feed the missus out on the porch while the rest of us were eating.

Chapter Eight

Can't say that our meal was very pleasant, what with Pa's brother eating like a hog, picking up his venison with his fingers and using his knife to shovel the potatoes into his cavernous mouth. Only Julie was oblivious to the tension around the table, happily playing with her string beans in between bites.

Eventually Pa asked the man, "What's wrong with your woman?"

"She's tetched."

"She always been that way?"

"No, she was fine 'til we settled out there on them plains. Something happened there."

"Like what?"

"Don't think it's the kind of stuff to talk about around the young'uns," Pa's brother said as he reached for more meat and potatoes.

I figured I'd best make up a plate for Ma before there wasn't any more food left. I placed it over on the trivet by the embers, then got a sucker for Matt and little George.

Pa told the boys if they were finished eating, they could go on outside to eat their sweets. Then he asked Ellie to take

Julie upstairs and put her to bed. After the young'uns were out of earshot, Pa urged his brother to continue the story.

"Happened when I was out hunting," Pa's brother said. "We had us a nice cabin. Found it abandoned out there on them plains. Didn't have no windows, but it had a good roof and a big hearth. Got a little stuffy in there if the fire was going, but we could keep the door open to get some air."

The old man leaned back in his chair, with a far-off look in his eyes. For the first time, I saw some semblance of humanity in him.

"Bunch of Indians must of came by that day. Just walked right in, from what I can figure. Mary and me, we had us two babies—a boy about the same age as your youngest son, and a girl just starting to walk. When I come back from my business, I noticed there was no smoke rising from the chimney. Got me scared for what I'd find."

Pa interrupted him, telling Benjamin to go out and set with the brother's missus so Ma could hear the rest of the story.

"I want to hear about it, too," Ben said, but he knew by Pa's look that there wouldn't be any debate about it.

He left the table reluctantly, telling Ma to come in. I got her plate from the hearth, while Pa filled her in on what she had missed of his brother's tale.

"So, like I was saying," George continued, "I knew I wasn't going to find anything good in that cabin."

The old man stopped talking, acting as if he were trying to get his emotions under control. He took a deep breath and cleared his throat, but for some reason he didn't spit.

Finally, he said, "I found Mary face down on the bed, covered in blood. Thought she was dead, 'til I saw her leg move. When I turned her over, she was cradling...she was cradling... our...boy..., and he was.... he was scalped."

The old man pushed his plate aside and put his head in his hands on the table, like he couldn't face what he had seen. Ma got up and put her arms around the old man's shoulders, tears in her eyes.

Will took himself outside to sit with Benjamin. I felt like I was going to puke, but I needed to hear what happened to the daughter. Pa sat there, stoic-like, though his expression showed that he was deeply moved.

"And your little girl?" Pa asked.

"Gone." Old man George raised his head. "I searched for her. Days, weeks. Couldn't find her nowhere. The damn Indians must a carried her off. Don't know if they killed her or took her for one of their own. She was a pretty little thing."

"And Mary's been like she is ever since?" Ma asked.

"Like she's in a trance," Pa's brother said. "Every one of them Indians must a had their way with her. Raped her and left her for dead with our boy. I buried him out there on them plains, then cleaned her up real good. I burned the mattress and tried to get them blood stains out of the floor, but I knew we couldn't live there no more."

"She been to see a doctor?" Ma asked.

"Didn't know of anyone who could help her. That's when I thought about coming east... coming home. I figured she might get better if she was around kindly people."

Ma informed Pa's brother about Mary's outburst before supper, when Mary seemed to think that Julie was her baby.

"Don't surprise me none," he said. "Only time she seems to focus on anything is when she sees a little girl. Other than that, she don't eat, she don't talk, leastways not much."

"I got her to eat some potatoes," Ma said. "I think we need to send for Doc Pyle in the morning. She's nothing but skin and bones, and if she doesn't get some nourishment, she'll be dying."

"Don't see how he'll be able to help her. The doc will see how tetched she is, and send her off to the insane asylum."

"She's hurting real bad inside," Ma said. "Maybe there's some medicine or treatment he can prescribe."

"I'm telling you, she does crazy things. Sometimes I wake up at night and find her walking outside, buck nekked. Other times, she don't know who I am, acting like I'm one of them Indians out to get her."

Pa got up to light the lanterns and candles, and motioned for me to clear the table. Shadows bounced off the walls creating eerie images. The only sound in the room became the cacophony created by me scraping remnants from the dishes into the pigs' slop bucket.

"We'll figure out what's to be done tomorrow," Pa said. Now that you smell better, you and the missus can sleep in Will and Ben's room. They can bed in the loft up them steps over there."

"That's where I slept as a boy," old George said. "Don't mind staying up there now."

"This part of the house is the old log cabin," Ma said. "It might bring back too many bad memories of what happened to Mary. Fact is, it might be why she didn't want to come in. I'll bring her around to the front door of the big house, and up the steps to the second floor. She can wear one of my clean chemises to bed."

The fireflies were out in full force when Ma helped Mary up from her rocker, suggesting that she first make a pit stop at the outhouse. While Ma was waiting for the woman, she told Matt and little George to wash up and go to bed. They must have been tuckered out, because they didn't complain too bad.

Ma explained the sleeping arrangements to Benjamin and Will, encouraging them to get anything from their rooms that they might need for the night. Then, she called for Pa to help lead Mary around the darkened stone house to the front stoop. I opened the latch of the heavy oak door for them from the inside, gave them a lit candle to take upstairs, then returned to my task of washing the dishes.

Pa's brother still sat at the table, his puffy features set in relief with the shadows of the room. Might be he was thinking of long ago, back when he was a boy, when the large rustic area served as the kitchen and living quarters for his entire family.

Now we have lots of counters that Pa built, with oak shelves for our dishes, and a pantry for dry goods. We've still got the old rocking chairs by the hearth but, most often, we just sit on the porch in the summer.

I filled the large dishpan by the window with hot water from the kettle, cleaning each plate with soap that I rubbed on my rag. Then I set the dish in the other tub with cold rinse water.

I wondered what was taking Ellie so long to return since she was supposed to be helping me. Guess I figured that Julie was being particularly uncooperative about going to sleep.

My reverie was interrupted by the uncle's deep, raspy voice. "You got any whiskey in the house?"

"Not since Pappy passed," I said.

"Damnation!" he yelled, banging his fist on the table. He muttered a string of curse words as he stood, his chair scraping along the hardwood floor.

The disgusting man gave me an ugly look, then stormed out the door.

Chapter Nine

After early morning chores and breakfast the next day, Pa told Will he should saddle up Bella, one of our mares, and ride over to Doc Pyle's place. The old man's missus was still up in bed, refusing to eat or get dressed.

"Tell him my brother's wife is poorly," Pa said with a nod to Ma as she poured him another cup of coffee. "See if he can come by and take a look at her."

"Mark my words," old man George said as he held his mug out for Ma to fill, "Ain't nothing he can do for her. Best to let the good Lord take her."

Ma gave him one of her looks as she placed the coffee pot back on the trivet. Seemed like she was about to give him a piece of her mind, but she held her tongue about it. Instead she told Benjamin to carry some hot water upstairs before he went out to the barn as she planned to give Mary a sponge bath. In the meantime, Ellie was to watch Julie and clean up the kitchen, while I gave Matt and little George their lessons.

"You remember how to thresh the wheat?" Pa asked his brother.

"Can't say I'm any good with farming. Never did like it."

"You're not going to just sit around here, one arm longer than the other. Best you earn your keep."

"You got a rifle? Had to sell mine to pay for the transport here. I can hunt."

"That'll do," Pa said. "Plenty of deer and rabbit in the woods. We got a shotgun in the barn. Powder's there, too."

"Out there on them plains I learned how to tan a hide. I make some good leather."

I could see that the uncle's statement had caught Will's attention. "Can you show me how to do tanning?" Will asked as he glanced at Pa's expression to find approval.

Pa's face didn't register any emotion. He just said, "Might be good for you to learn after you help with the farming, boy. Now, head on out and get the doc."

Pa stood up and stretched, then put his mug into the dishpan. "Let's get working. Benjamin. You can show your uncle where we keep the firearms after you bring up the water for your ma. Then meet me out in the wheat field."

Ma went upstairs to tend to Mary, bringing with her a bowl of porridge and a spoon. I cleared the table, setting the dishes on the counter for Ellie to wash, and told Matt and little George to get their slates.

"Best you first do any business in the outhouse," I said, "then meet me in the front den."

The way the big house is designed, we've got two large rooms on either side of the central staircase and hall. The room on the right is our parlor. It's set up somewhat fancy, with a cozy hearth and homespun draperies on the tall windows. There's plenty of respectable seating, even some upholstered chairs for when visitors come calling.

The den on the left is a mirror image in construction, but its function is less formal. It, too, has a fireplace and draperied windows, but we designate it as a workroom. A long wooden table with benches on either side can be used to roll out fabric for cutting and sewing, serve as a writing space, or function as a desk for teaching the boys their lessons. Ma's spinning wheel is set up in front of the hearth, and two rocking chairs are by the windows for reading or cogitating.

I was sitting on one of the benches at the table when Matt and little George traipsed in, looking like two hoodlums heading to prison. They took their appointed seats on the bench across from me.

This is my favorite chore. Ma says I took to teaching like a fish takes to water. Without a doubt, she instilled in me a love of learning, showing me that education can be enjoyable.

Matt's doing fine with the alphabet, but George still gets confused with some of the letters. Today I planned to focus on P and B, with practice writing upper case and lower case, then forming some words.

I gave each of the boys a chalk and rag for their slates, and had them start writing a row of P's. If it didn't come out just right, I instructed them to erase and start over.

We practiced the hard P sound, 'til the boys got silly trying to spray spit on each other as they pursed their lips to force air through them.

"Seems to me you got the sound of a P," I said, trying not to laugh. "Now, let's make some words. Take turns, one at a time. Matt, you go first."

"Pig," Matt said, without a second's hesitation.

"That's good. See if you can write it for me."

Clear as anything, Matt wrote p-i-g.

"Gold star!" I said, reaching over to draw a star in the top right corner of his slate. Matt painstakingly erased p-i-g, careful not to wipe off his reward.

"Your turn, George. A word beginning with P."

"Post," George said. "Like a fence post, Lizzie."

"Gold star for you as well," I said, drawing a star on George's slate.

"Hey!" Matt exclaimed. "Why's George getting a star if he didn't write the word?"

"George can't write words yet," I said. "Of course, if you write the word *post*, you can get another star."

Matt thought for a moment, then he muttered, "It ain't worth it."

"That's 'cause you don't know how to write it," George said. "I gotcha that time, Matt. I been thinking up some P words."

"I can write it if I want," Matt said sullenly. "I just don't feel like it."

"Give it a try, Matt." I encouraged. "Gold stars add up. Just sound out the word, letter by letter."

Matt took his time, concentrating on each sound. "Puh," he said first, making sure to spray George with spit, and writing the letter P on his slate. "O is easy," he said, writing the letter O. "Ssssss is S, and tttttt is T. P-o-s-t. There it is."

"That's excellent, Matt," I said as I drew another star on his slate. "Now I want you both to practice the letter P. Matt, you write on your slate as many P words you can think of. George, you keep writing P, capital and small."

A vigorous rap on the front door signaled the doctor's arrival. I told the boys to keep working while I took him upstairs.

Doc Pyle is of average height, with brown hair trimmed nice, and muttonchop sideburns. He wears spectacles, carries a black valise, and I could see the gold chain for his pocket watch around his neck. He's about the same age as Pa, even grew up around these parts but, when he came of age, he went off to study medicine at Columbia College, in New York.

"Good to see you, Doc," I said as I opened the door. I noticed his buggy parked on the drive out front by the hitching post.

"Likewise, Lizzie," he said. "Look at you, just about all grown up."

I guess I blushed a little, because Matt and George were giggling, catching the doctor's attention. "And look at these two fine young men," he said. "You must be having your lessons. What are you studying?"

"P words," Matt said.

"**P**erhaps you can **p**lay at the **p**ond after you **p**ractice," Doc Pyle said, with an emphasis on each P in the sentence. Matt and George smiled, nodding in agreement.

"Ma's upstairs with the woman," I said. "I'll show you to the room."

"Thank you, Lizzie," the doc said as we climbed the steps. "Will told me a little about what has transpired since yesterday."

"The woman's tetched. She doesn't talk much, just stares into space. And she's so skinny, a good wind could just blow her over."

"I'll take a look and see what we can do for her."

Chapter Ten

Ma had pulled over a chair, and was sitting there next to the bed. Mary was cleaned up good, hair brushed and braided, wearing a fresh chemise. I was surprised to realize for the first time that she isn't as old as I had originally thought, maybe not yet forty. But she was still just layin' there, looking at the beams in the ceiling.

"Thank you for coming, Doc," Ma said. "This here's Mary. Don't quite know what to do for her, except try to get some food into her belly. You can see she's all skin and bones, starving to death. I got her to eat three spoons of oatmeal just now."

Ma stood up to give the doctor her chair. He sat down and put his broad hand with slender fingers over Mary's bony one. "Glad to meet you, Mary. My name's John Pyle. Folks around here just call me Doc."

Mary didn't look at him, but she nodded that she heard what he had to say. Doc Pyle told Mary that he was going to do a physical examination, but Ma and I were going to stay in the room.

Mary shook her head vehemently. "Don't touch me," she said, almost in a whisper.

"I'm not going to touch you anywhere private," Doc said. "You'll stay dressed. I'm just going to listen to your heart, and feel your pulse. If you let me, I'll push on your belly to see if you have any pain. You tell me to stop, and I will. Is that all right with you?"

Mary hesitantly nodded her agreement, though I could see she was upset about it. I figured she could start screaming again, so I told Ma I was going to let the boys go on outside.

"That'll be fine," she said. "Tell them to do some more weeding in the garden."

Matt and George were quite ecstatic about their release from schooling. They quickly erased their slates and put them on the shelf before challenging each other to be the first to reach the yard.

When I returned upstairs to stand at the lintel of the doorway, I saw that Doc had Mary sitting up in bed, asking her to take deep breaths. Ma was telling him what we knew about her horrible ordeal out west. Mary didn't blink. Not once, the whole time I was watching.

The doc didn't seem like he was paying heed to what Ma had to say, though I know he was listening. He took his time looking in Mary's ears, nostrils, and throat, feeling the glands in her neck and under her arms, checking her heartbeat. Finally, he took both of her hands, and looked her in the eye. Mary didn't return the gaze.

"Look at me, Mary," Doc said in a gentle voice. "I need to talk to you." Mary did as he asked.

"Is that story true, what Jane Mitchell just told me?"

Mary slowly nodded her agreement, one little tear falling to her cheek. Doc wiped it away.

"You're not tetched, Mary. The only way your brain could keep your heart beating was to block out the suffering you experienced. You can live like this, leastways until your body gives out from starvation. Or you can choose to come back to life. It's up to you."

Doc Pyle gave Mary time to process what he had said. You could have heard a pin drop in the room, it was so quiet.

"What's it going to be, Mary?" Doc said. "You going to live or you want to die?"

At least ten seconds went by, and I wanted to shout that, of course, she wants to live. Ma knows me, and she gave me a warning glance to keep my mouth shut. Finally, Mary said real soft, "I don't know."

"That works for me," Doc Pyle said. "Means you need time to think about it, and you haven't been able to think since your brain shut down. So, this is what we're going to do. How about we give you a week to think on life or death?

Mary looked at Doc somewhat skeptically. Seems to me that's the first time I saw some expression in her face. Not much, but at least a little. The doc noticed it, too.

"I want you to stay up here for the rest of today. You can sleep in the bed or look out the window, whatever you like. Jane or Lizzie will bring you some tea, and give you some tonic that I'm going to leave with them. For supper, they're going to bring you a hunk of bread with jam. You must eat all of it, and nothing else. Will you promise me to do that?"

Mary hesitantly nodded her agreement. I couldn't help myself but to remind Doc that she was starving. Certainly, she needs more than a piece of bread.

"The woman hasn't eaten in quite a while, and her brain's been shut down," he said. "Her gut won't work if she gets too much food all at once. The bread's easy to digest, and the jam has fruit and sugar to help build up her strength. We'll take it one day at a time."

"What about tomorrow?" Ma asked.

"Start with a little oatmeal for breakfast, with cream and sugar on it," Doc said. "Maybe a roasted potato with butter for supper. That's all. Next day, same thing unless she asks for more. No overfeeding. And you'll be giving her a spoon of tonic three times a day."

"What's in the tonic?" I asked.

"It's a tincture of Echinacea, an herb that has medicinal value. They weren't too keen on homeopathic remedies when I was in medical school, but I've been studying about natural treatments on my own. In Mary's case, it seems to make more sense to prescribe the tonic, rather than the traditional use of bloodletting or salves."

"When should she come downstairs?" I asked.

"It's up to Mary," Doc said. "The fresh air would be good for you, Mary, if you want to sit on the porch. But when you feel the need to be alone, you come on up here and close the door. Your husband can be with you at night."

Mary suddenly squirmed, vehemently shaking her head. It was evident she wanted no part of being with Pa's brother. Of course, I don't blame her. I don't like him much either.

Ma and Doc locked eyes, both immediately recognizing Mary's aversion. "Perhaps your husband could sleep in the loft over the kitchen with Will and Benjamin," Ma said. "Leastways until you feel better."

Mary relaxed, and nodded her agreement. Doc Pyle put his equipment back in his valise, and brought out a glass vial of his tonic. Ma handed him the spoon from Mary's oatmeal, and he filled it to the brim with the clear amber liquid, telling Mary to open wide. The pungent concoction took her breath away as it went down.

"Don't leave this where the young'uns can find it," Doc warned. "And don't give more than three spoons a day. It has spirits in it, and it's meant only for Mary."

"Then you'd better hide it in your room," I said to Ma. "Pa's brother's been hankering for whiskey."

"Don't see why he'd need to know what's in it," Doc said as he picked up his bag.

"I'll be back in a week, Mary. You can be thinking about the answer to my question. Do you want to live or die?"

Chapter Eleven

It wasn't but a couple of evenings later when Ma and Pa were relaxing on the back porch, sipping their coffee after supper. I was washing the dishes, and Ellie had taken Julie upstairs to get her ready for bed. Matt and little George were romping in a pile of hay by the field, while Will and Benjamin got a tanning lesson from Pa's brother over by the barn. Looked to me like they were vigorously scrubbing the back of an animal pelt, possibly a raccoon.

It was a sultry dusk, after an unseasonably hot June day, the kind of day that made me wish we had a summer kitchen off from the house. I had the windows and door open to try to get some air circulating in the stifling cabin, and couldn't help but hear Ma and Pa's conversation from outside.

"How long you think Mary's going to need Will and Ben's room?" Pa asked.

"Don't rightly know. But it seems to me there's a slight improvement in Mary's condition. Wouldn't be surprised if she wants to start coming downstairs, maybe sitting out here for a spell each day."

"You think she's going to be well enough for me to tell George that they're soon going to have to get their own place?"

"Can't say that she will or won't. What's your problem with them staying here? Seems to me, kin need to care for their own."

"Couldn't swear on a bible that George is my brother," Pa said. I just about dropped the plate I was drying, because I've never heard Pa say anything about that. And I've been thinking the same thing.

"You're being obstinate, William," Ma said in her gentle voice. "Just because you don't remember him, doesn't mean he's not your ma's boy."

"There's nothing about him to make me think of my ma, or even my pa. He doesn't look like either of them. Even when Pappy took to drinking in his older years, he never acted like this one. It's like he was brought up in the wilderness."

"He's been wandering out west for nearly forty years. That's just about your whole lifetime. No telling what you'd be like if you lived among Indians and wild animals."

"It's no matter. If he's my brother, he was raised right, and you can't soon forget that. I don't want him influencing my boys, or hanging around my girls. Just think about it, Jane. Even if the man is come near 60 years old, he's still got needs. His missus doesn't want him in her bed, he's going to be hankering after Lizzie. She's almost a woman now."

"That's ridiculous, William. No man in his right mind would be thinking that way about his brother's daughter."

"I tell you, this man's not my brother. I know it as clearly as I know my own name. I want him out of my house and off my land."

"Well, Mary can't go anywhere right now. It wouldn't be the godly thing to do to send her and him off. There's a chance she'll get better. I won't hear tell of it, William."

They must have both been thinking, because there was suddenly no more talking as I put the dried dishes in the pantry.

After washing off the table, I lit the candles and lanterns, then lugged the big kettle to the counter and scraped out the residue from the bottom into the pigs' slop bucket. I poured the soapy dishpan water into it and sloshed it all around, perusing all the while about Pa's words.

How would anyone rightly be able to prove that this man isn't Pa's brother? Mary doesn't talk, at least not much, and even if she could, she wouldn't have known George's family. Maybe Ma was right that Pa was being silly. How else would this man know to say he was George Mitchell from Yellow Springs? He even spoke about sleeping up there in the loft when he was a boy. Can't say that we'll ever know the truth.

Finally, Pa said, "I can tell the man he's got to sleep in the barn. It probably won't make any difference to him."

"That wouldn't be right," Ma said. "But I have a notion. If we added a wall in the den with a doorway through to the hall, we'd have an extra room downstairs. We don't really need the den to be the whole length of the big house, and it wouldn't hurt to have an extra bedroom."

"Tarnation, woman! It's farming season. I don't have the time to be building walls or doors."

"We could hire it out to the Mennonite carpenters," Ma said. "Then, Mary can sleep there, and when she's ready, her husband can join her. In the meantime, Will and Benjamin can get back in their room and your brother, or whoever he is, can sleep in the loft."

Pa was quiet for a few moments, probably thinking through the details. That's just how he is before he makes any decision.

"Guess it wouldn't hurt to get a cost on building a room," Pa said. "But it only takes care of one problem. How do I find out if he is who he says he is?"

"We could have a pig roast for the 4th of July," Ma said. Invite all the families that knew your ma and pa, as well as your brothers. Most of the old folks are gone now, just like Mammy and Pappy. But their young'uns are grown up, even older than you, with most of them still living on their homesteads. Get them all talking around the fire pit. Surely someone would remember George as a boy."

"You know why I married you?" Pa said.

"Because I'm the prettiest girl you ever did see?"

"Surely so. But you're smart, too. Smartest and prettiest girl I ever knew."

Pa must have tried to kiss Ma, because she said, "You stop that right now, William Mitchell. I'll have you know that the children are around. In fact, where are Matt and little George? It's past their bedtime."

Pa tugged on the bell, and the young'uns came running out from the darkness of the field, into the glow of light from the kitchen. For that matter, Will and Benjamin also joined them on the porch, though I noticed that the old man was still sitting out by the barn. He must have lit up the small butt of a cigar, because I could see the flicker of a red ember on the end of it.

"You'd best visit the outhouse, Matt and George. Then go on up to bed," Ma said. "Ben will tuck you in."

"Already peed in the field," Matt said. "We found a toad out there, and we were seeing if it would hop away if it got piss on it."

"I don't want to listen to that kind of talk," Ma said. "If I hear it again, you'll get your mouth washed out with soap. Give me a kiss good-night. And don't forget to say your prayers."

The boys barreled by me, racing Ben to see who could be first up the stairs. I went out and sat on the rocking chair next to Ma.

"The kettle's ready to dump and rinse at the pump, Will," I said. He went in to do his chore, and Ma leaned over to say to me, "Guess you heard what Pa and I were talking about."

"I wasn't trying to eavesdrop, but I heard some of it."

"Don't be mentioning it to the boys. Most of it's between Pa and the man."

"I won't," I said. "But I agree with Pa. That old man isn't his brother. I feel it in my bones."

Pa reached over and put his hand on mine. "You're like me, Lizzie. We know how to listen to our gut. But, your ma, here. Now she's different. She listens to her brain and her heart more so. We need to learn from her."

"Don't you worry, Pa. We'll find out who that man is, one of these days. I feel certain of it."

Pa nodded. "I hope you're right, Lizzie. Guess there's a specter of truth in everything. We just need to watch and wait for its appearance.

Chapter Twelve

On Saturday morning after breakfast, Pa told Will and Ben they could go with him to Jacob Moser's place in the wagon. Moser's a carpenter and a Mennonite. Pa hired him to lead the construction on the big house some years back, and he'd be the best craftsman to now put up a wall in the den.

After determining the cost, and checking to see when Moser's available for the job, Pa and the boys planned to visit other homesteads to tell them about our Independence Day gathering. They'd also bring the grain they'd been threshing all week to the grist mill.

I wanted to go along, too, but Ma said I was needed to help with the pickling she'd be doing to get ready for the 4th of July festivities. My visit with Emily Price was evidently going to have to wait until after the holiday.

Matt and little George were sent out to pick cucumbers, beans, onions, and radishes from the garden, and warned that there'd better not be any shenanigans. Most of the crop were still immature, and Ma needed as many vegetables as the boys could harvest.

Pa's brother, or whoever he is, said he'd be hunting for the day, which was fine with me. He's not much good for doing anything else, and I'd be glad not to have to listen to his hacking or smell his stinking cigar.

While Ma went upstairs to feed and dress Mary, Ellie and I cleaned up after breakfast. Julie soon tired of sitting in her high chair, so I let her down to play in her corner. A couple of spoons, a pot, and a bunch of wooden blocks that Pa had made for her last winter kept her occupied, with enough clatter to wake up the dead. That's fine, though. Better to know what Julie's up to since she's now at that age you can't let her out of your sight.

I was bringing back fresh water from the pump when Ma returned to the kitchen. Surprisingly, Mary was following her, looking nice in Ellie's stays, petticoats, and apron, with one of Ma's caps over her braided hair. She still appeared peaked and so very thin, but her eyes had lost some of that glassy stare that we'd come to expect.

Ma noticed Mary's gaze toward Julie, and I wondered if seeing the baby would trigger another emotional outburst. Before there was any chance of it, Ma said to Mary, "This here's my baby, Julia Ann. We call her Julie. I was thinking you might want to help by keeping an eye on her for me."

"I had me a baby girl once," Mary remarked haltingly as she sat on Pappy's rocking chair. "I called her Bridget."

"That's a pretty name," Ma said softly. Mary nodded, but she didn't say any more.

Matt brought in a bowl of small cucumbers that I set about washing and slicing for pickles, while Ma made the brine and Ellie prepared the jars. "George ain't doing his share of the work," he complained, watching to see what Mary was doing, waiting to see if he got any reaction from the rest of us.

"Guess you're going to have to teach him how to do it," Ma said distractedly.

"I showed him where to dig for the onions and radishes. He seems more fixed on finding worms."

"Maybe you could play a counting game with George," I said. "See who finds the most onions or the most radishes."

"What's the reward going to be?"

Ma gave Matt one of her looks. "You don't get a prize for doing what you're supposed to be doing. Now go on out there and bring me what I need before you get a swat on your behind."

"I can help the young'uns," Mary said, hardly audible with all the racket that Julie was making.

"If that's what you want to be doing, that'll be fine," Ma said calmly, though her eyes showed me that she was surprised with Mary's offer. "You come in if you get tuckered."

So, that's how we knew that Mary was on the mend. Mind you, she still has quite a way to go to be well, but I figure, she must be choosing to live. Doc Pyle's going to be pleased that his tonic is working.

By the time we heard the lids ping, signaling that the prepared jars of cucumber pickles had sealed, Matt returned with the bowl of onions and radishes. The vegetables were immature and rather small, but still fine for pickling.

"That's all of them that's ready," Matt said as he handed the container to Ma. "The lady said so."

"You can call her Missus Mary," Ma said, examining the yield. "Is she doing all right?"

"Guess so. She ain't complaining. Leastwise, she's helping George get the beans that are ripe. Can we play now?"

"Not yet. You boys can go berry picking. There should be raspberries and blackberries on the bushes over by the tree line. The ones getting the most sun might be ready now."

"They are," Matt agreed. "George ate some yesterday."

"And you didn't?"

"Well, maybe one or two, but he had the most."

"Get as many as you can find that are ripe. And don't be eating them all or we won't be having a cobbler tonight. You can tell Missus Mary I said she should come in and set a while."

Ma dumped the vegetables from Matt's bowl on the table, wiped it out, then returned it to him for the berries. It looked to me that we'd only have enough onions and radishes to fill one jar, maybe two at best. I peeled the onions while Ellie washed the radishes, cutting the ends off them as we went along.

"How'd you learn to be such a good cook, Ma?" I asked.

"Same as you're doing. Watching and helping."

"It's not like that for me. You and Ellie seem to enjoy it. I don't." I rinsed off the onions and put them into the jar, ready for the brine.

"Just takes practice," Ma said as she poured the pungent liquid, almost to the brim. The aroma of vinegar, cloves, and peppercorns made my mouth water with anticipation for the tasty pickled vegetables. "Besides, you can't eat much if you don't cook."

"It seems like such a waste of time," I said. "A woman spends all her day in the kitchen, fixing the food, preparing the meals. Men-folk just come in and sit themselves at the table, waiting to eat."

"That's how it's supposed to be," Ellie said, somewhat righteously. "A good wife makes a home for the family."

"Don't know why it's got to be like that. Women can do other things besides cooking and making babies."

"You'll feel differently when you find a good man and settle down," Ma said. "Not many other choices unless you marry into wealth."

"I can make my own way. Don't need a husband telling me what to do and when to do it."

Ma shushed Ellie before she'd say something that would get me riled up. With a firm tone, she said to me, "While you're bellyaching about it, get some potatoes and carrots out of the pantry. We'll be making a stew for supper if your pa's brother brings back any suitable meat from his hunting. If he doesn't, we'll kill one of them chickens at the coop."

I would probably have sassed Ma about the misnomer of the old man, but Mary joined us with an apron full of beans. She dumped them on the table and began cutting off the ends.

"Why, thank you, Mary," Ma said, handing her a bowl of water to soak the vegetables. "Are Matt and George picking the berries like I said?"

She nodded in the affirmative, glancing at Julie. "Guess you know the babe is sleeping," Mary said.

All of us turned our attention to Julie, none of us realizing that she had curled up next to her blanket on the comforter, thumb in her mouth, and was sound asleep.

We were even more surprised to watch Mary get down on the floor with Julie, cradle her in an embrace, and close her eyes.

Chapter Thirteen

Independence Day dawned with barely a wisp of clouds in the sky, a pale sliver of the waning moon just visible over the tree tops. Pa and the older boys went out earlier than usual, starting the fire in the pit on the other side of the barn before doing their chores.

Late yesterday, Uncle whoever-he-is George took charge of killing the hog that Pa had designated, spending much of the evening gutting the innards and taking out the spinal cord, cracking bones so the pig would lie flat.

Matt and young George were mesmerized by the gory removal of glands and silver skin lining the ribs, even reaching their little hands into the center cavity to tug out parts that the old man said had to be discarded. The boys were disgustingly bloody before Ma eventually told them to get washed up and go to bed.

After breakfast, Pa, the old man, Will, and Benjamin went out to start the barbecue. Pa checked on the embers in the fire pit, pushed them to the side, and added additional hardwood for burning.

I watched from the kitchen window as the four of them lugged the hog from the springhouse, laying it on the ground in the rock encased pit, and surrounding it with red hot cinders.

Later, Will and Benjamin helped Pa carry out two long wooden work tables from the barn. Ma was directing where to place them in the yard for guests to put any side dishes they'll bring to the festivities.

Once Missus Mary's husband was out of the house, she came downstairs wearing her own dress and petticoats that Ma had washed for her. She dished herself a bowl of porridge and took it with her to the rocking chair that now has a permanent place by Julie's comforter.

Doc Pyle was pleased when he visited Mary the other day. In just a week, her eyes had lost that glassy stare, and there was some semblance of color in her cheeks. Doc told Ma she was doing right, letting Mary get used to being around us, not urging her to do anything she doesn't want to do.

I noticed that Mary takes herself off to Will and Ben's room upstairs if there's any chance her vile husband would be around. Not that I blame her. Strange thing is, only Mary, Pa, and I have such an aversion to him. Ma and Ellie show him kindness, and the boys appreciate learning the things he teaches them.

Young Julie seems to like that Mary sits with her just about every morning. Ma says it gives her peace of mind so we can do our work without worrying what trouble the baby could get into.

I've been thinking that Julie's chatter might somehow get Mary talking. Julie doesn't say much that can be understood yet, most of it being gibberish except for some simple words. But she likes nursery rhymes, often mimicking any action with her hands and arms. Of course, *Hickory, dickory, dock* is her favorite, but we can't help laughing when she stands up and falls down with *Humpty Dumpty.*

"Humpty Dumpty sat on a wall," I prompted as I dried the dishes. Julie stood up, hunching like she was going to sit. "Humpty Dumpty had a great fall." "Fawwl," Julie said as she plopped to the floor. "All the king's horses, and all the king's men, couldn't put Humpty back together again." Julie rolled around on her comforter, flailing her pudgy little arms and legs. Even Mary seemed to smile at Julie's antics.

After I washed out the kettle, Ellie began preparing the baked beans that had been soaking in water overnight. While the beans were boiling, she put the other ingredients together, adding brown sugar, chopped onion, dry mustard, salt, and pepper. Once the beans are cooked, she'll add molasses and the bowlful of spices to simmer all day in the hot embers of the kitchen fireplace. As soon as a ham hock is done enough to be pulled off the roasted pig, we'll add that to the pot.

Ma and Ellie made a few loaves of bread and two apple pies yesterday while I was giving Matt and George their lessons, so all that was left for us to prepare for the cookout was coleslaw and potato salad. I set out to cut the cabbage and peel the potatoes while Ma made the dressing.

"What time do you think folks will start arriving?" I asked as I got the potatoes out of the pantry.

"Your pa told them any time after noon," Ma said. "Not sure exactly how many will be here, but it doesn't really matter. There's going to be plenty of food with what we made and some they'll bring. Of course, the pig won't be ready 'til supper time."

"I can't remember when's the last time we had everyone over," I said while scraping a large spud over the slop bowl. "Maybe after the house raising?"

"Might have been," Ma said, looking out the window to check on the boys. "Didn't feel much up to it after Dan passed. Next thing I knew, three more babies came along. I'm finally getting my energy back. Couldn't do this, though, if it weren't for you and Ellie."

We were all surprised to hear Mary speak up. "You lost a boy?" she asked Ma.

"Two of 'em. Buried out back by the big oak tree."

The two women gazed at each other with an unstated understanding of what each had experienced. They were linked by the silent connection held by all who have lost a child, a bond etched in their hearts and souls.

"Don't know how you can ever get over that," Mary said softly, eyes holding deep regret.

"You never forget your babies," Ma said. "I'm lucky I've got mine right out there in the yard where I can feel the earth they're layin' in. Better than my ma and pa and brothers, fed to the fish in the sea."

"They got the pox on the ship to America," I explained to Mary. "Ma's whole family died. Sailors just threw them over the side after they stopped breathing. You got any kin?"

Mary shook her head. "Don't know if I do. But my boy is buried out there where we lived. His name was Jonathan."

Ma went over to Mary and embraced her. Quietly she said, "Tomorrow after all the hoopla, we're going out to the big tree and we'll make a grave for your Jonathan there. Then, you and me, we can sit out there on the grass and talk to our babies."

Mary nodded her agreement, and squeezed Ma's slender fingers in her bony hands. All the while I was thinking that it was a kind of blessing that Mary ended up here with us. Except for Pa, Ma never really had a friend, leastwise not after she was grown. Both women are about the same age, and life hasn't been easy on either of them.

How was Ma able to overcome her sorrows, I wondered, while Mary's whole body closed in on itself, locked in a cocoon of grief. I knew, then and there, that Ma would be the one to help Mary find her spirit.

"Now that Julie fell asleep," Ma said to Mary, "maybe you'd like to help Lizzie with the potatoes. When the folks start arriving and Julie awakens, I'd be grateful if you'll keep watch of her on the back porch. You don't have to be talking to anyone if you don't want to."

I went out to the pump to get water for the kettle, while Mary settled herself at the table. By the time I returned, she was scraping and peeling those spuds like there was no tomorrow. We must have done ten pounds of them, then cut up some onions and celery for when the potatoes were cooked.

Ma finished dressing the coleslaw, and told Ellie she could start making the barbecue sauce from butter, vinegar, brown sugar, salt, and pepper. I was to sweeten the tea and put the large pot of it on one of the tables outside, next to Pa's cider.

I no sooner had the beverages arranged when the first buckboard arrived with Joseph Holman, his wife Sarah, and their four boys. Pa went over to welcome them, and called for Will to help unload the barrel of corn whiskey they brought.

There was no doubt in my mind who would be the first to fill his mug, slurping his spirits while he watched over the roasting pig.

Chapter Fourteen

By mid-afternoon, twelve families had joined us for the festivities. Buckboards and buggies were parked all along our drive, while the horses were led to the back pasture to graze during their respite. Each of our guests brought blankets and stools to sit upon, food to share, as well as cups and mugs for their beverages.

Cheers were called with each new arrival, and I could hear the mothers remind their children to mind their manners. It didn't take the men long to pour themselves some of Holman's whisky and join Mary's husband at the fire pit.

Will and Benjamin were put in charge of organizing games for the boys to play. They started off by making two teams, even the younger ones being assigned, and got a match of kickball going.

Ellie took it upon herself to show the girls how she cards wool. She gave each a pair of carders, and they sat in the shade on a blanket, talking and brushing the fibers.

I told Ma that I'd take charge of putting out the food and refilling bowls so she could relax with the women-folk. Most of them, including Mary, had gathered on the porch, some with their babies or little ones on laps, to share any recent gossip they might have heard.

Chicken-chested Henry Harris saw me bringing out a plate of pickled vegetables, and bounded over to ask if he could help. Seems to me like a whole heap of new pimples pocked his peach-fuzzed cheeks, stringy black hair combed behind his ears. I wasn't trying to be rude, but I had no intention of having to be beholding to him.

"Don't think there's anything else that has to be done right now," I said as I made room for the dish on the table.

Henry pushed some of the bowls closer together, which wasn't a terrible thing, but it annoyed me. I guess he's about a year older than me, probably old enough to be out with the men-folk instead of hanging around here. He gave me a penetrating look and said, "You're looking mighty fine, Lizzie."

I knew that wasn't true, and didn't have anything to say about it. Still, I nodded that I heard him as I handed him a basket of rolls Mrs. Yeager had brought.

"If you want to be useful," I said, "you could take these over to the men. They might be getting hungry."

Henry declined, saying, "They're busy talking. I'll just stay with you in case you got anything else to take out."

"I'm going to set awhile with the women," I said. "There's no need for you to be hovering around me."

"You got anyone calling on you?"

"Don't see that's any of your business."

"Guess it is," Henry replied with a grin that showed crooked teeth already looking yellowed from a lack of brushing. "I'd like to come a calling."

"Don't waste your time," I said firmly, in a tone I might use when talking to Matt. "You'd best find someone else to call on." Then I turned on my heels, most likely leaving him to wonder what bee had crawled under my bonnet.

I took myself to the porch, finding a seat next to Missus Mary. She had been watching me all along, and reached out to rest her hand on mine.

"You can do better than that one," she said in a quiet voice, almost a whisper. When I looked at her, I could see the hint of a smile, and a mite of a twinkle in her eye.

"I know, but Ma's going to have a fit if she learns I was so mean and nasty."

"Sometimes a man don't listen unless you tell him your mind real strong like. You're going to be a fine woman, Lizzie."

Amazed that Mary had put two sentences together with such kind words, I gave her hand a squeeze. It felt as if we were kindred spirits, and there was so much I wanted to ask her.

I wondered how she could have let herself marry someone to the likes of the old man. Did she ever speak her mind with him, like she was just advising me to do? Had she actually agreed to move to the plains out west where she had no kin? As much as I'd like to experience life beyond Yellow Springs, I don't think I'd ever have the courage to do what she's done in her lifetime.

My ears picked up on some of the conversation between Ma and the ladies. Mrs. Emery was saying that folks have been deciding on a name for the crossroads with the general store and grist mill. Quite a few are in favor of calling the village Kimberton, in honor of Mr. Emmor Kimber.

"He's a fine man," she added. "A Quaker and a teacher. Starting a school for girls right there in Kimberton."

"Two of our girls are enrolled at the French Creek Boarding School for Girls," Mrs. Yeager said. "Rose and Amelia. Elsewise they'd have been here today."

"Aren't they too old for schooling?" Ma asked.

"Rose is about the same age as your Lizzie. But she wants to be a teacher. She'll get some more learning, and serve as a tutor. Amelia's only 10, and that's a good enough age to start."

"They don't have time off for the holiday?"

"Mr. Kimber believes that the students learn better if they're totally immersed in their lessons. They'll have some time off in August, then again in October and April."

"Speaking of Kimber, he's also going to be the new post master," busy-body McClure said with a hint of sarcasm. "Of course, if you ask me, he's got his hands in too many pots. Heard he's even planning to build a Quaker meeting house on his land." She clucked her tongue as if she didn't approve of all Kimber's involvements.

"Lizzie was at the crossroads a couple of weeks ago," Ma said. "Went with her brother when he took the grain for milling. She told me how nice it was to see you there, Lucretia." Ma always seems to have a knack for smoothing ruffled feathers.

"Yes," Mrs. McClure added demurely. "Unfortunately, we didn't have much of an opportunity to talk, I was so busy making my purchases, but she looked lovely in her finest dress."

I wanted to tell her what a liar she was, but some of the other ladies on the porch had been gabbing with her at the store, so they knew the truth. Instead, Ma said, "Lizzie told me the new store manager is a kind young man, hired by Mr. Kimber. Recently married, too."

"Let me tell you," the gossip monger said as she brushed a piece of lint from the front of her apron. "He had that sweet girl working in the store, waiting on customers. As if she were a harlot. I just don't understand this new generation. I'm sure the girl's mother would be appalled to know that all she had taught her daughter went right out the window. Of course, she's not from around here, so who knows how she was raised."

Some of the other women nodded their heads in agreement, murmuring similar sentiments. It was obvious that Lucretia McClure is highly respected in the township, and her words were well worth heeding. I knew that she had raised eight children, David being her youngest. Still, it wouldn't surprise me if her brood harbored embarrassment about her negativity and constant disapproval.

"Emily's from West Chester," I said, almost indignantly. "That's not so far as the crow flies. And her husband was taught by Mr. Kimber at the Westtown Quaker School. Mr. Kimber thought well of him as an honest man with a quick mind in mathematics. That's why he hired him."

"That's all well and good," Mrs. McClure responded, her dark, penetrating gaze piercing me. "I hold no ill will against him. I'm just saying that a good woman belongs in the home, not running a business."

Mary squeezed my hand, a warning that it was not the time to argue with the opinionated woman. Ma also gave me one of her looks and said, "Lizzie, would you mind seeing if your pa is ready for the barbecue sauce? You can take it out to him. When you come back, some of our visitors here might be ready for a refill of sweet tea."

As an afterthought she added, "The boys look quite hot in the field. Tell Will he can take them to the pond for a swim, but he and Benjamin must keep an eye on the young'uns."

Chapter Fifteen

I carefully removed the pot of sauce from the crane with hand mitts, and set it on the table while I gave the beans a stir. After finding a ladle, I carried the pot out to where the men had gathered around the pit, their tongues loosened with liquor. Couldn't say that any of them was drunk, but they were certainly under the influence.

Even Pa was talking up a storm, not likely in normal situations, leastwise not in my experience. He paused his story when he saw me approaching, and said, "That's mighty fine, Lizzie. You can leave your wares over there by the fire where your uncle's sitting."

Pa must have noticed my furrowed brow at his mention of George as his brother, so he continued. "Enid McClure and Thomas Phillips both remember him, so there's no question about it."

Sure enough, Mr. McClure and Mr. Phillips were both fully engaged in conversation with the uncle, heartily recalling stories of years gone by.

"You remember that bear you scared off when we was out hunting?" McClure asked.

"Damn near ten feet tall when he stood on his back legs," George replied, then cleared his throat and spat on the ground.

"You got a brain mixed with popcorn and honey?" Mr. Phillips asked. "That animal was a baby, somehow got separated from his ma."

"You wouldn't know," George said with a raucous guffaw. "You and Enid run off like two frigging bush pigs."

That got all the men laughing. One of them raised his mug and said, "Cheers!" The others followed suit with a chorus of cheers while taking another swig of whiskey.

"What was the name of that dumb dog of yours?" Mr. Phillips asked George. "We'd take him out to the woods to scout out the prey, and the stupid mutt couldn't never even find his way home."

"He wasn't so smart, but he could sniff out an animal half a mile away. I need to get me a good old 'coon dog like he was."

"We're not getting any dog, George," Pa said firmly. "Had one for a long time, and just about broke everyone's spirit when he up and died."

"Loosen your buttons, Willy," George said. "I'll be getting me a dog whether you like it or not."

This time I think it was Mr. Yeager who yelled, "Cheers!" And, once again, they all slurped their draughts. Even Pa took another mouthful, though he sure didn't look happy about his interaction with old man George.

I'd about had enough of the men's banter and wanted to take my leave, but not before I asked Pa to cut me a pig hock. Putting it in my apron pocket, I walked out to the field to give Ma's message to Will. He was relieved to be done with the game, and the boys did their own cheering when they learned they were free to romp in the pond.

By the time I returned to the porch, Ma was already bringing refills of beverages to the women. I told her I'd be out to help as soon I added the ham bone to the beans.

When I filled Mrs. Yeager's glass, I asked her about Rose. Though I hadn't seen her in a long time, perhaps since their barn raising several years ago, I remembered her as a quiet type. I couldn't quite imagine her as a teacher.

"She's doing fine, Lizzie. She likes tutoring, but she's now got a suitor. Between you and me, I think she'll end up marrying before the year is out."

I told Mrs. Yeager to give her my best wishes, then moved on to refill Mrs. Harris' glass. I didn't have much to say to her, which was fine since she was deep in conversation with Mrs. McClure. I thought it best to finish my task before she could turn her attention to me and expound on Harry's supposed good qualities.

^^^

As the late afternoon sun dipped behind the tree line, the hog was declared done, and the men began pulling the meat off the bones. I rang the supper bell, and the boys straggled in from their swim, most of them soaking wet from stem to stern. They didn't seem bothered by it, no doubt figuring they'd soon dry off, though each of them was told to clean up at the pump.

Ma asked Will to carry out the pot of beans, while Ellie and I brought out the salads and pie. Everyone heaped their plates with food, and sat wherever they had a hankering.

When the eating was done, the women began to gather up the bowls from what they brought, even sharing some of the leftovers. Ma encouraged all of them to take home more of the meat, so it wouldn't go bad.

The older boys were instructed to gather the bones from the carcass and bury them in the woods. Pa said he didn't want any wild animals carousing around our place looking for food.

It was dusk by the time the last buggy departed, and we were all about done in. Ma asked Benjamin to put Matt and little George to bed, and Ellie to do the same with Julie. Will and Pa doused the fire pit to be sure all embers were out, then brought the stools and tables into the barn. Ma and I took our leftover food to the spring house so it wouldn't spoil.

Old George lit up his stub of a cigar, took a few more slugs of whiskey, and leaned his back against the wall of the barn to watch the stars come out. The rest of us joined Mary on the porch when we finished our chores.

"Don't recall ever being so tired," I said mostly to myself but loud enough the others could hear. "I surely can understand why we don't have a big gathering very often."

"What did you say to Henry Harris that got him out of sorts?" Will asked. "He stood around talking to David McClure, watching the rest of us play, then they took themselves off to explore the woods."

"Didn't have much to say at all. Just told him I wasn't interested in having him come calling on me."

Pa and Will laughed, though Ma didn't think it was so funny. "I hope you weren't rude to the boy," she said. "Before you know it, you won't be having anybody calling on you, being so particular. Come on, Mary. Let's go on up to bed before I say something I'll regret."

"Don't worry about what your ma just said," Pa told me when Ma was out of hearing range. "She's tuckered out, and rightfully so. You got plenty of time before you need to find a man you'd like to keep company with."

"Lizzie's going to end up a spinster," Will chanted, teasing me. I swatted his arm for good measure.

"I got one thing to ask you, Pa," I said. "You really believe that old man setting by the barn out there is your brother?"

"Reckon I do now that it was confirmed by McClure and Phillips."

"From what I heard, he couldn't get any of the stories straight that he told. Didn't know much about the bear they said he scared away, and he couldn't recall the name of his dog from way back when."

"He was halfway to being drunk by the time you got there to hear what he had to say, Lizzie. Sometimes facts are more important than gut feelings. We may not like it, but George over there is my brother. No doubt about it."

Chapter Sixteen

I had been reminding Ma for at least two weeks that it was about time for me to go to the general store in Kimberton to keep my promise to Emily Price. Finally, Pa announced at breakfast that Will could drive the first of our corn to the grist mill after he helped with more of the picking. Ma said I could go along, but not until I gave Matt and George their lessons.

Construction has started for the new room on the first floor of our home. Jacob Moser and his crew framed the wall dividing the den last week, and cut out the doorway to the hall. That was the only door Ma wanted, but Moser suggested adding another entrance through the den to circulate heat from the fireplace during the winter months. She and Pa talked it over for a few days, finally deciding that it made good sense.

This week, the builders completed the lathing and first layer of plaster, which now must dry and set before they can continue their work. Matt and little George had been happy to postpone their schooling while the craftsmen were working, but not quite as enthusiastic to hear that they'd be back to task this morning.

As for Pa's brother, we don't see much of him except at supper or when he's tanning his hides out by the barn. Most days he spends hunting, selling his pelts, or visiting the local taverns, whichever he has a hankering for. That sets well for Mary, who likes to help Ma with chores or keep watch over Julie, and she seems more relaxed when he's not around.

Last week, as Ma promised, she and Mary piled some stones out under the oak tree, like we did to mark the burial place of our kin. Sometimes, Mary goes out there to talk to her Jonathan, but she didn't make a grave for Bridget. She told me that she believes her baby girl is still alive, living with Indians out on the prairie. Don't rightly know, but Mary seems to have come to terms with it.

Once Matt and little George got settled with their slates at the table, I told them we were going to practice short A words by making some rhymes. I started them off with a chant.

"Short A says aaaaaa, just like in caaaaat. My word is cat." The boys had to repeat it three times while I wrote the word *cat* on each slate.

"OK, Matt," I said. "Now it's your turn."

"Short A says aaaaaa, just like aaaaapple. My word is apple." He handed me his slate for his star.

"That's excellent, Matt, but you picked a hard word, and not a rhyme. Do you think you can write *apple*?"

He picked up his chalk and wrote a-p-l.

"You got some of the letters, but not all of them," I said as I wrote the word *apple* on his slate. Let's think of things that rhyme with cat. Your turn, George."

Thus, we continued, both boys trying to surpass the other for the collection of rhymes and their achievement of gold stars. I laughed at their antics, fueling the competition between them. And yet, they learned, having fun all the while.

"How'd you get so smart, Lizzie?" Matt asked while he copied the words I had written. "How'd you learn to read and write so good?"

"Ma taught me. She did the schooling for me, Will, and Benjamin. Even Ellie, once she was old enough. Ma went to a real Quaker school before she married Pa."

"Did Pa go to school?"

"Not likely. But he had his lessons at home, just like you."

"You should be a teacher, Lizzie. I mean, like, a real one in a school."

"I never thought it'd be possible since any teachers I ever heard about are men. Then I learned about Rose Yeager. She's my age, going to the new school for girls at the crossroads. Her ma said she's tutoring some of the students there. I've been thinking I'd like to do that as well."

"You should ask about it when you go to the general store today," Matt said as he used the rag to erase his slate.

"Don't know who I'd ask. Besides, it's not like I can go off to school. Ma needs me here."

My emphatic statement seemed to end the conversation, and I told the boys they could go out and help Ellie in the garden. While I put the slates and chalk on the shelf, I thought about Matt's advice to inquire about the new school. Emily might well be the best person to ask.

^^^

Will dropped me off at the front of the general store before he drove the buckboard across the street to the grist mill. I carried a basket of yarn that Ellie had spun, enough to barter for sugar and salt. With the other hand, I deftly lifted my petticoats so I wouldn't trip going up the front steps.

Emily was busy sweeping the far end of the porch, her underskirt pinned up to her waist so she could maneuver the broom under each rocking chair. I noticed her petticoat had been made of gingham, not plain muslin like mine, but the prettiest cobalt blue with white checks that matched the summer sky. Her stays were dyed a similar color, encasing her narrow waistline. Emily pushed some errant strands of blond hair back under her cap, then glanced up to see my admiring gaze.

"I've been wondering if you'd ever be back," she said with a smile that enhanced the dimples in her cheeks.

I always felt that my face would be much more attractive if I had a feature to distinguish it, rather than plain freckles across my upturned nose. When I smile, I'm left with chipmunk cheeks, leastwise it seems like it to me.

"We've been busy on the farm," I explained. "One of our cornfields came ready for harvest, and Will brought the first batch to get some cornmeal made for Ma. That's why I could come today."

"Well, let's go in and get a cup of tea," Emily said as she unpinned her petticoat, rearranging the folds to fall gently over her stylish leather shoes. "We've got some time before the next arrival of the stagecoach."

"I'd like that," I said, pulling open the large oak door. "I'll give Mr. Price my order and this basket of wool to barter."

"You must have read my mind," Emily exclaimed. "Two customers were looking for yarn just this week, and we had none. Now I know where we can get it locally."

"We have plenty of it. My sister, Ellie, loves to spin. I'll tell Ma you'll be looking for some more."

Emily politely interrupted her husband who was busy with a customer to tell him that we'd be in the back room after we made some tea from the kettle in the hearth. I told him I'd be needing sugar and salt to purchase, and placed my basket on the counter.

Other than two old geezers chewing the fat while sitting on the rockers by the large mantle, there was a definite lull in business since the last time I'd been here.

"Glad to see you back, Lizzie," Joe said with an earnest smile. "Emily's been hoping you'd be coming to visit."

Chapter Seventeen

Emily led me through the double doors in the rear of the store. The room is more like a large pantry or storeroom, piled high with cartons and barrels along the walls. In the center of the room, there's a square wooden table with two hardback chairs. Emily motioned for me to sit there.

"You came at a good time. Mornings are real busy, as well as late afternoons when the coach arrives. Joe set up this room for a place we can put up our feet if we get a chance to take a break."

"Did you get home for the 4th of July?"

"We did, but it was way too short a visit. Still, if it weren't for the kindness of Mr. Kimber, we might not have been able to go. The stagecoach was full, with folks wanting to go to the county courthouse for the fireworks. That good man lent us his horse and buggy for the entire day."

"You got a farm out there in West Chester?"

"Had one 'til my father got killed. Kicked by a stallion right in the heart. My mother sold most of the land, but kept the big house, not far from the center of town. She takes in boarders now, and makes baked goods for anyone who wants to buy them. She said she's making ends meet for herself and my two sisters still at home."

"Don't know what Ma would do if my pa wasn't there to provide for us. Of course, my brothers Will and Benjamin are getting old enough to do the farming, though Will doesn't like it. He'd rather be a businessman.

"How many children in your family?"

"There's seven of us. Two boys died young. So, now we got four boys and three girls. Little Julie's still a toddler."

"My mother never remarried after my father died. She said she was too busy raising three girls to be looking for a man. If you ask me, she's content with her independence. What about that uncle and his missus that came on the stage looking for your place? Are they any help?"

"That's a whole other story," I said, rolling my eyes. "Only thing good about it is Missus Mary. She was real sick, but Doc Pyle fixed her up with a tonic. She's still skinny, though she's eating now, and she helps Ma with chores to earn her keep. Fact is, she and Ma get along good. I've come to really like her."

"I didn't take to her husband," Emily said, sipping her tea. "Not just because he stunk like a polecat, but he didn't treat her nice at all."

"I still can't believe that he's Pa's brother. Pa didn't take to him either, but Mr. McCabe and Mr. Phillips said it was him. They remembered him from when they were boys. Pa told me I should just accept the fact."

"Does he help with the farming?"

"Doesn't lift a finger. Only thing he does is hunt for animals and tan their hides. Trades the pelts for whiskey. He's drunk as a skunk most nights."

"What's Missus Mary say about that?"

"She doesn't pay him any heed. Won't even let him sleep in her bed. Not that I blame her. I wouldn't let him come near me if I was married to the likes of him."

"Maybe she never shared a bed with him. Some women aren't interested, though I can't imagine why not."

"She must've been with him some time ago, because she had two children when they lived on the prairie out west. The boy got scalped, and the Indians took away the baby girl. That's why Mary wasn't talking. The doc said she wasn't tetched after all, just that her brain shut down, most likely because she couldn't bear to remember such a terrible experience."

"That's real sad," Emily said. "Is she talking more now?"

"Some. Not a lot. More to Ma, I think. One of these days, I'm going to ask her why she ever married George Mitchell. It doesn't make sense to me."

The little bell at the front door of the store tinkled someone's arrival, and Emily peeked through the double doors to see if she was needed. I took a last swig of my tea, and told her I should take my leave, but I first wanted to ask about Mr. Kimber's school across the road.

"I'm not the person to give you any particulars," Emily said. "But Mr. Kimber's daughter, Abigail, just came in. She and her mother, Susanna, both teach there. They call her Abby."

Abby looks to be about my age, maybe a year or two younger. She's dressed plainly, in the Quaker style, her dark hair parted in the middle, and pinned into a bun at the nape of her neck under her cap. She has wide-set eyes and a thin, straight nose, giving her an austere countenance. Yet her features soften greatly when she smiles.

"This here's Lizzie Mitchell," Emily said to Abby. "She has some questions about your father's school."

"I'm pleased to meet thee, Lizzie," Abby said warmly, reaching out to take my hand. "Art thou interested in the school for thyself or someone else?"

"I'm wanting to know how I can become a teacher or a tutor at the school."

"How much schooling have thee?"

"I was home schooled by my mother, who was educated at a Quaker school in Philadelphia. Now I give lessons to my two younger brothers."

"That's fine," Abby said. "What dost thou know of the French Creek Boarding School for Girls?"

"I know it's just been started by your father. Right there in the house across the road. Guess it doesn't matter about your faith to go there, because Mrs. Yeager said two of her daughters are enrolled, and they aren't Quaker. She said that Rose wants to be a teacher, just like me."

"I feel the same way," Abby said. "Like thee, my mother taught me. Now I help her at the school by teaching reading to the younger girls."

Several customers had entered the store, one woman standing by the millinery counter, trying on bonnets. I thought the one in her hand was the prettiest thing I ever did see, though I wasn't as impressed with the plain straw hat covering every strand of her braided auburn hair.

Emily excused herself, saying she'd best be getting back to work. I told her I'd be paying for my wares shortly, then I returned to my conversation with Abby.

"Would I be eligible to teach?"

"We have no positions presently, mostly since we don't yet have the enrollment to support hiring. My father teaches arithmetic, as that's his specialty. He wrote a classroom book on the subject. My mother instructs the students in grammar, composition, and penmanship. Among the three of us, we have the basics in reading, writing, and arithmetic. We hope to add sciences such as botany and astronomy through the year."

Abby must have noticed my crestfallen countenance, my pipedream of becoming a teacher crushed. As I was thanking her for her time, she interjected, "Quite honestly, Lizzie, the best opportunity to advance as a teacher would come from within our school. That's been my father's experience, and he plans to continue the precedence. If thou enrolled as a student, and demonstrated excellence in thy studies, thou could be asked to tutor the younger girls. Possibly even asked to stay on to teach when thou wouldst complete the curriculum."

"How much does it cost to attend the school?"

"Our fee is $75.00 per year. That includes thy room and board. Half is due upon enrollment, the other $37.50 during the first month at school."

"Oh, my!" I exclaimed. "That's quite expensive. I don't know that my father could afford it."

"It's quite reasonable considering it would provide an opportunity to advance thine own education. In time, should thou be hired as a teacher, there might be income to be sent back to thy family."

"When would I be admitted?"

"We'll be having a two-week break in August. I'd suggest waiting until after that time."

"You've given me much to think about," I said, wondering how I'd ever even approach the topic with Ma and Pa.

Abby must have read my mind, because she added that my parents could make an appointment to meet with her parents to discuss the admission requirements.

Once again, I thanked her and told her that I'd let her know, one way or another, whether I'll be attending the French Creek Boarding School.

I turned with the intention of collecting my order at the counter, clumsily bumping into a tall, strapping young man who was studying a saddle and bridle offered for sale. The intrusion caught me off guard, and I must have twisted in a way to get my underskirts wrapped around my legs.

Abby reached out to try to catch me but, before I knew it, I had literally fallen into the fine-looking fellow's strong arms. Blushing, I extricated myself, apologizing profusely for my clumsiness.

"That's quite all right," he said with a twinkle in his eye. "It's not every day that I have a chance to hold a pretty girl in my arms."

I studied his face as I composed myself. I wouldn't call him handsome, as a dandy might be. Rather, he's clean-shaven with nice features, most of all his hazel eyes. His hair and eye brows are dark brown, well-shaped, and his bottom lip has a bit of fullness to it. I'd say he's a couple of years older than I am, but not too much. I put out my hand to greet him.

"You're very kind," I said, somewhat awkwardly. "I'm Lizzie Mitchell from Yellow Springs. This here's Abby Kimber."

"Pleased to meet you, Lizzie. I'm Thomas Hawks. Please call me Tom. Abby knows me already, as I'm apprenticing with the blacksmith across the road."

"Good to see thee again, Tom. If there's time later, my father would like thee to take a look at our mare's hoof. He thinks she caught a pebble."

"Be glad to do so," Tom said, with a most delightful smile.

"I'd best be gathering my things," I said distractedly. My legs didn't seem to want to do my bidding, but I knew that Will was probably waiting for me out front.

I gave Tom my most demure pose, which wasn't very practiced, and said, "I'm very happy to have met you both. Enjoy the rest of your day."

Though Emily was still busy with the hat customer, she glanced my way and winked at me. Mr. Price told me that the wool had covered the cost of the sugar and salt, and he handed me a bag of each.

I was just hoping I could get out the door and down the steps without tripping.

Chapter Eighteen

I couldn't get Tom Hawks out of my mind. Decidedly, I was smitten, yet felt that he must think of me as a schoolgirl, and an especially clumsy one at that. In bed at night, I imagined every romantic scenario I could think of. He would ask where I lived, then ride his hefty steed with the exquisite saddle he was eyeing at the general store to come calling.

Of course, he'd have to ask Pa's permission, but he'd have done something nice so Pa would think highly of him. And Ma, who's always hospitable, would welcome him and invite him to set awhile, maybe offering him sweet tea on the back porch.

Perhaps Tom and I would walk through the woods hand in hand, like Ma and Pa sometimes do, stopping to toss pebbles in the creek or watch the sunset. We'd share our innermost feelings, and never run out of conversation.

During the day, however, my dreams faded like a specter that disappeared with the rising sun. Surely, Tom had seen that I'm plain, not as pronounced as Abby, but having none of the striking characteristics that Emily exhibits. Her lovely dimples, blond hair, and tiny waistline would attract any man, not that she flaunts her beauty.

I decided that the first thing I'd conquer is my unruly hair, and maybe my waistline. I could forego second helpings of stew, and eat fewer slices of bread with jam. I wanted pretty petticoats, not the ugly muslin variety that was the hallmark of a farm girl. Somehow, I had to convince Ma that we should buy the pretty pink gingham.

Lost in my thoughts, I shucked the corn for supper on the stoop of the back porch, tugging at the husks, then carefully removing all the strands of silk. The clean ears went into my basket, while the remnants would go to the fire pit for burning the next time Pa cooked a large hunk of meat.

I had to think of a way to earn money, first to make myself more presentable, then to pay my way to go to the French Creek Boarding School. Emily said her ma sold baked goods to make ends meet. I never took to cooking, but maybe I could learn to make sweet treats to sell at the general store.

Another possibility might be to practice spinning yarn. Ma had taught me long ago, but I found it to be a boring labor. Still, it might be worth taking it up again, if I could make money doing so.

"For heavens' sake, child," Ma said as she stood at the doorway to the kitchen. "What's taking so long with the corn? Your pa's going to be wanting his supper before it turns dark, and you're lollygagging out there."

"The corn's done," I said, standing to brush the silken threads off my apron.

"That's fine, then. Water's already in the kettle hanging by the fire. Put the cobs in and cover the pot, and be careful of your skirts when you're reaching over the flame. Mary and I are going to set awhile on the porch, the kitchen's so blasted hot. You can bring Julie out when you're done."

Ellie was making a vinegar dressing for the garden salad while I got the corn cooking. A whiff of the tangy apple cider, as she mixed it with a little sugar, herbs, and cooking oil, reached my nose. "That smells good," I said. "You'll have to teach me how to make it."

"It's the same as Ma's usual recipe. I just change out the spices to give it a different flavor."

"That's pretty smart. How'd you know to do that?"

"I like to try different ingredients to see how they taste when they're mixed together. Sometimes it's to my liking, other times not so much. I enjoy this combination the most."

Ellie seemed pleased about my compliment. A little sweet talk goes a long way when a person's looking for a favor, as I'll be when I ask her to let me spin some wool.

In the meantime, I told Julie to bring what she wanted from her playthings as we'd be going outside. She gathered her rag doll, and toddled with me through the back door, heading right over to hand it to Mary. It wasn't long before Julie settled on Mary's lap, twirling her hair and sucking her thumb. I sat in the rocking chair next to Ma.

"What's making you so dreamy eyed?" she asked while swatting a fly that landed on her apron. "You've been brushing that hair of yours 'til it's about ready to fall out."

"Nothing. Just trying to make it look nice."

"It'd do better if you let me braid it for you."

As a child, I hated the time it took to stand still while Ma fixed my hair. Eventually, she tired of clashing with me about it. It might not be a bad idea to let her try it again.

"I don't want braids hanging down. Can you do them up for me like you wear yours?"

"Go get the brush and pins. We've got time right now."

So, there we sat, Ma brushing and twisting, taming the wayward strands into an attractive and more mature style. "I need to earn some money," I said as she yanked and tugged.

"What for?"

"I want to buy some of that pink gingham for a petticoat."

"What's gotten into you? Ever since you went to the store the other day you've been acting strange. Is that girl you met putting notions in your head?"

"Emily's real nice, Ma. You'd like her. She never said a word about my appearance. I just noticed it myself. I'd like to wear pretty clothes, like she does."

"You can't be fashioning yourself into someone else," Ma said. "You've always been your own person. That's what makes you so special."

"I met another girl at the store, a little younger than I am. Abby Kimber. Her pa runs the boarding school."

"And you want to be like her, too?"

"No. She's Quaker and dresses plain. Her features aren't real attractive until she smiles. Then she looks kindly."

"So, you decided that you'd rather be seen like Emily, not Abby?" Ma asked with another tug on my hair.

"I guess so. I never paid any heed to what I look like, except knowing I'm not pretty like you. I'm not trying to be like Emily or Abby in looks, but I'd like to be stylish."

"Ladies like Mrs. McClure frown on ostentation."

"That doesn't mean anything to me. Like you said, Ma, I should be myself, and dress the way I want to. But I know I'd have to pay for something I'm hankering for. That's why I was thinking I'd have to earn money."

"What are you going to sell?"

"I was thinking maybe sweets, if they're not too hard to make. Emily's pa was killed by a horse, and her ma sells baked goods. I'm not very good at baking, but maybe I could make brittle and sell it at the general store."

"You'll need to make a lot of it to buy the fancy fabric."

"That's what I was thinking. But I also need $75.00."

Ma must have been taken aback, because she suddenly stopped braiding my hair, and turned me by the shoulders to face her. "Saints preserve us, child! Whatever do you want that kind of money for?"

"I'd like to be a teacher, but to do that, I'd have to get more schooling first. That's how much it costs to go to the French Creek Boarding School for Girls."

Ma gazed out over the fields, seeming to sort her ideas before she responded. I wondered what she was thinking to be taking so long, her face expressing an emotion I wasn't sure about. She brought herself back to the moment, released my shoulders, and finished braiding.

"There now. Look in the glass and see if you like it."

I walked over to the window, adjusting my stance to find a reflection. Ma had made two braids and arranged them across the top of my head in a very appealing manner. Even when I donned my cap, I looked older, like a woman, not a schoolgirl. I knew this was the appearance I was hoping for.

I gave Ma a hug, and told her that it was perfect. Even Mary smiled her approval.

"It's hard for me, Lizzie, to think of you as all grown up," Ma said. "I wasn't but a few months older than you when I married your pa. Now I know how my mother must have felt when I left home."

"It won't be the same with me. I'll come home on school breaks. Then, when I get a job as a teacher, I'll live close enough to help you out."

Ma slowly nodded her agreement. She turned to Mary and asked what she thought.

"You raised Lizzie good. She's old enough to set off on her own, even if she don't have a man. Fact is, she's probably better off. I'll tell the husband to give me some money from selling his pelts to put toward what she needs for the school."

"That's mighty kind of you," Ma said. "I'm guessing that her Pa's not going to be too keen on the idea, but I'll talk to him. Just don't be saying anything about it, Lizzie. Leastways not until I approach the subject with him."

"Abby said that you and Pa can meet with her parents to find out more about the school. I wouldn't be enrolling until the end of August, if you decide I can go. In the meantime, I'll start making some brittle, if you show me how. Every penny I earn will go in the tin can."

"Don't get your hopes up just yet," Ma said. "Your pa can be stubborn, and you're his favorite child. It's not going to set well with him, you going off on your own."

"I love you, Ma."

"I love you, too. Now go help Ellie get the food on the table. The men will be ready for supper before you know it."

Chapter Nineteen

Kimberton, Pennsylvania

August 1821

It was a sultry Sunday afternoon that Emily Price and I chose to spend together, along with her 14-month old baby girl, Rebecca. The humidity was dreadful, the leaves on the trees as still as stones piled in a grassy field. The sky was overcast, a pale silvery gray left as residue from the morning rain, perhaps a portent of an evening shower.

Emily and I sat on the wooden bench under a large maple behind the general store, Becca playing with her toys on the blanket spread in front of us. Some of the younger girls from the boarding school across the road were frolicking in the side yard, occasionally waving to me or trying to get my attention with their antics. I'd see them soon enough tomorrow morning in class, once the school week began. I intended to keep today for having my own enjoyment.

"How was your visit at home?" Emily asked, retrieving the ball that had rolled out of Becca's grasp.

"It was delightful, though we were busy with canning and preserving much of our summer harvest. Nonetheless, having two weeks' vacation from school was refreshing. Mr. Kimber's considering eliminating the August break, which I think is a mistake, especially when some of the girls are needed to help their families during this time of year."

"I heard Susanna Kimber talking about it," Emily said. "She feels that too much time is lost from the girls' studies."

"Might be better to eliminate or shorten the October holiday. That's just my opinion, though. I don't have much of a say in the schedule."

"It makes sense. You excited about starting your second year of teaching?"

"I am. I can't say my first year was easy. After I finished a year of studies and was hired to stay on as an instructor, I had all kinds of notions about being a woman of the world, earning my own wages, setting my own rules. But, in reality, that's not how it is. Though my room and board are included in my salary, the pay is minimal. And, of course, I must abide with the regulations, always setting a good example. Even Tom's not very happy with my lack of freedom."

Becca crawled over to Emily, attempting to climb up to her lap. "Speaking of Tom," Emily said as she reached down to pick up Becca, "where is he today? I thought the two of you would be spending time together."

"He and Will rode to Manavon for the afternoon. They want to see if there might be notices of business opportunities at any of the taverns in town."

"You going to see him later?"

"Maybe. Just depends."

"On what?"

"We had an argument recently. He wants me to quit my teaching job so we can wed."

"You can be mighty stubborn. That's the second time you've turned him down. I thought you were in love with him."

"I do love Tom. Other than you, he's my best friend."

"That's a good basis for marriage," Emily said. "I'd say the same about Joe."

"I don't disagree, but look at you. You're like motherhood personified. Becca sleeping in your arms, you with that glow about you. It wouldn't be like that for me."

"It's the best feeling in the world," Emily said as she brushed Becca's forehead with a kiss. "And I think I'm expecting again."

"Honestly? That's wonderful! Have you been to see Doc Pyle?"

"Not yet. I haven't even told Joe, though he's probably wondering why I've been so emotional lately. I just want to be sure before he gets his hopes up."

"I'm really happy for you. But don't you see? That's my problem. I thought when I'd find the man of my dreams, that I'd be happy to settle down and raise a family. I don't have one bit of a desire to be a mother. It wouldn't be fair to Tom for me to lead him on. Best we just stay friends."

"He's not going to wait around forever."

"I'm aware of that. But I want to be assured that he's the right one for me. How did you know you wanted to wed Joe?"

"I'm not sure. I just felt it. It was as clear as sunlight reflecting off glass."

"Same with Ma," I said, feeling gloomy that I haven't had the same experience. "Strange as it sounds, I had that feeling the first time I laid eyes on Tom. But then I got so busy with my schoolwork, and now my teaching, that I'm just not convinced any longer."

"Maybe it's your environment holding you back," Emily said in a gentle tone. "I mean, except for Sundays and rare holidays, you never get away from your work. And, quite honestly, the Quaker life isn't for everyone. Have you considered living at home and driving to work each day? Your homestead's not that far away."

"I thought about it, but we start our school day at 5 a.m. I don't want to be maneuvering a buggy over hills and through the woods before the sun rises."

Emily nodded her understanding of my predicament. She gazed across the road, not seeing, but thinking, all the while gently rocking Becca. Finally, she smiled, dimples creasing little lines in her flushed cheeks.

"I have an idea. We have storage rooms above the store, next to our quarters. Joe and I could clear the boxes in a couple of them. There's still plenty of space for them on the second floor and attic. Maybe Mr. Kimber would allow you to move up there near Joe and me."

"Gosh!" I said, feeling that Emily's suggestion has merit. "Would Joe consider such an arrangement?"

"He thinks highly of you, Lizzie. Besides, we'd each have our own living space. The bigger question would be if Mr. Kimber would give his approval, or even if your father would agree, you being unmarried and all."

"Pa's not the one I'm concerned about," I said with a chuckle. "He told me just the other day that he's worried I'll be turning Quaker. Not that it's an awful thing. Just that he doesn't set with some of their beliefs. Mind you, I'd be happy not to go to Meeting every week. Emmor Kimber can be cantankerous, ranting on and on about this or that. If it weren't for Mrs. Kimber's good spirits, I wouldn't be able to stand it."

"Well, then, let's hope Mr. Kimber's in a positive frame of mind when you ask him. I'll be happy to put in a good word for you. How's your father feel about Will rooming above the livery while he's working at the grist mill?"

"Pa's gotten used to the idea," I said. "He so much wanted for Will to follow in his footsteps, one day taking over the farm. But Will has never enjoyed working the land. Problem is, Will doesn't know what he wants to do. He tried learning how to tan hides from the uncle, but Will said it's a stinking job. He doesn't like milling the grain, nor does he want to learn a trade like what Tom does as blacksmith. Quite honestly, I think he was happiest when he was helping me sell my candies a couple of years ago."

"Nothing wrong with being a vendor or merchant. How about running the business side of the farm? He could start a market what with all of the goods your family produces."

"Our land is mostly on high ground, not really conducive to folks coming to buy. Besides, Will's now 18 years old. He wants to be off on his own. Guess we're both the same in that matter, not like Benjamin or Ellie. Ben's probably going to be the one to take over the farm someday. And Ellie? Well, she's got her eye on every eligible male she sees. Truth be told, I think she's set her sight on David McClure. God help us."

Emily giggled with the thought of David with Ellie. We both knew that David would be a fine suitor. His mother's the problem. If Ellie's lucky, the old witch will meet an early demise.

"Seems to me that Will's got to think beyond what hits him in the face," Emily said. "You know, Joe never thought of himself as a store proprietor until Mr. Kimber offered him the position. The job fits him to a T. Maybe Joe can give him some guidance."

I was thinking on Emily's words when Becca stirred, somewhat fussy. I tried to catch her attention with some of the nursery rhymes like those that would settle down our Julie when she was a baby, but nothing seemed to work. Emily said it would be best to take her in, change her diaper, and get her something to eat.

"You're welcome to join us," she added. "Can you stay for supper?"

"I was going to prepare my lessons, but I'm not yet in that frame of mind. I can help you with the vegetables."

I gathered up Becca's toys and shook out the blanket, folding it neatly to put in Emily's bag. We were heading to the side door of the general store when Emily spotted Emmor and Susanna Kimber walking through their grove by the stream across the street. She waved to them and nudged me to go ask Mr. Kimber about the possibility of new living arrangements. I didn't have long to consider what I would say, as they changed direction to come and greet us.

Emmor Kimber is an imposing man in his mid-forties, tall and large-framed, with muttonchop sideburns and thick eyebrows. Susanna is also tall, but slender. She's a year or two older than her husband, a fact I know because she teases him that she's wiser because of her age.

Susanna wears her hair parted in the middle, with some curls at her forehead. The rest is put in a bun in the back. Today she's wearing a simple frock, dark cerulean in color, and a plain bonnet. Her warm smile brings out the brightness of her eyes.

When they reached us on the walkway, Susanna leaned over to give Becca a kiss on her forehead saying, "How sweet thou are, little one. Thy mama's taking fine care of thee."

To me she added, "It's good to see thee back, Lizzie. I trust it was an enjoyable time at home."

"Very much so," I said. "Ma and Pa send you their best."

"Such a lovely family," Mrs. Kimber said as she brushed a mosquito from Becca's leg. "I've seen Will a few times now that he's working at the grist mill."

"Yes, ma'am. He appreciates the job, though I think he'd be better suited as a merchant."

"He's still young. Plenty of time for him to decide what he'd like to do in life."

I nodded my agreement. "Of course, Pa would prefer for Will to be working on our farm, but he's come to terms with the fact that Will doesn't like farming, not like my other brothers."

"Each child is different," Susanna said. "We see that with our own brood. Abby and Mary, even Patti, enjoy teaching, but Gertrude marches to her own drummer."

Becca was getting impatient, fussing all the while. Emily was probably wondering when I'd get to the point of asking Mr. Kimber about the upstairs rooms, so she took the bull by the horns.

"I was thinking, Mr. Kimber," Emily said, "that you might be able to enroll another student at the boarding school if you had an extra bedroom. Joe and I would be willing to move some of the storage items from the second-floor above the general store, such that Lizzie might have her own room there."

Emmor and Susanna gazed intently at each other, their eyes connected by similar thoughts. I noticed that Mrs. Kimber gave a slight affirmative nod, almost imperceptible.

"That's a fine idea," Mr. Kimber said. "The missus and I were talking about the need to increase our enrollment. In time, we may put an addition on the house, but an extra room would do for now. Art thou sure that thy mother and father would agree to the arrangements, Lizzie?"

"Quite certain, sir," I said, hoping my delight wouldn't be betrayed by my expression. "Being that I'd be living just across the street, I could still help with the children when needed."

"The terms of thy employment would stay somewhat the same," Mr. Kimber said. "The room will be included in thy salary, as well as breakfast and mid-day meal at the school. Since the workday will end with the last lesson of the day, thou may find other means for your supper."

"That's very reasonable," I said, keeping my enthusiasm at bay. "I can move my personals tomorrow evening, unless you have a preference in the matter."

"We'll need to provide a bed and dresser," Susanna said as a reminder to her husband.

"No need to worry," Emily said. "I've noticed one of each in the far room at the end of the hall. Of course, both are covered with cartons."

"Then that should be my room," I said. "We'll find a place for the storage items."

"Well done," Mr. Kimber said as he took his wife's arm to depart. "Let us know if there is need of anything else."

Chapter Twenty

The recent housing arrangement is working quite well. I like that there's closure to my teaching day, and I've enjoyed having supper with Emily, Joe, and Becca each evening. I'm no longer required to attend the weekly Meeting, led by Mr. Kimber, nor do I need to assist with chores at the school beyond my scope of work.

A few times each week, Emily invites Will and Tom to join us for a meal in the back room of the mercantile. Joe added a larger table, three more hard-back chairs, and Becca's high chair to accommodate all of us. Our conversation is lively, with each of us telling stories about our day or sharing local gossip we'd heard.

"Your uncle came by the store today," Joe said. "Wanted me to buy some of his pelts. If it weren't that I'm always able to sell them, I wouldn't take them off his hands. Soon as he gets the money, he heads out to find the nearest tavern."

"Probably finds himself a loose woman, then gets drunk as a skunk," Will muttered with a look of disdain. "Did he bring that mangy mutt of his?"

"Didn't see any dog. Must have left him at your farm."

"Pa said if the mongrel kills any more of our chickens, he's going to shoot it," Will noted. "Seems to me, he means his word."

"Maybe your uncle left the dog home so he could do his whoring," Joe said. "Left him to play with the young'uns."

"Ma don't let any of them play with the dog. He's full of fleas and ticks from hunting with the uncle. Ever since Ma found a tick on Julie, she won't let that dog in the house. Don't think her word counts for much, though. When she goes to bed, the uncle brings the hound up to the loft with him."

"Your uncle's still sleeping in the loft?" Emily asked as she handed Becca a corn cob to suck on.

"Mary won't have any part of him," I said. "She's got her own room on the first floor of the big house, and locks both doors whenever she goes in there."

"Don't you think that's strange?" Tom asked, soaking his bread in gravy.

"Not if you know him," I said. "If you ask me, Mary hates her husband. I asked her about it once. She told me she doesn't remember what he ever did to her, but she abhors him even being near."

"Maybe, in time, it'll come back to her," Emily said. "You mentioned she's talking more now."

"She talks some, especially to Ma and to Julie. Mostly she helps with the cooking, churning, and washing. She and Ma have become bosom friends."

"I'm just glad we don't have to live there anymore," Will said. "Pa's got as much animosity towards his brother as Mary does. Ben told me that Pa barely gives the uncle the time of day."

"Just as well," I said. "You'd think after three years being there, he'd have got his own place by now."

"He's biding his time," Will replied. "He wants the farm, says it's his by right. If he didn't spend all his money on liquor, he'd probably have enough to buy some of Pa's land."

"I know you don't like farming," Joe said to Will, maybe trying to change the subject, "but I've been thinking that you're missing out on some mighty big opportunities with what your Pa has going."

"Like what?"

"Like making deliveries," Joe said. "Don't know if you've noticed this, but there's a ton of new people in the county. Look at Manavon, just three miles from here. The Phoenix Iron Works employs a lot of folks making nails. None of them are farming, so they need to buy food and dry goods."

"You looking for a delivery boy?" Will asked.

"Not necessarily. Business here is good, especially when the farmers are waiting for their grain at the grist mill. I'm saying you could start your own business. All you really need is a horse and wagon, and the goods your mother and father already have. Instead of them bartering, you can charge a fair price and give your folks a share of the proceeds."

I watched Will's expression, his brow furrowed as it does when he's concentrating. I actually thought that Joe's idea was brilliant, connecting Will's desire of having his own business with our family farmstead.

After several moments of reflection, Will replied, "Don't think I've seen anything like that around these parts. Besides, I don't own my own horse or buckboard."

"There's a gentleman with such a business in West Chester. Emily and I saw him last time we visited her mother. He carries a barrel of milk, butter, fresh produce, jerky, and jars of jams or preserved foods. You could do the same thing. Add some of Lizzie's nut brittle, maybe some yarn, and you've got yourself a traveling store."

"Pa's already lending you one of the mares," I said. "Maybe he'd also let you borrow the wagon until you can buy your own."

"I don't know, Lizzie. You think Pa would approve of such an arrangement?"

"Can't see why not. Present the concept to him as a partnership in business. *William Mitchell and Sons,* or something like that. You can drive to the villages around here where folks aren't farming. There's Manavon, Charlestown, Uwchlan, even Malvern."

"I can help you with the business side," Joe said. "You'll need to maintain ledgers with your accounts. It can be tedious, but it's not hard if you keep up with it."

"It sounds good to me," Tom said. "You don't like working at the grist mill, breathing in all that dust from the grains. Wouldn't hurt to try it."

Knowing Will, he needs time to process Joe's suggestion. I told him he should think on it. I also said I'd go with him when he wants to talk to Pa about it. In the end, that was his decision. To cogitate.

Seeing it was getting late, Tom and Will helped me clear the table and take our plates to the back counter in the store for washing. Emily took Becca upstairs to put her to bed, while Joe lit the lanterns and swept the floor of the storeroom, leaving it in good order.

After we stowed the dried dishes, Tom, Will, and I chose to sit awhile on the front porch. Joe went upstairs to spend time with Emily. It was a balmy evening, a light wind from the west helping to evaporate the sweat we had worked up.

I was seated between my brother and Tom, gazing at the shimmering stars, half hidden by the branches of towering trees swaying in the breeze. At the inn across the street, a few candles flickered in upstairs windows. None of us had much to say, each of us tired from the day's work and knowing we'd have to be up with the morning birds. Still, there was a comfortable stillness amongst us.

Tom broke the silence by saying, "I like you living at the store, Lizzie. We're all like family now."

I looked at Tom, light from inside the store casting a glow on his handsome face, shadows on his broad shoulders. His smile always gives me delight, especially as his full bottom lip broadens, and delicate lines form in the creases of his alluring hazel eyes. I put my hand over his, both resting on the arm of his rocking chair. That's my way of saying that I know being part of a family is important to him.

Tom has no kin, as far as he knows. As an only child, the firstborn, his parents succumbed to a yellow fever outbreak in Philadelphia. Initially, he was taken in by the Philadelphia Orphanage, then sent to a foster family who moved to Chester County in 1803. No longer able to care for the young boy, Tom was returned to the local almshouse until he was put into indenture. At the age of 18, he was released to apprentice with the blacksmith at the crossroads in Kimberton.

Despite his shoddy upbringing, Tom's a fast learner and has a positive outlook. I like that about him. He takes what he's given in life, and makes the best of it.

On the other hand, I think Tom could do better than shoeing horses and grinding axes. Not that there's anything wrong with being a blacksmith. It's a good skill to have in these parts. But Tom's smart. With a little more education, he could advance his status.

We talked about that once, but it didn't set well with him. I've never mentioned it again because it's his own business. Sometimes I wonder if that's another reason, somewhere deep inside of me, that I've turned down his wedding proposals.

Will suddenly stood and stretched, announcing that he needed to hit the sack. Tom agreed, albeit reluctantly, and he gave my hand a squeeze. Then he leaned over to kiss me, a soft touch, as delicate as a butterfly, right on the lips.

I glanced at Will to see if he noticed Tom's indiscretion, or my blush, but he had already begun his descent on the steps. Tom hurried after him as I called, in scarcely more than a whisper, "Goodnight to the both of you. Sweet dreams!"

Chapter Twenty-One

The following Sunday, Will, Tom, and I drove to Yellow Springs for a day with the family. Mr. Kimber was kind enough to lend us his buggy, and Emily sent a yard of muslin to Ma to barter for some yarn. Will and Tom planned to help with the seemingly never-ending harvest, while I'd assist in the kitchen.

I figured Ma would be surprised to see me, especially since I'd been there just two weeks prior. But Pa would be grateful for the extra field hands. Besides, Will and I had things to discuss—my living over the general store with Emily and Joe, and Will's proposition for a business venture with Pa.

The day was sunny, hot, and humid, typical for the end of August. Tom took the reins, while Will and I sat in the seat behind him, all the while giving him directions despite his having been to our homestead before.

From Kimber's stable, Tom turned right onto Hare's Hill Road, and another right onto the road to Uwchlan. Both are major thoroughfares, with the dirt packed solid under the mare's hooves, both roads having many curves and hills.

Tom maneuvered the buggy expertly, and I enjoyed the pastoral scenery. We passed through Yeager's farmland, their stone house on the knoll above the road, then crossed Clover Mill Road and Pikeland Road, making a sharp left onto Yellow Springs Road, just past the culvert over Pickering Creek. Our farm drive is about a quarter mile from there, on the left, not far from where the road merges along Pine Creek.

Five-year-old Julie came running to meet us, barefooted and sassy, pigtails swaying with every broad stride. Tom unhitched the mare and led him to the field for grazing, while Will lifted Julie and twirled her around, until they were both dizzy. Once she regained her balance, Julie grabbed my hand and pulled me to the back door.

"Look who I found, Ma!" she called.

Ma wiped her hands on the rag in her apron pocket, and said with her generous smile, "Lordy! What a surprise. I hope you can stay awhile."

"We have the entire day. Will and Tom will help with the crops, and I can work with you in the kitchen. Here's some muslin from Emily to trade for whatever yarn you got."

"Ellie can put some in your buggy when she finishes making the biscuit dough. Mary's peeling potatoes, so I'll have her add a few more to the pot. I just mixed up a batch of sweet tea, if you'd like to get some. We can all go out to the porch for a while."

It wasn't long before we settled ourselves in the rocking chairs, except for Julie playing hopscotch on the path. Mary brushed a strand of her graying hair back under her cap, wiping the perspiration on her forehead with the back of her hand. I noticed she's filled out some, no longer skin and bones.

Fifteen-year-old Ellie is petite, like Ma, and has all the curves of a young woman. She greeted me warmly, saying she likes my Sunday dress. I must admit, I'm partial to this modern style with the higher waistline and fitted bodice. The skirt's not as full, almost A-line in fashion.

"Don't see how you can do much work in the kitchen looking all fancy like that," Ma said. "You allowed to wear such finery when you're teaching?"

"I'll use an apron, like I do at school. Mrs. Kimber has no objection with the cut of the dress, so long as it's modest and the color is plain. I save this one for Sundays."

"It's mighty pretty," Ellie said. "I especially like the small flowered cotton print and the puffy short sleeves. Maybe if we do well with our harvest this year, Ma will buy one for me."

Ma raised her eyebrows and said, "We'll see about that. Did you put your biscuits on the embers?"

"Not yet. It's so blasted hot in there. We need to get us a summer kitchen."

"You certainly are anxious to be spending a ton of money, what with new dresses and out buildings, young lady. When you get wed, you can buy all the things you're hankering for. In the meantime, you can make do with what we have."

Ma sounded disgruntled, but she really wasn't. I could see from the twinkle in her eyes that she was teasing Ellie. Quite honestly, I knew she'd be wanting the same things. From the time I was a child, Ma always told us that we can't always have what we want.

"I have some exciting news to tell you," I said, changing the subject. "Mr. Kimber let me move to a room above the general store so he can enroll more boarders at the school."

"Mercy, child!" Ma said. "You're not married, though you should be considering it by the way Tom swoons over you. Are you sure it's proper to be living on your own?"

"The world is changing, Ma. I'm 19 years old, soon to be 20. The arrangements are no different than if I still lived at the school or in a boarding house. Besides, if I marry, I'd need to resign from my teaching position. That's the rule, and I must abide by it."

"I'm not sure your pa's going to like this, you living by yourself."

"I'm not alone. I'm just down the hall from Emily, Joe, and their baby. It's quite respectable."

"They're not kin. Folks might not approve, the way it looks. Already I can hear Lucretia McClure's tongue wagging."

"I could care less what that busy-body thinks," I said, shaking my head in dissent. "The Kimber's wouldn't permit anything improper, Mr. Kimber being a Quaker clerk and all. I'm happy about the arrangement. My work day ends with my last lesson, and I have supper with the Price's. Even Will joins us just about every evening now."

"It's good that Will's watching over you. I'll tell that to your pa. What do you think, Mary?"

"Don't know why a woman can't live by herself if she wants. Wish I'd done that instead of marrying so soon after my husband died."

Mary's statement gave me the opportunity to question things I'd been wondering about. I honestly couldn't fathom why she'd agreed to wed the uncle, let alone move far west with him.

"What was your first husband's name?" I asked, rather abruptly, just out of curiosity.

"I been thinking on that," Mary said after a few moments of silence. "Reckon it must've been Jonathan, same as my boy. 'Twas his seed that made him."

"So, you had one child with your first husband? And you had a farm in Ohio?"

"That's what I been remembering. It weren't real big, not like your pa's land. We had us a log cabin by a stream that flowed through the woods."

Mary appeared to be pondering about years long past, memories clouded by the atrocities she had experienced when living on the plains. She continued. "Jonathan cleared the land, a little more each year, with the help of an ox we got from a couple heading back east. They was tired of trying to make do on land that had a mind of its own."

I sensed that Mary was getting lost in the few memories that had begun to surface, and Ma was giving me one of her looks, warning me that I'd best not be upsetting Mary. Still, I continued. "How did your husband die?"

"A bear got him," Mary said. "I run and took Jonathan's rifle and shot it dead, but it was too late." Two tears escaped from the corner of Mary's eyes before she wiped them away with the back of her hand.

"You done good remembering that," Ma said gently. "I can't imagine how you survived, what with a little boy and a farm to run on your own."

"It's why I married George Mitchell," Mary said. "He was different back then, from what I recollect. Not like he is now. But he wasn't a farmer, leastwise not like Jonathan. We was about starving to death. That's why I agreed we should sell the land and go west. Besides, living there in that cabin, trying to make something of our land, I was troubled by Jonathan's memory. It weren't fair to George. At least that's what I was thinking."

"Then you had a baby girl by George?" I asked

Mary nodded. "Out on them plains," she said. "Bridget was the prettiest thing you ever did see. She had a liking to your Julie when she was a baby."

"That's not so strange when you think that George is Julie's uncle," Ma said as she stood and straightened the folds of her petticoats. It was obvious that she was bringing conclusion to my questioning.

"We'd best get back to work. Ellie, get one of your aprons for Lizzie. Then you both can go down to the spring house and bring me some butter and milk."

I waited on the porch for Ellie to return, just in time to see Pa's brother emerge from the woods with his scruffy dog, carrying a dead raccoon. He threw the carcass by the side of the barn and walked to the pump to wash his hands.

Seeing me, George seemed to forget what he was about to do, and said, "Look what we have here, Dawg. Our pretty woman has come to see us. Give your old uncle a kiss, Lizzie."

George grabbed my face with his bloodied thick fingers and kissed me on the lips. I pushed him away with all my strength, and spit out the disgusting moisture he left on my mouth.

"Don't ever do that again," I said with clenched teeth. "You ever come near me, you'll be the sorriest man in these parts."

I bolted off the porch to wash my face at the pump, still hearing his guffaws echoing in my mind.

Chapter Twenty-Two

We were crowded around the kitchen table for supper, but it didn't seem to bother anyone. Ma and Pa sat at either end, with the boys on one side, Pa's brother, Mary, and the girls on the other. Mary and I made sure we were far separated from her husband, both avoiding any possibility of looking at him.

I didn't tell anyone about the repulsive kiss I received earlier. I'm not sure why, except I knew it would upset anyone who heard about it. Besides, I handled the situation myself, and I felt certain that I was perfectly clear in my admonition to the disgusting man.

Young George and Matt were clowning around as usual, still picking on each other and telling tales. Nonetheless, Pa stated that they've both been helpful with the harvest, and have what it takes to be a farmer, as does Benjamin.

Matt's now 9 years old, and does quite well with the sickle to break down the corn stalks. Young George, at age 7, uses the grass hook to assist with clearing the field. When the two of them get tired of those jobs, they sit in the shade and shuck corn to prepare the ears for the sheller that 16-year-old Ben operates.

"We've got a lot of corn ready to go to the grist mill," Pa noted. "You think you could take it back with you, Will, to get it ground for us?"

"I can do that, Pa. Fact is, I could take the cornmeal you don't need and sell it for you."

"Why would you think to sell the grain? Your ma uses the flour for baking."

"You said yourself that we're having a good yield this year," Will said, trying to set up his business proposition to Pa. Maybe he mentioned something to Benjamin about it, because Ben got into the conversation.

"Couldn't hurt to put some aside for selling, Pa. You know Ma's been wanting that summer kitchen."

I had to admit that Ben's ploy was a good one. Pa would do just about anything he could for Ma, and vice versa. Besides, even eating supper in the kitchen was sweltering this evening, despite the door and windows being open.

"We can use the extra for bartering, like we always do," Pa said as he reached for another helping of venison stew. "Don't need to be fixing something that ain't broke."

"Joe Price at the general store told us there's a lot of new folks around these parts who aren't farming," I said. "There's a man in West Chester who's a traveling vendor selling milk, butter, eggs, flour, and just about anything you can think of."

"Missy's got a good point," old George said. "I seen him when I was there. Carries a big barrel of milk in his wagon so folks just buy what they need."

"What were you doing in West Chester?" Pa asked. The frown on his face expressed great consternation.

"Checking on the deed to our land at the county court house," the uncle said while reaching for another hunk of bread. He didn't seem fazed by the question.

"Tarnation!" Pa yelled as he pushed away from the table, the loud scraping noise startling Julie.

Through clenched teeth, he added, "If you lifted a hand to help around here, I'd give you some of the land. Hell! You'd have enough money what with selling your pelts that you could pay to have a house built on it, except you waste it on whiskey."

On that note, Pa turned on his heels and stormed out to the yard. Even the uproar didn't seem to bother the uncle none. He put a big pat of butter on his bread and spread it around.

Ma excused herself, and went out to walk with Pa. The rest of us finished our meal in silence. I felt sorry for Will. He never got a chance to ask Pa about starting a business, though I had a feeling Pa wouldn't have been open to the idea anyway.

Once old George left the table to work on his tanning by the barn, the tension amongst the rest of us began to dwindle. Matt and little George imitated the uncle's revolting eating habits, one pretending to wipe his beard with the crux of his arm, the other picking carrots out of the stew after licking his fingers. All of us were laughing, but I knew Ma wouldn't be pleased with the rudeness, making fun of another.

I began clearing the table, while Ben set up the dishpans, and Ella prepared the leftovers for Will and Tom to take to the spring house. "Enough of your shenanigans," I said to the two younger boys. "Take Julie out with you and play a game until bedtime."

"We'll catch fireflies when they start lighting up," Matt said. "Get your jar, Julie. We'll see who can find the most."

Mary offered to wash the dishes, so I dried and put them away. "It rightly saddens me to see how much upset the husband can cause," she said, handing me the large serving bowl.

"Why doesn't he want to make a home for you?" I asked, swishing the towel around, inside and out.

"Don't know about that. Reckon I'm not much of a wife."

I let that comment settle awhile, and took the bowl to the pantry. Growing up, I hadn't had many opportunities to observe the special bond between a man and wife, like I notice with Emily and Joe Price. Except for Ma and Pa. They've always been totally united. Surely, they had some disagreements through the years, but they solved problems together. I'd never witnessed such open animosity as displayed by the uncle and Mary. It made me wonder if other marriages could be so flawed.

"Seems to me it goes both ways," I said when I returned to dry the knives and forks. "It makes me want to be absolutely sure that I dearly love the man I marry."

"Tom seems like a good man," Mary said, handing me a plate to dry. "He don't got much to say, but nothing wrong with that."

"Sometimes he says plenty," I said with a chuckle. "I can't see myself loving anyone else, but I still don't know for sure if we should wed."

"You'll know when the time is right," Mary said, lugging the dishpan out to the yard, dumping the dirty water on the flower bed.

I finished putting all the dishes away, and gave the table a final wipe. Sweating like a polecat, I went out to get a cup of water at the pump. Ella, Will, Tom, and Ben had joined Mary on the porch.

The young'uns were running around, Dawg nipping at their heels. Ma and Pa were walking hand in hand, coming back from their walk in the woods. I could see that Pa was settled down, even laughing at something Ma had said to him.

"You ready to get going?" Will asked me. "I'd like to get Mr. Kimber's buggy back before dark.

"Guess so. Don't you want to continue your conversation with Pa?"

"Not tonight. I planted the seed. He'll need time to think it over. Let's get the horse hitched, Tom."

Ben went to get the bags of corn to put in the buggy, while Ellie fetched some of her yarn from the parlor. I said my farewell to Mary and leaned over to give her a hug.

Mary squeezed my hand, but she didn't have anything to say. I knew she had said more to me today than I could ever remember.

Ma and Pa walked with me to the buggy. Ma had her arm around my waist; Pa matched his paces with ours.

"Drive careful, Tom," Pa said. "Will, you take care of your sister. Don't be letting folks wag their tongues about her living over the general store."

Pa's comment surprised me, but only for a second. Ma must have told him of my new living arrangements in a way that set right by him. I gave Ma a kiss, whispering my thanks in her ear.

Tom helped me into the buggy, then hopped up front to take the reins. Will hugged Ma, and shook Pa's hand.

"Thanks for your help today," Pa said. "You can sell that cornmeal, Will. Bring back some money for your Ma."

Chapter Twenty-Three

My assignment at the French Creek School changed as the academic year got into full-swing. Mrs. Kimber placed her second daughter, Mary, into my former role of teaching phonics to the younger girls. Abby Kimber will assist her mother with the development of the curriculum. I'll now be providing reading instruction at all levels, a task I'm rather pleased about.

We didn't have many books at our farm. Most everything I had read came from Ma's bible. Since I've been at the school, however, the Kimber's have been adding to their library, even permitting me to borrow books that I can read in the evenings. I love Jane Austen and Elizabeth Meeke, even Mary Shelley. My favorite story, thus far, is *Pride and Prejudice*.

Of course, to teach reading, I must also instruct diction and the proper use of grammar. This was one of my biggest challenges when I first came to the school three years ago. It still doesn't come easy to me, and I sometimes revert to the way we spoke at home.

My communication is more proper when I'm surrounded by those who are more educated. In fact, I don't understand why Ma picked up some of Pa's colloquialisms. After all, she was schooled before she ran off with Pa. Nonetheless, recitation has been helpful for me, and I'll use the method with the girls in my care.

I use Webster's *Speller* as the primary text for every level of reading, though I sometimes refer to Murray's *Grammar* for the older girls. Just as Ma taught me to do when I gave my brothers their lessons, I begin with a review of the alphabet, word construction, and rhymes with the younger girls—aspects emphasized by Webster. Developing sentence construction is a more difficult task, especially using the correct pronouns after a preposition.

Mrs. Kimber showed me a useful trick to help the children recognize prepositions. With my quill pen, I printed each of the words on brown paper, and tacked them to the walls above the chalk slate in our classroom. Each day after lunch and recess, I have the girls recite the words. *About, above, across, after, against, among, around, at, before, beside, between, by, down, during, except, for, from, in, into, near, of, off, on, over, through, to, toward, under, up, with.* I chuckle to myself every time I hear my students' recitations of the prepositions through the open windows as they jump rope in the yard.

I was sharpening quills during my break one afternoon when two of the middle level girls interrupted my reverie. Surprised to see them standing in the doorway, each looked like the proverbial cat that swallowed the canary.

Both are about the same age, though they're different as night and day. Anna is 13, tall and lithesome, with dark curls protruding from her bonnet. Esther is 14, large framed and muscular, freckle-faced with long red hair she typically wears in braids.

Anna and Esther enrolled at the school last year, and have become the best of friends. I'd say that Anna is the more cultured of the two, perhaps because of her vast travel experiences as the daughter of a well-known statesman from Philadelphia.

Esther, on the other hand, hails from Charlestown, a village not far from my home in Yellow Springs. Her family has a large farm, similar in size to ours, and she's the youngest of eight brothers and sisters.

"What are the two of you up to?" I asked, as Anna giggled and Esther blushed. "I'd have thought you'd be enjoying this lovely afternoon outdoors. At least until recess is over."

"I have a problem," Esther said. "I guess it's not so awful since my ma told me it would happen sooner or later. But I'm bleeding. Down there."

Esther pointed in the general vicinity such that I knew she was experiencing her first period. Anna was watching my expression, not certain whether Esther was making up a story or in need of medical assistance. She seemed relieved when I congratulated Esther on becoming a woman.

"Did your ma tell you how to take care of it?" I asked.

"She said I'd need to wear a rag, but I don't know how to do it. Do I just... you know, bunch it up under there?"

"Some women do. You'll figure out what makes you most comfortable. I'll show you where Mrs. Kimber keeps the rags first, so you can fix yourself. Then, we'll go see Emily at the general store. She stocks contraptions that will hold the rag in place. I got one for myself, and it works fine."

Anna tentatively followed us to the rag bag in the back shed where we do our laundry. It was evident that she hadn't been privy yet to the mother-daughter conversation about the birds and the bees.

Esther, on the other hand, had certainly seen animals in heat, and learned at an early age the intricacies of nature. Anna and I waited outside while Esther cleaned up and arranged her clothing.

"Do all girls experience this?" Anna asked skeptically.

"We do," I said. "We just don't know when the first time will come. It's a sign that our bodies are ready to nurture a child. Once a month, if we're not pregnant, the blood will be shed."

Anna's brow furrowed as she reflected on my words. Suddenly her expression changed, as she gazed at my smiling face. "I know about this," she exclaimed. "My mother would take to bed each month, and my nanny would tell me she had the curse. I surely never wanted the curse!"

I put my hand on Anna's shoulder, hoping my positive attitude would dispel the negative associations she had formed. "There's nothing to fear, Anna. Our monthly experience is not an affliction or scourge. If anything, it's a nuisance to wash and bleach the rags. We don't retreat to our rooms. Rather, we live our daily lives no differently. With that in mind, I'd like you to take my class when the girls come in from recess while I go with Esther to the mercantile."

"What will I tell them?"

"Explain that I have an errand. The younger girls must each write a grammatically correct sentence. The older ones will create a short story from the sentence of their choice. When I return, the students can recite their narratives."

"I'd rather go with you and Esther."

"I need you in the classroom. And I promise we won't be long. Will you help me?"

Esther must have heard our conversation as she opened the shed door and emerged, still straightening her petticoats. "Miss Mitchell's idea is a good one," Esther said. "Leastways, no one will think the two of us have been gadding about, losing track of time or missing the bell signaling the end of recess."

"All right. I'll do it, but only if you promise to hurry back. And tell me *everything* after supper this evening."

I knew I should probably notify Mrs. Kimber where I was going with Esther, but searching for her would delay me from my task even longer. If we hurried, we'd be back before anyone would know I was missing.

^^^

Emily Price waved when Esther and I entered the store, though she was busy cutting fabric for a customer. Joe, too, was deep in conversation with a patron, apparently helping the young man determine which size nail would be best for his construction project. I kept Esther occupied as we rummaged through the button box. She whispered to me that she didn't have any money to make a purchase.

"We'll put it on my account," I said quietly. "You can pay me later."

Esther nodded, her serious expression confirming her nervousness. My own anxiety was a result of the unanticipated delay, and I was relieved when Emily was finally able to wait on us. Before long, Esther had a small wrapped packet that she had discretely placed in her deep pocket.

"You come back if you need any assistance with your procurement," Emily said to Esther. Her smile was particularly reassuring.

"I will. Thank you for your help."

"I'm glad you were here," I said to Emily. "On the way over, I had a thought that you might be trying to settle Becca for her nap."

"You escaped that part," Emily said with a chuckle. "She's now sleeping soundly in the back room. I've rigged a bell to her ankle so I can hear when she stirs. By the way, you also missed your brother. He stopped in to get a few things for your mother since he's returning your father's wagon."

"He's not working at the grist mill today?"

"Apparently not. He filled the buckboard with his wares and spent the morning as a traveling vendor. If you ask me, he was quite pleased with the outcome. Will might not have left yet, as he still needed to hitch his own horse to the wagon so he has a way to get back. He said he won't be joining us for supper."

"Speaking of getting back, Esther and I can't tarry for a moment longer. We certainly appreciate your assistance."

As we made our way across the road, Esther turned and looked at me with a questioning gaze. "Did I hear you right? Will from the grist mill is your brother?" A pink hue was spreading from her neck to her cheeks.

Pretending I didn't see her blush, I said, "Why, yes. Will Mitchell is my brother. I'll have to introduce him to you one of these days."

"Oh, we've met," Esther said with a wide grin. "I think he's rather fine-looking."

Chapter Twenty-Four

Several evenings later after supper, Will, Tom, and I sat on the front porch of the general store with Emily, Joe, and Becca. Dusk brought out the fireflies, which captivated Becca, while the west sky caught my attention with its splendid fusion of crimson, lavender, and cerise.

A finely-attired couple were animatedly chatting as they emerged from the inn across the street and strolled along Hares Hill Road. I wondered if they were staying the night as they awaited the morning stagecoach or, perhaps, exploring the village to determine if the boarding school would be a suitable environment for their daughter. By the time they rounded the bend on the hill, my imagination had crafted a captivating story of who they were and why they were visiting.

Will, on the other hand, was discussing his expanding clientele, obviously seeking additional input from each of us. I know he values Joe's business acumen and Tom's knowledge about horses and wagons because their chatter during our meal was all about the things that would affect Will's bottom line on a ledger sheet.

"So, what do you think, Lizzie?" Will asked.

Will's question startled me from my reverie, and brought me back to his conversation. "About what?"

"Partnering with the uncle. Weren't you listening?"

"Are you crazy?"

My outburst brought a round of laughter from all except Becca. She toddled over to me, smacked my skirt, and exclaimed, "Bad girl!"

I reached down to lift Becca to my lap, but she squirmed away. "I'm not bad, sweetie. Will's naughty for teasing me."

"I'm not kidding, Lizzie. Uncle George said he'd buy the horse and wagon, and we'd share the profit 50-50."

"What's Pa say about it?"

"Don't think he knows that his brother wants to join my business venture."

Though the lanterns inside the store gave some ambient light to where we were sitting, Will's facial expression was hidden in the shadows. Joe picked up Becca, and walked along the porch rail, obviously musing as he said, "Do you trust him?"

"It's not so much *trust*," Will said. "He's got money from selling his pelts, and I need a wagon with a strong horse. Can't be wasting time returning Pa's buckboard every time I make deliveries."

"Comes down to whether it's worth being in commerce with the man," Joe said, glancing at his daughter whose head was now resting on his shoulder, eyes closed. "You'd have to make it clear to him that you're the boss, and that doesn't sound like what he has in mind."

"You made $38 last week," Tom said. "With that kind of income, you'll soon have enough to buy your own wagon. I told you, I'm keeping my eyes open for a good deal on one, as well as a strong work horse."

"Most of that money went back to Pa. It's his goods I'm selling."

"Then, maybe, you need to change your business plan," Joe said. "You're not working for your pa; you're partnering with him. That's where the 50-50 split should be, if that's the course of action you want to take. I'd suggest that you buy your pa's produce, milk, and eggs wholesale. Then the profit's yours."

Will was obviously reflecting on Joe's advice. I could almost detect the furrowed brow that was an indication of Will's concentration.

During the break in conversation, Emily yawned quite loudly while I watched the visiting couple return to the inn. They walked hand in hand, carefully stepping around rocks and pebbles along the road that were barely discernable in the descending darkness.

"Don't let old George put ideas in your head, Will," I said when the inn's guests were safely inside. "I'll give you some money toward the cost of your wagon. Listen to Joe. He knows what he's talking about."

"You don't have to do that, Lizzie. I know you don't have a sizeable salary as a teacher. And you're still paying Ma and Pa for the cost of your education."

"I want to help. I'll even make more nut brittle you can add to your wares. Every penny adds up. You don't need the uncle."

Joe walked over to Will's rocker, Becca sound asleep in his arms. "Emily and I need to get this child to bed, but I want you to stop by tomorrow, Will. We have some money saved, and I'm willing to make you a loan with low interest. You give it some thought, then we can talk about it."

Emily stood and rubbed her hand across Joe's shoulder. She must have noticed Will's reticence before she said, "Don't be disagreeing with my husband, Will. He's a good and honest man. His offer is sincere. Now, we'll bid each of you a good night."

I told them that I, too, was heading upstairs and echoed Joe and Emily's farewell. As I was departing, Tom asked me to wait a moment. "I need to talk to you, Lizzie."

"Tonight? I'm mighty tired, Tom."

"Guess it can wait, then."

"How about Saturday afternoon?" I suggested. "Perhaps we could walk to French Creek and bring a picnic lunch."

Tom hesitated for a moment, then said, "That's fine. I'll stop by the store around noon."

"Add some vittles for me," Will said as he bounded down the front stops. "I'll chaperone."

Chapter Twenty-Five

It was a fine mid-September Saturday afternoon when Tom and Will arrived at the general store. Though it was warm, there was no humidity, and the cool northerly breeze was refreshing. I had packed a basket with leftover grilled chicken from last night's supper, a loaf of freshly baked zucchini bread, and a decanter of sweet tea.

Emily had teased me all morning that I should prepare myself for another marriage proposal, yet I still wasn't sure what my response would be if Tom popped the question again. Two nights of tossing and turning, pondering what I want in life, didn't ease my angst.

Will was in a carefree mood, carrying his fishing pole and gear, oblivious to the dark circles under my eyes. Tom took my basket in one hand, and crooked my arm in his as we set off up the hill on Kimberton Road. When we got to Seven Stars Road, Will directed us to cut through the field and bypass the pond until we reached the wooded bank.

Tall oaks and maples, as well as beech, poplar, and hickory trees, densely line both sides of French Creek, yet one fallen oak is perfectly arranged for seating. Someone had taken an axe to the side branches, and removed the bark, making for a comfortable perch. The top of the tree protrudes halfway over the creek, which Will claimed as his spot for trout fishing.

"How ever did you find this place?" I asked Will as I pinned up the front of my skirt.

"I can't take the credit. Tom found it some time ago. It's a pretty good fishing spot."

"Figure it must have once been a Lenape camp site," Tom said. "I found a bunch of arrowheads, even some broken pieces of pottery."

The three of us arranged ourselves on the log, while I distributed the chicken and cut each a piece of bread with the knife that Emily insisted I put in the basket. Luckily, she threw in three cotton napkins we could use to cover our laps.

"I think I found you a horse and wagon," Tom said nonchalantly as he gnawed the rest of the meat off a wing bone.

"You serious?" Will asked. "How much?"

"Eighty-five bucks for both."

"Sounds like a bargain. What's wrong with them?"

We all laughed at Will's skepticism, though I knew he was right to have some misgiving. "A fellow from Manavon brought in the wagon. His name is James Moore. The front axle needs some repair, but I can fix it for you. The horse could use a little fattening, though a week in your pa's field should give him some nourishment."

"Why's he getting rid of them?"

"He wants to purchase a Saddler gelding. Says he plans to head out west."

"You think I ought to buy his wagon and horse?"

"Yeah, I do. You won't get anything better for that kind of money."

"I can give you $20 to put towards it," I said, wiping my fingers and mouth with my napkin. After taking a few swigs of tea, I passed the decanter around.

"I got $40 saved from my work at the grist mill," Will said. "That means I'd only have to borrow $25 from Joe. Once I have my own source of income, I should be able to pay him back pretty quick. And you, too, Lizzie. Tell the guy he's got a buyer."

"I already did," Tom said with a grin that lit up his face.

"When's it available?"

"Tomorrow afternoon, or as soon as you can get the cash together. I've already started soldering the axle."

"Wow!" Will exclaimed. He jumped off the log and did a little jig before grabbing his fishing pole to bait the hook. "That calls for a celebration tonight. Fried trout anyone?"

Tom and I were still laughing as Will hopped back up and shimmied along the fallen tree until his legs were dangling over the creek. He cast his line, now fully engrossed in his endeavor.

"That was real nice," I said to Tom, brushing off the crumbs on my bodice. Now that Will was occupied, I felt certain that Tom would feel more comfortable to tell me whatever it was that he wanted to talk to me about.

Tom reached over and took my hands in his. As I gazed into his eyes, I had no doubt why I love this man. He's gentle and kind, and treats me as an equal. Didn't I once tell Will that those are the qualities I'd want in a husband? Suddenly, I knew what my answer would be when Tom asks me to wed.

Tom cleared his throat nervously, and squeezed my fingers as if to reinforce that we're meant to be together.

"I got something to say, Lizzie," he said with a quixotic smile, looking more anxious than any of the other times he asked for my hand in marriage.

"Well, say it," I said, glad to finally come to terms with what Tom's been wanting.

"Our friendship is very special."

"I agree."

"You know I love you."

"Without a doubt. And I love you, too."

"I'm going west with James."

My heart stopped beating for a second, I'm sure. But, then again, perhaps I didn't hear correctly. "What did you say?"

"The fellow from Manavon. James Moore. I'll be traveling with him. Maybe to Texas."

I felt the tears begin to form as I slid from my perch on the log. Wiping them quickly before Tom could see my distress, I said, "How long will you be gone?"

"Don't know. Might settle out there if I like it."

My hands trembled as I unpinned my skirt and shook out the folds. I didn't know what to say, nor did I think I'd have the strength to respond. My chest felt like the time I'd been thrown by our mare, my breath caught somewhere deep inside of me.

Tom must have taken my silence for needing more information, or maybe he was just nervous. "They say it's not for the faint of heart," he rambled. "There's Indians out there and they can be savage."

"I know."

"The journey won't be easy."

"Probably not."

"But I'll never have a chance like this again. James has already done all the research and he has maps, rudimentary as they are."

"Of course."

"So, you think I should go. Right?"

"If that's what you want."

Our conversation was halted by Will's hoots as he tugged his line out of the water. "It's a whopper!" he yelled.

Tom grabbed our basket and ran to the edge of the creek. Will drew the fish in slowly, maneuvering its gyrating body over toward Tom. Tom quickly grasped the line and called for me to hand him the knife.

Will scrambled off the tree when the huge trout was disconnected from his pole, and the two men worked to gut the fish. Once the entrails were thrown back into the water, we gathered our things to head back to the store.

Tom and Will both lugged a handle of the weighty basket, while I trudged with a heavy heart behind them.

Chapter Twenty-Six

Will, Joe, and Tom sat out back at the fire pit, while I helped Emily prepare the slaw and make biscuits. Becca was somewhat fussy, most likely teething. The child settled down once Emily rubbed a little whiskey on her gums, finally falling sound asleep on Emily's lap.

I kneaded the dough vigorously, much more than was necessary, then pounded it out on a floured board before cutting circles with a mug. My irritation didn't go unnoticed.

"What's bothering you?" Emily asked, with an expression of genuine concern.

"I don't want to talk about it."

"Must be you turned Tom down again."

For some unknown reason, that unleashed a torrent of anguish in me. I plopped on the rocking chair next to Emily, sobbing uncontrollably. The handkerchief I found in my apron pocket was of little comfort, though it was a help when I loudly blew my nose.

"Did you and Tom argue?" Emily asked, obviously not sure what she could do to console me.

"No." Once again, I blew my nose and dabbed at my eyes. "Tom's leaving. He's going out west."

"You can't be serious!" Emily exclaimed. "That's why he wanted to talk to you?"

I nodded in the affirmative, then said, "The thing that's so upsetting is that I planned to tell Tom that we could be wed. I suddenly realized that my love for him is deeper than the friendship we have. But it's all for naught."

"Did you share your feelings with Tom?"

"Not about his travel. What purpose would that serve? We have no commitment other than friendship. I'll not act like a whining brat, nor will I beg him to stay."

"You can be so stubborn," Emily said gently. "It wouldn't hurt to let him know your sadness."

"I won't," I said emphatically. "And you dare not tell him of it. I'll immerse myself in my teaching, perhaps furthering my education. In time, Tom will only be a distant memory."

Emily sorrowfully shook her head, gazing at me with unsaid regret. "Then go wash your face, and use some powder on your nose. If you take Becca upstairs, I'll finish the supper preparations. When the potatoes and fish are brought in, I'll call you."

"Thank you," I said as I lifted Becca from Emily's lap to my arms. She stirred slightly, but quickly returned to her restful slumber. "You're a good friend."

"An honorable companion would help you see the error of your ways. You're making a big mistake by not telling Tom how you feel. I'll honor your wishes, but it's against my better judgment."

^^^

"Have another piece of trout," Will said, passing the platter to me. "There's plenty here, and the rest is drying on the low embers outside so Tom has some jerky for his trip."

"I won't be taking too much of it," Tom said. "You'll be able to put some on your wagon for selling. I'm sure there'll be plentiful streams for fishing along the way."

Quite honestly, I'd rather have stayed upstairs, but it wouldn't have been hospitable of me. My stomach was queasy, not so much that I felt sick, but enough that I had no appetite.

The entire conversation at supper centered around Tom's impending journey and Will's anticipated purchase of the horse and wagon. Even Becca's impishness was barely noticed as Tom expounded on his plans.

"James Moore and I will leave on Thursday. We'll travel first to Pittsburgh, then follow the Ohio river all the way to the mighty Mississippi. We hope to reach St. Louis by Thanksgiving. That is, if we can manage to ride 30 miles a day." Tom rubbed his rump for good measure and we all laughed, including me.

"Will you stay there for the winter?" Emily asked as she buttered a slice of bread for Becca.

"Guess it all depends on the weather. James said we should take a southern route from there if we decide to travel on to Texas."

"Why Texas?" Joe asked.

"Land grants. And I mean a lot of land, for pennies on the dollar."

"Makes sense if you want to be a rancher," Joe said. "You have a hankering for that?"

"Don't know. I'll keep my options open. Regardless of where we end up, I can always find employment. I'm a pretty good blacksmith."

"That you are," Will said. "You should see what Tom's done to fix up the wagon I'm buying tomorrow. It'll be as good as new."

"You saw it already?" I asked.

"We walked over to the shop before we cooked the trout. I'll buy some paint, if you want to help me with the advertising on it, Lizzie."

"Sure," I said, reaching into my apron pocket for the money I'd promised Will. Luckily, I'd remembered to bring it downstairs after I had composed myself. "Here's my $20 for the wagon. I have stencils at school for the lettering."

"That's great," Will said, his smile a sign of his elation. "Too bad you're not able to join Tom on his travels, but he said you encouraged him to go."

I felt my cheeks flush, more from annoyance than embarrassment. Obviously, Tom had taken my statement of *"if that's what you want"* as support for his decision. Still, I was determined not to seem like a jilted woman, despite my broken heart.

"This will be a wonderful opportunity for Tom," I said. "He can write letters so that I, too, can experience his journey."

"Without a doubt, Lizzie," Tom said. "And you can send mail back to me so I know what's going on around here."

"We can share one tidbit before you leave," Joe said as he gazed lovingly at his wife. "Emily and I are expecting our second child, due in April."

"Oh, my goodness!" I exclaimed amidst congratulations from the others. "That's wonderful news. How are you feeling?"

"Tired," Emily said with a chuckle. "But fine now that the morning sickness has ended."

I had totally forgotten that Emily told me she suspected her pregnancy back in August. In fact, I was kicking myself for being so self-centered that I didn't even realize her distress the past few months. "I never thought...," I began.

"You see?" Emily said with a chuckle. "I *can* keep secrets." Our eyes met, both of us recognizing the depth of our friendship.

"On that note," Tom said, "Will and I are going to work on the wagon until dark. Do you mind if we take our leave?"

"Not at all," Emily said. "We'll have a special supper on Wednesday, in your honor, Tom."

"Much appreciated," Tom said as he stood to shake Joe's hand. He kissed Becca on the forehead and Emily on the cheek as he prepared to depart. As a second thought, he bent down and kissed me on the lips.

"Let's go, Romeo," Will said, opening the door to the evening breezes. "We've got things to do."

Chapter Twenty-Seven

The following Saturday after lessons, I enlisted Anna and Esther's services to help me paint the signage on Will's new buckboard. The girls selected the largest, fanciest script from the carton of stencils we had lugged from the art room, and I agreed that *Mitchell & Sons* should be painted in black on both sides of the wagon.

Esther surprised me by suggesting another smaller logo on the back frame with Will's name as proprietor. I have no doubt that she was hoping my brother would be overseeing our endeavors, but Will had been asked to work overtime at the grist mill, what with the end of harvest season drawing nigh.

I found it best to keep occupied since Tom's departure. Moments alone leave me despondent and prone to tears. Esther has a pleasantness about her, seeming to find the good in any situation. She makes me smile.

Anna is also kindhearted, though a bit naïve despite her world travels. It's evident that she was coddled as an only child, protected from difficulties by over-watchful nannies. Her friendship with Esther is enabling Anna to be less anxious about every little thing. In fact, they tease and joke until I'm laughing with them. I enjoy their company, and it serves to suppress my sadness.

Using a yardstick and chalk, we carefully measured vertical and horizontal lines for our lettering. Esther and Anna placed the stencil in the proper location, holding it straight while I dabbed the black paint. In short order, we had one side of the wagon finished and stood back to admire our work.

"Your brother's going to like this, Miss Mitchell," Esther said as she moved at various angles to observe how the light played on the wording. "It's looking quite fine. Perhaps he'll take us all for a ride later this afternoon."

Anna nudged her, laughing. "We can see through your ploy, you know."

"What ploy?"

"You want to flirt with Miss Mitchell's brother."

"I do not!" Esther retorted, though her statement ended with a giggle.

"You try to catch his attention whenever you see him."

"That's not entirely true. But, I must admit, he is rather fetching."

"Enough, the two of you," I said with a chuckle. "Let's finish the other side."

Once again, the girls held each stencil, while I carefully dabbed the paint. I almost smeared the lettering when Esther suddenly asked, "Do you ever flirt, Miss Mitchell?"

I pretended to be engrossed with my task, wiping extra paint off the stencil with the rag from my apron pocket. "I don't believe I do," I said.

"Perhaps because you already have a suitor," Esther said.

"Keep the stencil straight. We don't want to smudge the paint. If you're referring to Tom Hawks, he has departed to make his way out west."

"When did he leave?"

"Two days ago."

"Awww, Miss Mitchell. That saddens me. I felt sure that you would soon wed. I told Anna just last week that we would be your bridesmaids. Didn't I, Anna?"

Anna nodded, then signaled to Esther to move the stencil for the last L. As I dabbed the final letter, Esther continued her dialogue.

"Maybe he's just sowing his wild oats. That's what my mother said when one of my brothers did the same thing. In no time at all, he came back home, tail between his legs. Told us the grass isn't greener, if you get what I'm saying. Why didn't you go with him?"

"How could I leave my classes in the middle of a term? Besides, he didn't ask me to join him. He probably knew I'd decline the offer."

"Obviously, you didn't flirt," Esther said with a hint of humor in her voice. "I shall have to teach you a thing or two."

"Pray tell, where did you learn to be so worldly?" I asked as I stepped back to observe our work.

"You know I'm the youngest of eight children, Miss Mitchell. Surely one discovers many interesting tidbits when watching older siblings. The trick is not to seem too flirtatious. Honorable men aren't attracted to a hussy, but they *do* like a woman who's playful and engaging."

"And have you honed this skill?" I asked teasingly.

"Not quite. I still need practice."

Anna and I both laughed, especially when Esther feigned a coquettish stance. "And you plan to gain proficiency with my brother?"

"I believe so."

"She has already started," Anna said with a giggle.

"Well, I only initiate a conversation if I see your brother when Anna and I are out walking. Just being cordial, you know."

"Definitely," I said while looking through the carton for an appropriate smaller set of stencils for the back of the wagon. "And does Will take the time to converse with you?"

"Occasionally. Of course, he's never rude. But he's quite busy, working at the mill as well as starting his own travelling mercantile. I'm impressed that he's so industrious."

I didn't want to burst Esther's bubble by pointing out Will's flaws. Besides, this was evidently a school girl infatuation that would dissipate like snow melting on a sunny field when she completed her studies.

"It's true that Will has his focus on the new business," I said. "But I'm sure he enjoys socializing with you. What shall we stencil on the back of the wagon?"

"I think it should read *William Mitchell, Proprietor,* using the lettering you've selected," Esther said. "Anna can hold the stencil, while I dab the paint. You can take a rest."

I spread my skirts and sat cross-legged on the grass, using my rag to wipe off residual paint from the stencils we no longer needed. Though Esther took charge of the design on the back of the wagon, both girls worked in tandem. I thought to myself how lucky they were to have developed such a delightful friendship at a youthful age. Were it not for attending school together, their paths might never have crossed.

"Do you think you'll ever see your beau again, Miss Mitchell?" Ester asked, still carefully dabbing black paint.

Her question gave me pause, and I wasn't sure how to respond. I watched two squirrels chasing each other across the dirt roadway, one with an acorn in its mouth. They haven't a worry in this world; playful, while still busy hoarding food for the winter. Why have I not found such balance in my own life?

"I doubt it," I said after some silence. "Tom and I are very different. "He's content to enjoy what life has to offer."

"And you?"

"I seek something more."

"Like what?"

"I want to keep learning, embracing knowledge that I can share with my pupils. I love teaching, and I can't quite see myself doing anything else."

"But you can't marry if you're a teacher," Anna said.

"Perhaps someday I'll feel the urge to have a family. For now, I've found my niche. What about the two of you?"

"My father will arrange my marriage," Anna replied. "He plans to find the most fitting partnership for me, one that will benefit my status in the world."

"My pa said he's learned to stay out of it," Esther said with a chuckle. "He aimed to select the best match for three of my oldest sisters, even striving to extend the boundaries of our farm by marrying them off to sons of our neighbors. It didn't work."

"Why not?" Anna asked.

"He's got a passel of grandkids always hanging out at our place. He said it's just more mouths to feed. If you ask me, Pa's plumb tuckered out. Besides, he knows I've got a little more gumption than my sisters."

"Maybe you'll be a teacher, too," I said, laughing. I often felt that Esther was somewhat like me, wanting more in life than following the traditional establishment of a woman's place in the home.

"Perhaps I will," Esther agreed as she stepped back to eye the completed advertisement on the back of the buckboard. She walked entirely around the wagon, nodding her approval of the finished product.

"Your brother's going to be quite pleased," she said with delight. "Let's go tell him that his traveling store is ready for the road."

"The paint must dry first," I said. "We should wash up and return our supplies in the condition we found them. It will soon be time for your supper, and you'd best not be late."

Seeing Esther's decided disappointment, I added, "I'll ask Mrs. Kimber's permission for the two of you to join Will and me for a Sunday afternoon drive tomorrow, if Will is agreeable."

"That's perfect, Miss Mitchell," Esther agreed, practically dancing as we gathered our things.

Chapter Twenty-Eight

There was a refreshing westerly breeze and a cloudless cobalt sky as Will shook the reins to nudge the new draft horse along Hare's Hill Road. He sat proud as a peacock on the front seat, along with Esther who made sure she got the coveted place next to him. After repairing the wagon's axle, Tom had crafted a wooden side bench from stem to stern to hold Will's smaller wares. It made a sturdy, albeit inflexible, seat for Anna and me.

As we passed the boarding school, Anna and Esther waved to a few of the younger girls playing in the yard. They, too, probably yearned for an outing, and I reminded myself that I should make short trips available to all of the boarders on a more regular basis. Pending the Kimbers' permission, of course. Perhaps it's time for me to start saving to purchase a buggy, rather than frittering my hard-earned money on frocks and sundries.

Will planned to stop at our farm to collect additional goods to sell and, of course, to show off his travelling store. We turned south on the road to Uwchlan, then Esther pointed out the turn for her home in Charlestown. I chuckled to myself when

I heard her tell Will that the next excursion could be to her farmstead.

My brother was quite content to engage in conversation with Esther, seemingly unaware that she was using feminine wiles to garner his attention. I had to admit that she has a knack of bolstering his ego without being pretentious.

"How ever did you train your horse to follow every command?" Esther asked.

"He's pretty smart," Will acknowledged. "Of course, I'm an experienced driver, and I know this road inside and out."

Given that Esther grew up on a farm in our locale, I had a strong suspicion that she, too, could handle a wagon. No doubt, she knows her way around these parts.

"Have you named him yet?" she asked coquettishly.

"My horse?"

"Of course. Surely he's deserving of a fine name to suit your expanding enterprise."

"Hadn't really thought about it. He's brown. Guess I could call him *Chocolate*. Get it? Chocolate like the sweets?"

"That's very clever of you, Will, since you can peddle chocolates from your wagon. I was thinking of something more regal sounding, like *Admiral* or *Prince*, maybe even *Jupiter*."

"I like the name *Prince*," Will said. Perhaps it was my imagination, but Will seemed to sit taller in his seat as he nodded his approval. "Yes, ma'am. *Prince* it is!"

It took everything in me not to roll my eyes. There's no doubt about it. Esther learned more than cooking from her older sisters.

As we turned left on Yellow Springs Road, Will explained that turning right would have taken us to the sulfur springs that George Washington and his troops bathed in during their battle respites. "There's even a hospital built there," he said.

"I'd love to see it, Will," Esther said. "Several of my uncles fought in the Revolution. Could we go there some time?"

"My grandfather also fought in the war," Will said. "His leg was badly injured. He came back to his farm to recuperate, though he never did walk good after that. Pappy always said that my grandmother was the best nurse he could have had. Of course, he was no spring chicken when he was in battle. Must have been at least in his forties. His older sons had already headed west, and my pa was too young to fight. Anyway, I could probably take you to see the place."

I noticed Will was doing a lot of talking today. He and Esther shared tales about family members from days gone by, and tidbits about life on the farm. Fact is, I don't think either of them took much of a breath during the entire excursion.

Will directed Prince to turn left at our drive, then urged him to take the hill slowly. "This is our road here," he said to Esther, pointing out local landmarks such as the huge beehive in the large oak tree on the right and the birch tree near the curve with his name carved into it.

Esther responded appropriately as she pushed some errant strands of red hair back under her bonnet. I figured she wanted to make a good impression on the family.

Pa and Benjamin were in the barn when we pulled up. Ben came running over, calling "Hey Pa. Come see the lettering on Will's buckboard!"

By the time Pa joined us, Esther had jumped down from the front seat and I had helped Anna out the back. Will was unhitching Prince and leading him to a bucket of water.

I gave Pa a kiss on his stubbly cheek, uncharacteristically unshaven for a mid-afternoon even if it were a day of rest. "This is Esther and Anna," I said. "They're two of my students and they helped me paint the advertising on Will's wagon."

"Nice to meet you," Pa said. "It looks fine, Lizzie. Mighty fine. Let me see that horse you got, Will."

Pa pulled open the gelding's mouth, checking his teeth, then lifted each hoof to examine underneath. "He looks good, though a mite thin. Put him out in the field for a while. Not too long. Don't want him to colic."

"His name is Prince," Will said. "Don't you think that's a fitting name for such a handsome steed?"

"Definitely. How did you afford him and the wagon?"

"Tom Hawks found them for me. A gent heading west sold them—only $85. Needed some repair to the axle, but Tom was able to fix the wagon before he saddled up to leave town."

"Where's he going?" Pa asked, with a sideward glance to me. Esther put her hand in mine.

"Probably to Texas," Will said. "He left last Thursday."

"Jilted your sister?"

"Don't think so, Pa. She told him he was free to go."

"Miss Mitchell's pretty shook up about it," Esther said. "Of course, you know she'd never say anything to hold him back from what he wanted to do. That's just how she is. Look at the dark circles under her eyes. You can tell she's not been sleeping well."

Pa took a good look at me, as did Will and Benjamin. I could feel the flush of my cheeks, as I kicked a rock in the dirt away from one of the wagon wheels.

"I'm quite fine, Esther. I'll take you and Anna to meet Ma and Mary."

"Your ma's a little upset," Pa said. "Coyote got another one of her sheep early this morning. We could hear the ruckus all the way to the house."

"Is that why you didn't shave today?" I asked.

Pa rubbed his hand across his bristly chin as he replied, "Been busy trying to fix the breach."

"How'd it get through the fencing?" Will asked.

"Rails were knocked out of their posts and wire's been cut. Not the first time, either. Bet my bottom dollar, that no-good bastard brother... Excuse my language, ladies. Take the girls to meet your mother, Lizzie. I want to show Will the damage."

Chapter Twenty-Nine

As I knew she would be, Ma was very hospitable to Anna and Esther. She invited them to sit on the porch with her and Mary while they carded wool, and suggested that I ask Ellie to bring everyone a glass of sweet tea.

Ellie was already a step ahead of me in the kitchen. She had filled six glasses with her refreshing mint-laced concoction, and the two of us managed to carry three each without spilling them.

"This is my sister, Ella Sophie," I said as Anna and Esther both took a glass of tea from my hands. "We call her Ellie most times. And you met Ma and Mary. Ellie, this here's Anna and Esther, two of my students at the school."

"I'm pleased to meet you," Ellie said, most likely noting that both girls were close to her in age. "Are you from Pikeland?"

"My family farm is in Charlestown township, not too far from here," Esther said, taking a sip of tea. "I'm the youngest of eight, and the luckiest of all my siblings to be able to attend the French Creek School."

"And I'm an only child," Anna said. "My parents travel often, though we maintain a home in Philadelphia."

"Anna's father is a diplomat," I added. "She has traveled all through Europe. Isn't that quite an accomplishment?"

"What country did you like best?" Ellie asked.

"I'm most comfortable in Britain, as we have a home there as well. But I enjoy visiting France, especially Paris. It's a lovely city."

"Someday, I hope to travel," Ellie said, glancing to see Ma's reaction. "Of course, first I need to see Philadelphia and, perhaps, New York. I shall visit all the fashion houses."

"How do you know of those?" I asked.

"I read about them in Pa's newspaper, the *Village Record*. Paris sets the trend for all of the latest fashions."

"Ellie will need to marry well," Ma said with amusement. "No man will be able to keep her in the finery she so desires."

"Have you any other children?" Esther asked Ma.

"Yes, two younger boys and a girl. They're fishing at the pond this afternoon. Most likely, Matt and young George are teasing little Julie mercilessly. I hope they come home with more than mud on their clothes. And, of course, you've met Will and Benjamin."

"Yes, we have," Esther said politely. "They've gone with Mr. Mitchell to examine the broken fence. We sometimes have a similar problem with the rails on our fences. On occasion, we'll find a few of our cows grazing in a neighbor's field."

"I suppose it's not so unusual," Ma said, handing Mary another pile of wool. "But, in this case, we have wire to reinforce the slats. It's evident that the wire has been cut, giving easy access to coyotes."

"Pa thinks it's his brother causing trouble," I said, looking to see if Mary agrees with me.

"The uncle gets blamed for everything gone wrong around here," Ma said. "If you can't say something kindly of someone, don't say it at all. Ellie, why don't you and the girls take a walk to the pond? See what the children are up to."

Esther was content to have the opportunity to explore our homestead. Anna didn't seem as enthusiastic, probably recognizing that she'd have to step around chickens and pass by the pigs' pen. Nonetheless, Ellie enjoyed acting as the hostess, and I'm sure she was looking forward to hearing more about Anna's global excursions.

"They seem very sweet," Ma said as we watched the girls head to the woods. "It's nice for Ellie to make friends. She doesn't have much companionship."

"It's Esther who wanted to come," I said with a chuckle. She's smitten with Will."

"Glory be!" Ma exclaimed. "She's a mite young for Will, don't you think?"

"A schoolgirl infatuation. Will hardly realizes that she seeks his attention. I must admit, though, Esther's older sisters have evidently taught her about womanly charm."

"A lesson you might do well to learn. Where's Tom? Usually he's with you and Will on a Sunday afternoon."

I felt my eyes misting, but I didn't want Ma to see how upset I've been. "He went to Texas, or some part thereabouts."

"How long will he be gone?"

It took me several moments to swallow my pride before I could respond. "Maybe forever."

Ma reached over to take my hand, and that triggered the waterworks. "Oh, Ma! Tom was my best friend, save for Emily. Whatever will I do without him?"

Ma handed me the handkerchief from her apron pocket and I noisily blew my nose, then wiped the tears from my cheeks. Finally, I said, "Tom didn't even ask me to go with him." Of course, that brought another crying spell.

"I know for a fact that there's nothing I can say to soften your grief, sweetie. It's a passage of life that's terribly difficult. In time, Tom may return or another beau may catch your fancy."

Blowing my nose again, I said, "I shall be a spinster, for sure. There will never be a kinder, more gentle man than Tom. I won't let myself experience what Mary did by marrying the uncle after her husband died."

"I had a child to raise and a farm I couldn't manage on my own," Mary said quietly. "I'm sorrowful that Tom is gone from you, but he ain't dead. Might be, he just needed to get the wanderlust out of his soul. Better to know that now, not after you got a passel of kids to feed."

"I know," I said, still sniffling. "That's what I tell myself, not that I see motherhood in my future. I'm going to stay busy, and perhaps further my education."

"I don't believe Henry Harris is courting yet," Ma said, once again brushing the wool fibers in her lap. "I could ask Mrs. Harris..."

"Ma, I'm not interested in Henry," I interjected before she could finish her sentence. "He could be the last man walking this earth, and I still wouldn't consider him a match for me."

"That's fine, then. I won't mention him again. Go wash your face at the pump before the girls return. I'm sure you don't want them to observe your distress."

As I wiped the cool water from my face with the bottom of my apron, I noticed that Pa, Will, and Ben had returned from the sheepfold. They took some time to load bags of grain and jars of jam into Will's mobile mercantile before joining us on the back porch.

"You have anything else you want me to sell, Ma?" Will asked.

"There's some eggs in the basket on the counter, and some venison jerky in the pantry. Mary pickled some cucumbers last week. You can take all but two of them jars."

"Do you have any yarn made up?"

"In the den. You can have five skeins. When you get some money from selling, I'll be needing a bag of sugar."

"I'll bring it by tomorrow afternoon, after I finish my deliveries."

"That'll be fine. You want to stay for supper?"

"Not today, Ma. Mrs. Kimber expects the girls back to the school by then. Where are they?"

The words were no sooner out of Will's mouth before we saw Julie skipping ahead of Ellie, Esther, and Anna. Ellie and Anna were deep in conversation, but I could see that Esther was keeping watch over Julie.

Will got Ben to help him retrieve all that Ma was willing to sell and load it into the wagon. Once Julie saw me on the porch, she came sprinting to wrap her short arms around me.

"Hey, Lizzie. Did you come to see me?"

"I sure did, pumpkin! How many fish did you catch?"

"Not one. Matt and George made me look for worms in the mud. But they each caught a catfish."

"That's good," Ma said. "I was hoping we'd be having a fish dinner tonight. Are the boys coming home soon?"

"They're trying to catch another one," Ellie said. "I told Matt to hasten because Pa would be wanting to start cleaning them."

"No hurry," Pa said with a twinkle in his eye. "I'm going to sit out here with your ma for a while, maybe even grab a little snooze."

"And we're going to take our leave," I said as I gave Julie a pat on the rump and a kiss on her cheek. "Looks like Will's got Prince hitched and he's ready to go."

"Tell Will to drive safe," Pa cautioned. "You girls come back any time."

"Thank you, Mr. and Mrs. Mitchell," Esther said. "It was a pleasure to meet you, Missus Mary. We had a lovely visit."

"I hope to see you again soon," Ellie said. "I want to hear more of your travels, Anna."

"I promise there will be more stories to share the next time we meet," Anna said with her engaging smile.

I had a feeling that Ellie and Anna would become the best of friends. Esther has her sights on Will, so I don't think she'll miss out on any of the camaraderie.

Chapter Thirty

In preparation for our fall break, the final week of September was a demanding one at school. The curriculum included compulsory testing in all major subjects, so additional study time was necessary. And, since the students would be gone for two weeks, they were required to wash their bedding, clean their dorms, and scrub the floors in the classrooms and dining room.

Most of the girls would be taken home by their parents, but those who lived at a distance were permitted to stay with the families of those who lived close by. Since Anna's parents were traveling, they gave approval for her to spend the time at Esther's farm.

Each evening, I stayed late to grade papers and assist the younger girls with their packing. They were to take home their summer frocks, and return with warmer clothing for the winter. Remarkably, there was no grousing about the added duties, as a sense of anticipation draped the halls and bolstered everyone's spirits.

Departure day was planned as a festival of sorts, with games, a treasure hunt, and a barbecue picnic. I thought it was quite kind of Susannah Kimber to suggest that I invite our Julie and Ella, and very generous of Will to offer to transport them.

Saturday of the first week in October dawned with just a nip of chill in the morning air, portending the imminent change of seasons. After dressing, I wrapped a wool shawl around my shoulders, put a few last-minute items into my valise, and tip-toed down the steps lest I awaken Becca too early. Joe and Emily knew I planned to stay with my family during the school break, and we had said our farewells last evening before going to bed.

First, I crossed the road to find Will's buckboard where he parks it behind the grist mill. Not a living soul was yet up and about, though I noticed a candlelit room in the hotel as I passed by. The air smelled decidedly of chrysanthemums, sage, and hydrangeas, while a light mist clung to the morning grass.

After I placed my valise under the front seat of Will's wagon, I proceeded to the side door of the school, near the kitchen. Still half asleep, Abby and Gertrude Kimber were bringing butter and jam to the dining room, while Mary and her mother prepared oatmeal porridge. I offered to slice the bread before ringing the bell to signal that breakfast was ready.

When we finished eating, the students completed their morning charges. Some of the older girls had kitchen duty, while the younger ones swept the dining room or carried clean dishes to the pantry. Since there would be no morning lessons, time was not of essence. We teased, bantered, and laughed, fully enjoying the first day of our vacation.

When I told Esther and Anna that Ellie and Julie would be spending the afternoon with us, they could barely contain their delight. "Perhaps Ellie might enjoy helping us organize the treasure hunt," Anna said. "Do you think she would?"

"I'm sure of it," I replied with amusement. "And Julie will want to be involved. What will you have the girls find?"

"Mostly flowers, leaves, and nuts," Esther said. "Anna and I made a list of plants we learned about in botany class."

"It sounds delightful," I said. "I'll be helping with the cooking. Will you be able to keep an eye on little Julie?"

"Of course. Though she may also want to play tag or hide and seek with the younger girls."

"Send her over to me if she becomes too overbearing. What time will you be leaving?"

"Late afternoon," Esther said. "One of my brothers will come for Anna and me. Perhaps you'll be able to meet him."

"That would be lovely. Does he still live at home?"

"No. He has his own farm just down the road. Well, it was part of ours, but Pa gave him some land as a wedding gift. He offered to pick us up since he needs some sundries in town."

"I'll keep my eye out for him. Perhaps you'll be able to introduce your brother to Will if they both arrive at the same time."

I'm not sure what possessed me to make such a remark, for it only served to encourage Esther's infatuation with my brother. Nonetheless, my words elicited a comical grin as she and Anna hooked arms before setting off to complete their next tasks.

I helped the younger girls make their beds with fresh linens before doing a double check that they hadn't forgotten to pack anything of importance. One by one, we carried satchels to the front parlor, lining them up like soldiers along the side wall, ready for the taking at the end of the day.

Before the girls could go out to play, I sent them to the kitchen to carry something to the yard. We needed cutlery, dishes, platters, and condiments, all of which could be brought out by small hands.

Finding several large watermelons ripe for picking in the garden, I lugged them, one at a time, to the picnic table by the millrace. Moments later, I noticed that Will had arrived with Ellie and Julie, and already they were surrounded by a bevy of schoolgirls. I made my way to the throng, observing that Esther and Anna were at the head of the pack, welcoming my sisters and inviting them to join us.

"We're here, Lizzie!" Julie exclaimed. "This is the most exciting day of my life."

I laughed, but thought to myself that it probably is the first time Julie's been to the crossroads. I took Julie's hand, and helped her jump from the front seat of the wagon to the ground, making sure her petticoats didn't trip her. Ellie waved to me as she took off with Esther and Anna.

"Thanks for bringing them, Will," I said. "Stop by later for pork barbecue."

"Might do that. What time do you think you'll be ready to leave?"

"I'll need to help clean up. Just depends on when parents arrive for their daughters."

"That's fine. I'm going to work at the mill for a few hours. Be back later."

"Well, go on," 5-year-old Julie said to Will, giving him a little push. She was obviously eager for her fun to begin.

"You remember what Ma told you before we left," Will cautioned. "You keep Lizzie or Ellie in sight at all times. And you use your best manners."

"I know," Julie said, tugging my hand impatiently.

As Will pulled away, I introduced Julie to a couple of the other primary level girls and encouraged her to join them in a game of hopscotch. Ellie was already helping Esther and Anna set up their treasure hunt table off the side porch, giggling with them as they decided what prizes to offer.

Parents began arriving around 3 p.m., and one by one the students departed with full bellies and their horticultural finds.

When Will returned, he made a plate of pulled pork and finished off the baked beans. I munched on a slice of watermelon while he ate, both of us watching Julie jumping rope with several of the remaining children.

"Julie's going to sleep well tonight," I said with a chuckle. "She's had a glorious day."

"Ellie seems to enjoy the company of Esther and Anna," Will remarked. "She's probably been bending their ears about fashion and style."

"No doubt about that. Though I daresay, Esther is more interested in books than clothing. Nonetheless, the three get along well."

"Definitely. Can we leave soon? I'd like to get back to the livery before dark."

"If you wouldn't mind helping me take things into the house," I said, noticing Susanna and Abby Kimber talking to a few of the parents on the front lawn. Gertrude, Patti, and Mary, no doubt, were washing dishes in the kitchen.

"More hands make light work," Will said. "Let's get the rest of the children to carry what they can."

In short order, the yard was spotless, food had been put away, and tables were carried to the storage shed. Esther called out that her brother had arrived, and I went to meet him as she and Anna gathered their belongings.

"I'm Lizzie Mitchell," I said, reaching up to the front seat of the buckboard to shake his hand.

"Pleased to meet you, Miss Mitchell. I'm James Kingsly. We've heard all about you."

Ellie and Will were assisting Esther and Anna with their bags, while Julie followed closely behind. Once everything was loaded in the back of the buckboard, Will helped the girls up to the front seat. Esther seemed to hold onto his hand a tad longer than necessary, and a deep flush rose to her cheeks.

"This is James," I said to Will. "Esther's brother."

"Glad to make your acquaintance," Will said. "I see you have the same duty I have. Let's get these girls home."

"They'll probably all be up half the night, giggling with excitement," James said.

"No doubt," Will agreed with a chuckle.

We said our farewells as they drove off, then I made sure to thank Mrs. Kimber for inviting Julie and Ellie. I let Ellie sit in the front seat of the wagon with Will, while Julie and I sat on the storage bench in the back.

By the time we turned onto the road to Uwchlan, Julie was sound asleep with her head resting on my lap. Ellie, on the other hand, told us every single detail of each thing she did for the entire day. It was enough to make me sleepy, too.

The late afternoon sun was low on the horizon, peeking through the vibrant fall leaves as we made our way south. It wouldn't be long before they'd be turning dingy brown and falling from their branches. The changing seasons never fail to amaze me, providing a sense of anticipation for what lies ahead.

Julie stirred as Will directed Prince to turn up our long drive, and I suggested that she should wake from her nap. As we reached the top of the hill, it seemed eerily quiet.

No one was on the back porch, the barn door was open but the barn was empty inside, and none of the lamps were lit in the kitchen. Will glanced back at me to see if I noticed anything awry.

"Where is everyone?" Ellie asked.

"I don't know," I said, feeling a deep perception of dread in the pit of my stomach.

Will pulled up to the barn, and called, "We're home!"

Ellie echoed in a louder voice, "We're home! Ma? Pa? Anyone here?"

I was relieved to see Matt and young George sprinting from the trees near the cow pasture. The look on their faces, though, was frightful.

"Come quick," Matt yelled. "Pa's been hurt. Real bad!"

Chapter Thirty-One

Will jumped from the wagon, bounding across the yard and through the trees ahead of Ellie, Julie, and me. Matt led him to the pasture, but little George stood there crying. He threw his arms around my waist and sobbed into my apron. Grabbing him by the shoulders, I got down on one knee and asked, "Are you hurt, as well?"

George shook his head vehemently. "No, but I think Pa's going to die. We can't get the trap off his leg. He's bleeding bad."

"Go get me some towels," I said. "Ellie, can you help him?"

"I want to go see Pa."

"Please, Ellie," I yelled as I turned to run toward the field. "Get lots of towels. You, too, Julie!"

I was shocked to see the amount of blood that had soaked through Pa's pant leg and covered Ma, Ben, and Mary. Someone had removed his work boots and placed a stick between Pa's teeth before he had passed out from his injury. His face was contorted in pain and as pale as a ghost.

Ma held Pa's head in her lap, her arms holding him tight under his armpits, tears streaming from her eyes to her bodice. Mary had wrapped her apron around his leg, just below the knee, and was holding it firmly to stop the flow of blood. Will and Ben were both tugging with all their strength at the jaws of the iron trap that had literally clamped into the bone of Pa's lower leg.

"Dear God!" I exclaimed at the horrendous sight. My belly heaved, but I managed to regain control. Will gave me a look that I knew signaled a dreadful outcome.

"Go fetch Doc Pyle," Ma said to me in a low, restrained voice. "And get some whiskey. I don't know how much longer your father can endure the pain."

I dashed to the buckboard, jumped up to the seat, and grabbed the reins. Ellie and George were scurrying from the house, their arms full of cloths, Julie trailing behind them. Not wanting her to see Pa's torment, I told Julie to climb into the wagon with me.

"Is there any whiskey in the house?" I asked hurriedly.

"Might be some in the uncle's loft," Ellie said.

"Go see. Bring it to Pa. Whatever you can find. I'll take Julie with me to fetch Doc Pyle. And, Ellie, brace yourself. It's not good."

With a click of my tongue, Prince led us down the drive and onto Yellow Springs Road. I wasn't nearly as cautious as Will, urging his gelding to travel the distance as quickly as possible. I breathed a sigh of relief to find the doctor at home.

"You've got to come quick, Doc," I said when he opened his front door. "Pa's been hurt with an iron trap, and he's bleeding horribly. There's no time for you to saddle your horse. Please come with me right away."

Doc Pyle grabbed his medical bag, and threw it in the back of the wagon. Then he stepped up to the front seat, scooting Julie to the center. He was no sooner settled in before I set off at a clip. I told him what I knew as we made our way to the farm.

"Is your pa conscious?"

"No. He's lost a lot of blood. Will and Ben are trying to get the trap off his leg, but it's in there deep."

"Is he in the house?"

"No. He's in the field. Can't imagine why there'd be an iron trap in the pasture unless the coyote's been after the cows."

"We have to get him into the house," Doc said. "The night air will be too chilly for him if he's in shock. Take me directly to the field, then bring some lanterns. It'll soon be dark."

I pulled the wagon as close as I could get to the pasture gate, and yelled that the doctor had arrived. Ellie ran over to lead him to Pa, while I urged Prince back to the barn.

"Help me carry lanterns, Julie," I said after assisting her down from the buckboard.

"I'll get the matchsticks," she replied in a remarkably calm voice that belied the terror in her eyes.

By the time Julie and I got back to the field, Doc Pyle had used his sharp tool to cut the wire holding the clamp's tension, then extricated its iron teeth from Pa's bone. He directed Will and Ben to make a pallet so they could carry Pa into the house.

I ran back, grabbing Julie by the hand, to light every candle I could find in the kitchen. Ellie followed me, and by the time the others arrived with Pa, we had lugged a mattress from the loft, and got a fire going in the hearth.

Doc Pyle led the entourage into the house and began giving orders. "Lizzie and Ellie, start filling every kettle with water and put it on the fire for boiling. Julie, you can get me a glass of drinking water for your pa. Matt and George, drag the mattress into the front parlor, close to the fireplace. Mary, stir the embers and add some logs. And, I need the room well lit. The rest of us will carry your pa on the pallet, then carefully transfer him to the mattress."

After moving the first pot of water onto the crane and over the flames in the kitchen hearth, I bounded upstairs to get a clean sheet and pillow for the mattress. Pa moaned terribly when he was positioned so that his left leg was easily accessible. I put my right arm around Ma's waist as we watched Doc cut the fabric of Pa's trouser and stocking, and gently remove them.

"You'd best keep the children out of the way," Ma said to me in a shaky voice. "They can stay in the kitchen, unless any of 'em want to go to bed. But keep pumping water. Doc's going to need a lot of it."

I caught a glimpse of the deep, raw wound in Pa's leg as Doc Pyle used tweezers to painstakingly remove bits of fabric, dried blood, and rust from the torn skin. Julie handed me the glass of water, which I gave to Ma before ushering her back to the kitchen.

While the boys formed a water brigade, I gathered clean rags from the laundry. The first kettle had not yet boiled, but it was hot enough to be used for washing. I lugged it to the parlor with the cloths, and Will set the next kettle on the crane.

One by one, all seven of us children had finished the imminent tasks and settled ourselves at the kitchen table. We were a gloomy bunch, not sure what to do next, and frightened about whether Pa would survive his injury.

"How is it possible that there was a loaded trap in the pasture?" Will asked. "Pa would never have placed one there. Did one of you boys set it to catch the coyote?" Each vehemently shook his head, denying the possibility.

"What about the uncle?" I asked. "Where is he, anyway?"

"He wouldn't be that stupid," Benjamin said. "Any one of us could have stepped on that thing—or the cows, for that matter. Besides, he told us this morning he'd be away a few days."

"Where'd he go?"

"Not rightly sure. Up north to hunt beavers, I think."

The whole thing set uneasy with me, but I didn't want to alarm the young ones. I just hoped there weren't any more traps set in any location on the farm.

"I'm hungry, Lizzie," Matt said. "Can you fix us something to eat?"

"Of course," I acknowledged, racking my brain for what we could prepare at this late hour. It didn't take but a moment for Ellie to spring into action. She brought a loaf of bread from the pantry, as well as butter and jam. I noticed the basket of eggs on the counter, probably being saved for Will's enterprise, and began breaking them into a bowl for scrambling.

"More water!" the doc bellowed "Hot and cold."

Will immediately lugged a hot kettle to the parlor, and tossed the bloody residue from the previous one into the garden. Ben put another kettle on the crane to boil, while Ellie began cooking the eggs. I brought in a bucket of well water and put it on the floor near Ma. She was again cradling Pa's head in her lap.

"He's burning up, Lizzie. Give me a clean rag soaked in the cool water. And get the quilt from my bed."

By the time I returned with the blanket, Pa was shivering to the likes I'd never seen. Mary was assisting Doc Pyle, holding Pa's leg still while he continued working on the ugly wound.

I stood there for several moments, mesmerized with the dreadful thoughts running through my head. Life is so very fragile. At any moment, it can be snatched when we least expect it. What would we do without Pa's steady protective guidance? It took all my power to set aside such horrendous notions while I prepared another cool cloth for Ma.

"Best make a pot of coffee for Doc Pyle and Mary," Ma said. "And bring another glass of water for your pa."

"You want anything to eat? Ellie's cooking eggs for the boys."

"No, but thank you. And Lizzie, ...I'm glad you're home."

I had tears in my eyes when I returned to the kitchen, but set about making the coffee so none of the others would notice. Though Ellie had made a plate for me, I couldn't begin to put anything in my stomach. Instead, I divided my eggs between Ben, Matt, and George since I knew they hadn't had any supper, then joined them at the table.

"How's Pa?" Ben asked.

"He's got a fever."

"Is he going to die, Lizzie?" Matt asked.

"I don't know. Reckon we should say some prayers."

We sat there with nary another word to say. The only sounds were the occasional popping of a log and the hissing of boiling water in the kettle.

It seemed like hours had passed, but it was possibly only thirty minutes when Mary passed through the kitchen to wash up at the pump. When she returned, she poured herself a mug of coffee and sat with us at the table.

"Your horse is still hitched, Will," she said in a quiet voice. "You might want to put him in a stall."

"Forgot all about Prince," Will said, grabbing a lantern for his walk to the barn.

"Be careful where you're walking," Mary added. "Could be more traps set."

"You know anything about them?" I asked.

She slowly shook her head right to left. "No. But I got a bad feeling."

Julie moved her chair closer to Mary's, then leaned over to rest her head in Mary's lap. Mary gently rubbed Julie's back, softly telling her that everything would be all right. In no time at all, Julie was in a sound sleep.

"Doc will be wanting some coffee in a minute," Mary said. "He's finishing up the bandages and talking to your ma."

"I'll get it," I said as I went to retrieve another mug from the pantry. I had no sooner poured a cup and put it on the table before Doc joined us in the kitchen.

"I need to wash up first," he said. "You got any soap and hot water?"

When he was done, Doc took a long sip of his coffee, then removed his spectacles and placed them on the table. He looked at each of us, sadness in his eyes.

"Your pa's sleeping now. I gave him a pinch of opium in a sip of whiskey. That should last a couple of hours."

"Can we go see him?" Matt asked.

"You can stand in the doorway. Your ma's lying with him to help him stay warm."

"Will he be better by tomorrow?" George asked.

"No. He's still in danger. I'll stay through the night."

"You going to have to cut off his leg?

"I hope not. But don't know yet."

"Why not?"

"Don't know how much of the bone was damaged. And there could be other problems."

"Like what?"

"Like an infection, or maybe even tetanus."

"What's that?"

"Lockjaw."

"Do people die from that?"

"Yep."

Will came back to hear the end of the conversation. I caught Mary's eye, and it's as if her gaze was preparing me for the worse. It was evident that Doc Pyle wanted us to know the seriousness of the situation, but his lack of detail indicated that he didn't want us unduly worried.

"Then we should all get some sleep," I said decisively. "I'll take Julie up to bed. Matt and George, brush your teeth and hit the sack."

I offered the loft to Doc Pyle but he declined. "I'll snooze on the upholstered chair in the parlor. Your father might need more medication through the night."

"Go on, all of you," Mary said. "Give us some peace."

Chapter Thirty-Two

Pa made it through the night, but only by a thread. No doubt, his stubborn nature put the pearly gates on hold. Doc was examining Pa's wound when I came downstairs with Julie. Ellie was already preparing breakfast, while the boys were feeding the animals and collecting eggs from the hens.

"You need any hot water?" I asked Doc, while watching Ma hold Pa's leg still. Her face was drawn and haggard, the front of her skirts stained black from yesterday's dried blood.

"Mary had been fetching it through the night. As the sun began to rise, I told her to go to her room and get some sleep. Yes, Lizzie. I could use a fresh batch. Might be some heating on the crane."

"Sure, Doc. I'll bring it to you."

Doc gave me a grateful glance and nodded. I noticed the dark circles under his eyes and his stubbled cheeks. "Bring a glass of cold water, too."

I led Julie to the kitchen, despite her wanting to stay with Ma, and suggested that she help Ellie by setting the table. Ellie had just lugged in a kettle of fresh water from the pump, and the two of us lifted it to the crane. I ladled boiling water from the other kettle into a smaller pot to bring to Doc. The rest she'd use to make the oat porridge.

I made two trips to the parlor, first with the hot water, then with a bowl and a cup of fresh water from the well. Ma turned to me, knowing it was part of my nature to want to assist my pa. "Doc said we need to give your father sips of water as often as possible. The fever and loss of blood cause dehydration. You could do that, Lizzie. And bathe his face and chest with the cooling rag."

I sat as Ma had done yesterday with Pa's head in my lap, gently caressing his forehead and shoulders. He was sleeping fitfully, occasionally moaning as Doc tugged on the dressing that had stuck to his leg. Pa's face was pale and yellowish, his cheeks and chin stubbled with bristles. He still had a fever, but it wasn't as bad as last night.

Bile rose in my throat when the bandages were removed and I caught sight of the ugly, festered injury. Doc warned Ma to hold Pa's leg tight, because he was going to bathe the wound with tincture of iodine—a rather new medication that greatly stings, but helps with healing.

Pa screamed in pain with the initial application, then settled back with a low keening. Using a hunk of cotton, Doc spread the dark orange liquid in and around the deep laceration before wrapping a new dressing.

"That's as much as we can do for now," Doc said. "I'd be grateful if Will could take me home. I'll return before dark."

Ma nodded, but looked fearful at the idea of having no ready access to the doc's assistance should the tide turn worse. I had the same feeling.

"I'll leave the vial with the opium-laced whiskey," Doc added. "He can have a sip for his pain each time he wakens."

"Thank you, Doc," Ma said wearily. "I appreciate your kindness."

"It's important for you to eat something and get some rest now, Jane. Let Lizzie watch over William."

"I'll be fine."

"I insist," Doc countered. "If you fall ill, it will be quite detrimental for your husband and your children."

Doc Pyle's a smart man. He knew the exact words to convince Ma that she needed to sleep before continuing her watchful care of Pa. Doc stood and retrieved his bag.

"I'll see myself out," Doc said. "And I'll have Will purchase more whiskey before he returns. It'll bring merciful relief for William during these first few days."

That sounded hopeful to me—that Pa would be all right if he could make it through today and tomorrow. Little did I know how tenuous that would be.

^^^

Ma relieved my watch by mid-afternoon. She had washed up at the pump after her nap and had changed her clothing, even ate a piece of bread with jam. She brought a cup of coffee with her to the parlor, and sat on the upholstered chair next to Pa's mattress.

"Did he awaken?"

"Only twice," I said. "I gave him a sip of the medicine each time and he quickly returned to slumber."

"And the fever?"

"It's getting worse as the day progresses. The cool water compresses don't seem to do a thing."

"I'll keep on it. Do we need fresh water?"

"Mary brought some just before you came downstairs."

Ma nodded and took another swig of coffee. Her gaze never left Pa's face, and I could see by her expression the immense love she feels for him. It was a reminder to me that I would never vow myself to another without the same deep, unrelenting passion.

"The children will need supper soon," Ma said after she took the last sip of her coffee.

"I'll help Mary and Ellie. They've already started making a stew. The boys are tilling the soil to prepare for planting the winter wheat."

"That's good. You hear that, William? Your boys are working the field."

The flutter of Pa's eyelids indicated that he heard our conversation. Ma, too, recognized that Pa was listening.

"You tell the good Lord that you aren't going to heaven yet," Ma said with tears in her eyes. "You've got a family that needs you. You fight with all your strength. You hear me, William?"

I noticed the smallest, faintest nodding of Pa's head. Ma handed me her empty mug, and said to me, "You go on now, Lizzie. I'm going to lie down here with your Pa. And you tell the others not to worry. I'm not letting my husband leave this earth. Not while I'm living and breathing."

Chapter Thirty-Three

I wish I could tell you that Pa was on the mend. For three days, he was in and out of consciousness, in excruciating pain. Doc Pyle arrived morning and night to disinfect the wound and change the dressing on Pa's leg. Ma rarely left his side, only relinquishing her self-imposed duty to grab a bite to eat, use the outhouse, or take a nap. For those times, she'd permit Mary, Will, or me to sponge Pa with cool compresses.

Pa's fever never really departed that first week. It would lessen in the mornings, but always spiked at night. Doc seemed worried, but didn't say much about what could be done. He did, however, encourage small feedings of chicken broth, which Mary prepared fresh daily.

Ma was spooning warm broth into Pa's mouth when Doc entered the parlor this morning. We had gotten Pa into a sitting position with his back supported by the wall and four pillows, but the feeding was a messy job. Each time Pa attempted to swallow, much of it would dribble out the corner of his mouth. Doc Pyle observed the scene with a decided frown.

"Good morning, Doc," Ma said, without looking up from her task. "William's being a good patient, trying to follow your instructions. He's consumed nearly half of his allotted broth."

"Looks to me that most is on his lap," Doc said. "What's going on here, William?"

Pa gave a slight movement of his shoulders, like he was trying to shrug but fell short. "_y _out_ doan _ork."

"Your mouth doesn't work?"

Pa nodded his head in agreement. At least it seemed like a nod. Ma stopped feeding Pa and looked at Doc, for the first time noticing the concern in his eyes.

"Let me take a gander," Doc said while signaling for me to leave the room.

I took Pa's cup of broth from Ma's hands, then poured myself a glass of tea before sitting at the kitchen table. Mary was kneading bread and Ellie was making a batch of muffins.

"Why so morose?" Ellie asked.

"Something's wrong with Pa."

"Obviously."

"No. I mean something else. He can't move his mouth."

"He's had a lot of opium and whiskey," Ellie said. "The uncle gets like that when he's been drinking."

"I guess that's possible. But Doc looked worried. He's examining him now."

"Might as well make yourself useful and peel some taters," Mary said. "Can't do nothing 'til we hear it from the horse's mouth."

Forty minutes later, Doc Pyle took the soap from the counter and walked out to the pump. After washing his hands, he returned to the kitchen and plopped into Pa's seat at the head of the table. Mary handed him a cup of hot coffee, and sat next to him. "Everything all right?"

He shook his head, running his fingers through his hair. "No. I suspect he has tetanus."

"I don't really understand what that is," I said, trying to think if I ever knew of anyone who had the disease.

"It's a very nasty condition," Doc said. "We don't know what causes it, and it's almost never cured."

"Is there no medication for it?" I asked.

"No, though the opium in spirits has been used. There is one experimental treatment that has shown some limited success."

"We'll do whatever need be, no matter the cost," I said. "What is it?"

"I've never tried it. Most folks don't survive tetanus, but I read of a recent cure by soaking the patient in hot water for hours at a time. We'll need the tub brought in by the fire, like you have for your baths."

"I don't understand," Ellie said.

"Tetanus causes paralysis," Doc said. "First of the face and mouth. Then it works its way down the body. If, or when, it reaches the lungs, the patient suffocates."

"Oh, my goodness!" I exclaimed. "How does hot water help?"

"I don't know. But it's the only treatment I've heard that has any chance of success. The opium just keeps the patient calm. It's not curative. The lengthy soaking in hot water may repress the nerves from reacting to whatever causes the paralysis."

"How about the water from the sulfur springs?" I asked. "Even George Washington and his troops bathed in the water from Yellow Springs for its medicinal purposes. We could fill kettles and pots with the water and bring them back in Will's buckboard."

"It's not a bad idea, Lizzie. I don't have a better one."

"Then I shall go immediately. Do you want to help me, Ellie?"

"Of course. But we should use Nellie and our own wagon, not Will's, especially since there's no time to ask permission."

"That's fine. I'll carry some kettles out now, and hitch up Nellie. You gather all the containers you can find and meet me out there."

"I'll set up the bathtub, and start heating some of our well water," Mary said, wiping her hands on a towel.

"Hurry," Doc said as he rolled up his sleeves. "I'll pump water from the well. Now that we've decided this course of action, we can't delay."

Chapter Thirty-Four

A week passed before we saw any noticeable change in Pa's condition. Doc kept him in a state of stupor for the first 5 days, and insisted that the water in Pa's bath be maintained at a constant 90 degrees. The house reeked of the smell of rotten eggs, no doubt because of the sulfur content of the water from the springs.

Benjamin and Will alternated with Ellie and me to fetch water from Yellow Springs, while the younger boys filled every vessel they could find with water from our pump. Mary and Ma made sure that there were always kettles heating in the fireplace.

Every morning, Doc arrived to help transfer Pa out of the tub and back to the mattress where he attended to Pa's injury. The boys would then dump the dirty water in the yard and wash out the tub before returning it to the kitchen. After supper, the entire process would begin again. It was no easy task.

On the sixth day of the hot water baths, I watched as Doc removed Pa's bandage. He prodded and poked before he dabbed the vile tincture of iodine into the wound. Pa attempted to yell, but no sound emitted from him. That didn't set well with me, but

Doc didn't seem fazed. In fact, he seemed somewhat pleased with the condition of Pa's leg.

"It's looking good, Lizzie. I think we'll leave it uncovered today."

"It's healing?"

"Definitely. Your pa's not out of the woods yet, but he won't lose the limb."

"That's a relief. What about the tetanus?"

"That's another story. I was hoping there would be some improvement by today."

Doc lit a candle and used its light to examine Pa's eyes. Then he pounded on Pa's chest, immediately placing his ear to listen for internal sounds. Using his fingers, he flicked Pa's skin to check for reflexes. Ma stood at the doorway watching, as I did, to see if there were any changes in Pa's condition.

Finally, Doc looked up at the two of us, smiling for the first time in days. "We'll begin to decrease the opium and spirits today. Continue the hot baths. Sips of water as often as possible."

"What about nourishment?" Ma asked. "He hasn't eaten for quite a while."

"He can't swallow yet. At least not to the extent that's required for eating. But I'm seeing an improvement in his breathing and his reflexes. The baths are working."

"Thanks be to God," Ma said with tears in her eyes.

"You can lie with him awhile, Jane," Doc added. "William draws comfort from the touch of your body. Lizzie and I will prepare the next bath, and I'll stay to help the boys carry him to the tub."

^^^

On the seventh day of the baths, opium was no longer added to Pa's whiskey. In fact, Pa had started to refuse the spirits. When

Doc arrived to help transfer Pa to the mattress, we were amazed that Pa was able to slightly move his arms to help boost himself from the water. Spittle was no longer dribbling from his lips, and his eyes had lost their glassy stare. I knew, without a doubt, that Pa was going to live.

Ma stayed with Doc during Pa's examination while I sat at the kitchen table with Mary. Ellie was giving Julie her lessons in the den; the boys were working in the field after cleaning the bathtub and returning it to the kitchen. When Doc finished with Pa, he washed his hands, then gratefully took the cup of coffee that Mary had prepared for him.

"We're going to skip the daytime bath today," Doc said as he seated himself at the table. "And we'll try some clear both for nourishment."

"I was hoping you'd say that," Mary said. "Already killed and cleaned a young hen this morning. It's in the pot."

"Good thinking," Doc said with a chuckle. "You've been a godsend around this place, Mary. Now that I'm thinking about it, where's your husband?"

"Don't know and don't care."

"Ben thinks he went hunting up north. Left the morning of Pa's injury," I said.

"That's near about twelve days ago," Doc said. "Hope he's all right."

Neither Mary nor I responded to Doc's statement. I figure we were both thinking the same thing.

"Will Pa need the bath tonight?" I asked, changing the subject.

"Not sure yet. We'll see how he does without it today. If your Pa continues to improve, it won't be necessary."

"I think the Yellow Springs was the cure," I said.

"You might be right, Lizzie. The sulfur content definitely contributed to the healing of your Pa's leg. Must have also put an end to the progression of whatever caused the paralysis. We doctors don't know much about tetanus—just that it's deadly. Seems to me, we're witness to a miracle."

"You're the miracle worker, Doc. You restored Mary, and now my Pa."

"Couldn't have done it on my own. You think you'd ever want to be a nurse, Lizzie?"

"No. I have no doubt that teaching is my calling. I find medicine fascinating, but that's because I like the science of it."

"If you ever change your mind," Doc said as he brought his mug to the counter, "you let me know. I could use a good assistant like you."

"Thank you, Doc. But don't count on it. Will you be back after supper?"

"I'll be here. Now, let your ma slumber with your pa this afternoon. And get some rest yourselves. Both of you."

Chapter Thirty-Five

Once Doc said that Pa no longer needed the hot water baths, Mary offered her room on the first floor for his further recuperation. Ma thought that was a very kind and considerate suggestion as Pa would still be close to the kitchen, but more comfortable sleeping in a bed.

Ellie and I stripped the sheets in both rooms, while Julie assisted Mary with the washing and hanging on the line. With Ben's help, we transferred all of Mary's goods up to Ma and Pa's room, and all their things to the downstairs bedroom. By the time the bedclothes were dry, we were able to make up the beds and gently transfer Pa.

After their morning chores, Matt and George foraged in the woods for a fallen branch that could be used as a crutch. They spent a good part of the day on the back porch, trimming and sanding the sturdy limb, until we all agreed that Pa would be quite pleased with their accomplishment.

Will returned to work at the grist mill when we knew Pa was out of danger, promising to bring me back to the school on Sunday afternoon. The more I thought about the end of the fall break from classes, the more convinced I became that I couldn't desert Ma when she most needed me. After Pa was settled in his new room, sleeping soundly, Ma, Mary, and I rested on the back porch.

"I'm not returning to the school tomorrow," I said as I watched Julie playing with Matt and George on a haystack.

Neither Ma nor Mary responded immediately, though I noticed them glancing at each other from the corner of my eye. Finally, Ma said, "Your pa's going to be all right, Lizzie. We'll be fine."

"I've given it a lot of consideration, I'm needed here."

I have to give Ma credit for recognizing that my words expressed my deep anxiety about not being around Pa, of not having him by my side. The thought that we almost lost him was more than I could bear. "*I* need to be here," I added.

Ma reached over and put her hand over mine. And that's how we sat, rocking in the shadows of the waning afternoon sunlight. Ellie interrupted our reverie when she stood at the kitchen door, asking if Ma wanted her to make biscuits for supper.

"That would be fine, Ellie. Is your pa still sleeping?"

"He awoke to use the chamber pot, but he's dozing now."

"That's good. Let us know when he stirs. I think he'd like Lizzie to read to him before supper."

I gazed into Ma's beautiful eyes, pools of mesmerizing wisdom and understanding, reflections of immeasurable love. "How do you do that?" I asked her. "How do you know innately what each of us needs?"

"I carried you within me, gave you life, and nurtured you these many years—just as I have with all nine of my children, though two are no longer with us. I know you, Lizzie. Through and through. You wouldn't be happy giving up teaching. In time, you could resent that you felt the necessity to abandon your dreams. You *will* return to school tomorrow, but we'll figure out a way that you can spend time with your pa every day until he's well."

I nodded my understanding of Ma's words. "Perhaps Mrs. Kimber would permit me to shorten my school day. Then I could come home to read to Pa before supper."

"That's an excellent idea," Ma agreed. "Take Bella back with you so you can come and go as you see fit. We won't be needing the mare now that the harvest is done. It'll be good for her to get some exercise."

I felt the weight of a heavy burden being lifted from my shoulders. All the pent-up emotions from the past two weeks came rising to the top, like steam emanating from a boiling kettle when the lid has been removed. Suddenly I wanted to dance, to yell, to cry, and to laugh all at once. I stood and did a little jig, then bent over to envelop Ma in my arms.

"I love you, Ma!"

"I love you, too. Now go get the *Village Record* that Ellie's been hiding in her sewing basket and take it in to read to Pa. He won't realize it's old news."

^^^

True to his word, Will arrived home mid-morning on Sunday. First thing he did was put $18 in the tin can from his sales, telling Ma that he'd managed a visit to his customers yesterday. Then he went looking for Pa in the parlor.

"Not there, Will," Julie said, taking his hand. "Pa's got a new room, where Mary used to be. I'll show you."

Pa was just lying there in bed, eyes wide open, his left leg hanging out of the covers, two weeks of scraggly hair growth on his face. He gave a wan smile to see his children at the doorway, and managed a gravelly, "Good to see you, Will, Could you give me a shave?"

"Sure can, Pa. You want to sit up?"

"Yeah, I do. What day is it?"

"It's Sunday, Pa. I'm here to take Lizzie back to school later."

"Well, help me up. I'll sit on Mary's rocker in the kitchen. Where's that crutch that Matt and George made for me?"

Ma had wrapped some wool and rags around the top of the branch as a cushion, and Julie ran to get it for Will. "We're going to take Bella back with us," I said to Will as we helped Pa to a sitting position, maneuvering his legs over the side of the bed. "Then I'll be able to help Pa whenever I have free time."

"That's fine, if Pa says it's all right," Will said.

"Her ma said it's what she needs to do," Pa replied. "Be careful of that dang leg, for God's sake!"

Pa tried using the crutch to stand, but he couldn't hoist himself up. Instead, Will and I sat on the bed on either side of Pa, and placed each of his arms on our shoulders. Then we slowly stood, so that Pa was standing between us. He divided his weight between the two of us, concentrating to get his balance. Slowly, he moved his right leg forward and took a tentative step. Though he only had to go about fifty paces to reach the rocker, he was exhausted by the time we got to the kitchen.

"You think you're well enough to be setting in Mary's chair?" Ma said as she wiped bread flour from her hands with her apron.

"My butt's got blisters from lying in bed." Both Matt and George started laughing, especially thinking Pa had said a cuss word.

"I'll put salve on it tonight. You want some coffee?"

"Don't mind if I do. Will, get my shave kit."

"You didn't use your crutch," Matt complained.

"Don't have the strength yet. But it's a mighty fine one. I thank you boys for making it."

"Let your pa have some peace," Ma said, getting a mug from the pantry. "Matt, get some water for your brother. Then you can all go see if Benjamin needs help in the barn."

Will lathered up Pa's face, and reached for the blade in Pa's shaving kit. "Sharpen it with the strop," Pa advised. "And go with the grain. Don't matter to me if you miss some whiskers. Just be careful not to cut my throat."

I watched as Will's brow furrowed in concentration while he slowly removed the hair from Pa's neck and chin, every so often rinsing the blade in the bucket of water that Matt had placed at Pa's side. I paid close attention, in case I'd be needed to assist with Pa's care when Will wasn't around.

"Best tell me what happened to my leg," Pa said. "A bear chomp down on it?"

I glanced over at Ma, and she nodded her approval for me to answer Pa's question. "You stepped on an iron trap."

Pa lurched in his seat, nearly causing Will a slip of the razor. "Hold still, Pa! Shaving another person ain't easy, you know."

"Where was it?"

"In the cow pasture."

"Why the hell would a trap be in the pasture?" Pa shoved Will's hand away, then wiped his face with a towel.

"I'm not done, Pa."

"Who in tarnation would set a trap for our cows?"

"We thought maybe you set it for the coyotes that's been after Ma's sheep."

Pa rested his head on the back of the rocker, seeming to try to recollect the events preceding his injury. Ma came over and knelt at his feet, taking his hands in hers. "We don't know who would do such a thing, William. It was a freak accident. But you're going to be all right now."

"Where's that no-good brother of mine?" Pa asked, eyes closed like he was in a trance.

"He went up north long before your accident," Ma said gently. "He's not been here in over two weeks."

"Doesn't mean he didn't set the trap," Pa said, opening his eyes and looking intently at Ma.

"You can't put blame on a person just because you have a dislike for him," Ma said. "Now, calm down and let Will finish the shaving. You've had enough time setting out here."

As usual, Ma can calm Pa with just the right words. He sat still, motioning for Will to lather the other side of his face.

"Guess I was pretty sick," Pa said.

"You had tetanus, Pa."

"People die if they get tetanus."

"Doc Pyle cured you with the water from Yellow Springs. And Ma. She brought you back to life."

Pa nodded and closed his eyes while Will removed the last of his whiskers. Finally, he stated, "Your ma knows I ain't going anywhere without her. Not even walking through those pearly gates."

Chapter Thirty-Six

Will and I helped Pa to bed as soon as his shave was done. We no sooner had him tucked under the covers before Pa was sound asleep, snoring as if to wake the dead. Without his facial hair, Pa was mighty pale; his ordeal leaving him looking peaked and fragile.

"I should have combed his hair," I said, more of my own musing than making conversation.

"It doesn't really matter," Will replied. "You know Ma will be caring for him."

"Of course. No doubt about it. Do you think the uncle set the trap on purpose to hurt Pa?"

"I don't know what to believe," Will said as we returned to the kitchen. He reached into his pocket and pulled out a tri-folded paper, rumpled and bent at the corners, a seal of wax on the back. "By the way, you had mail at the post office. Looks like it might be from Tom."

I took the letter and looked at it carefully, running my fingers over the address, some of which was smeared. Perhaps the ink hadn't fully dried when Tom sealed the page, or maybe raindrops had invaded his saddlebag to smudge the print. My mind wandered, wondering whether Tom had reached Texas, or if he was still en route.

"Aren't you going to open it?"

My hand shook as I sat in Mary's rocker and broke the seal. Eyes blurring, I scanned the words, making sure it was, indeed, a letter from Tom. It was dated only 16 days ago, posted from western Pennsylvania.

"Tom says they arrived safely in Pittsburgh," I said, handing the brief note to Will for his perusal. "They'll continue their journey, following the northern side of the Ohio River until it reaches the mighty Mississippi."

"Tom must still be smitten with you," Ma said as she put a pan of bread dough on the embers, "to send you a letter from his first stopping point."

"He even signs it *'Your Affectionate Friend,'"* Will teased. "Got to admit, ever since I've known him, Tom's had a soft spot for you, Lizzie."

"He'll soon forget me when he reaches his destination."

"Not if you write back to him," Will said as he returned the letter to me. I put it in my apron pocket.

"Can't very well do that without knowing where to send it," I said. "I suppose I'll just have to wait until he's settled."

"Maybe I should have gone with him," Will said. "It must be a whole new world out west."

"Ain't what you're thinking it is," Mary said, wiping her hands on a towel after cleaning the kneading board. "It's an untamed land."

"Furthermore," Ma said with a chuckle, "you like the finer things in life. You just need to find yourself a pretty girl and make a home for her."

"Don't think I'm ready for that, Ma. I need to earn enough money to settle down. I got plenty of time."

"Reckon you're about the age of my first husband when we got wed," Mary said. "Jonathan and me, we didn't have two cents to rub together. But we was happy."

"Did you grow up in Ohio?" I asked.

Mary stood there at the table for a few seconds, seeming to reflect on the past. "No. Can't say I did. Where your Tom sent his letter from. I remember that name."

"Pittsburgh?"

"That's what they took to calling it. We had a cabin near the fort. Fort Pitt."

"Seems like you're remembering your kin," Ma said. "What was your surname?"

"McBride. I was Mary McBride," Mary said with certainty. "And I wed Jonathan Hughes."

"Sounds Scott's Irish to me," Ma said.

"I reckon."

"Maybe you've got family living around those parts."

"Doubt it. My mama died in childbirth when I was still a young'un. Papa married a widow lady with her own brood, then he was killed in a skirmish. Guess I was more trouble than I was worth. When I overheard my new mother saying she was going to indenture me out, I hooked up with Jonathan and we took a flatboat down the river. Found us our own place."

"Tom was indentured," I said. "He was an orphan, and when he got old enough, the court ordered his indenture."

"It weren't going to happen to me. I made sure of that." Mary poured herself a cup of coffee and sat at the table.

"So, you and Jonathan found a campsite in Ohio?" I asked.

"Right down that there big river. A couple days' worth of travel. We found a nice piece of land by a stream. We was able to buy it because Jonathan's mother gave him some money, and the parcel was cheap. Even had a small cabin on it. But them woods was full of bears."

"Were there Indians?" Will asked.

"Some. But not like when George and I sold the place in Ohio and traveled far west. Guess the white folks kept pushing them out of there."

"What was George like when he was young?" I asked.

"He weren't so young when I married him. Probably near forty. I was but half his age. Still, he was kindly. Stubborn as all git out, like your Pa. In time, I came to love him. Then, suddenly, he was different once them Indians had their way with me."

"How different?"

"Don't know that I've figured that out yet. His hair's a mite thinner on top; his beard's bushier. That's not so strange. But George had good manners, as if his mother taught him to be respectful. That land out west can do bad things to a person, especially when you was scared for your life so much. Maybe living on that prairie took away all he had learned when he was young."

"Was he gone for prolonged periods of time, like he is now?"

"George was a hunter, no doubt about it. But he didn't wander off too far. Told me he'd always keep the smoke from our chimney in his line of sight. Made me and the young'uns feel safer."

"Enough questions of Mary," Ma interrupted. "If you're going to get back to the village before dark, you'd best be loading up your wagon, Will. You can get Bella saddled while you're at it."

"I hate to leave you, Ma," I said.

"You'll be back as soon as you're able. I don't have any fear about that."

^^^

When we arrived at the livery, Will arranged for a stall for Bella next to Prince and scooped feed into buckets for each. We filled their water troughs, then covered Will's wagon after retrieving my valise.

The two of us walked to my place in the late afternoon shadows to have supper with Emily, Joe, and Becca. We waved to a couple that I recognized as one of the students' parents, before trudging up the front steps of the general store.

"You're a sight for sore eyes," Emily said when she saw us, all the while stirring sausage gravy in the cast iron pan on a trivet. Becca toddled over to me, putting up her arms for a hug.

"Will was here the other day and told us of your father's ordeal. You must be exhausted."

"We're just relieved that Pa's recovering." Even as I said the words, I knew that Emily hadn't been so lucky. She lost her father after a freak accident. "What can I do to help?"

"You could make a pot of coffee. Joe's working on his ledgers, but he'll be down shortly."

Will made himself useful by fetching water from the pump out back, then he strolled through the store to see if there were new wares that he might want to add to his inventory. By the time Joe joined us, Emily had Becca settled in her high chair while I set the table.

"Serve yourselves," Emily said. "There's some biscuits in the warmer, and the gravy's hot."

"What's new around here?" I asked, reaching for the butter.

"Not too much. It was pretty quiet while the students were on break, though I noticed a great deal of commotion over there today as the girls straggled back."

"I almost didn't return," I said. "I didn't want to leave Pa."

"Understandable," Emily replied. "Nonetheless, I'm glad you're here. I missed you."

"Pa let me bring our mare so I can visit him whenever I'm able to do so."

"That's good. I'm sure he'll be getting stronger each day. When Will told us that your Pa was recovering from tetanus, I just thanked the good Lord that Doc Pyle knew what to do for him."

"The hot water baths were novel as a treatment, and certainly experimental. Usually the baths must be continued for weeks before improvement is noted, but the fact that Doc initiated them as soon as he suspected the cause of Pa's paralysis made for a speedier recuperation."

"Does he believe it was caused by his leg injury?"

"No doubt, though the medical profession doesn't know the actual cause of tetanus. Given the pour outcome for those who contract the disease, it seems imperative that scientists study the source of the illness."

"Perhaps you should study science. You said you'd like to further your education now that you're not distracted by Tom."

"Possibly," I said, reaching in my pocket for Tom's letter. I handed it to Emily saying, "He's continuing his journey along the Ohio river route. I do hope he remains safe."

Emily read the missive, careful not to get it within reach of Becca's sticky hands. She passed it to Joe, who remarked that he remembered studying geography in school. He told us that the Ohio River is becoming a very important waterway for our great land. It's difficult to even imagine since the only river I ever saw is the Schuylkill, down near Manavon. And that's fairly easy to cross at a number of fords.

"Your uncle could probably tell you about the Ohio River," Joe said while adding gravy to another biscuit. "I'm sure he used it to guide his way west."

"Wouldn't know," Will said, following Joe's lead to take another serving. "We haven't seen hide nor hair of him in a couple of weeks."

"He's a strange one, that old coot," Joe replied, bringing an end to that part of our conversation. "If you have time tomorrow, Will, I can work with you on your ledgers."

Will agreed that he could use some assistance with the books, and told Joe he'd be over toward the end of the day. He first needed to work at the grist mill, then visit his regular customers with the items in the back of his wagon.

I told them that I hoped to ride out to our homestead mid-afternoon, if Mrs. Kimber gave her approval. I'd make it a quick trip and planned to be back by supper time.

"We got a couple of newspapers left from last week," Joe said. "Take a copy of the *Village Record* to your Pa. He might enjoy catching up on the news."

Chapter Thirty-Seven

Loud chatter permeated the school dining room despite the early breakfast hour. Each student vied for the opportunity to recount her daily vacation activities though, for some, they amounted to the typical mundane tasks at the homestead. Those who traveled home by stagecoach enjoyed sharing more exciting adventures, telling us about the hustle and bustle of an ever-expanding city of Philadelphia.

Anna had the girls laughing with her escapades on the farm with Esther. She had never experienced the gory slaughter and plucking of a chicken or the rigorous burden of churning butter, as servants had always assumed those responsibilities in her household. Nor had she ever been permitted to work in the kitchen. Her favorite chore while visiting Esther's family was preserving apples after their harvest.

Before my first class, I had the opportunity to speak with Mrs. Kimber privately. I told her of Pa's injury and horrendous ordeal and, as I felt certain she would, she encouraged me to visit him often during his recuperation. She even offered to take my last class so that I could leave when the students began their afternoon recess.

"Dost thou need transportation?" she asked.

"Our mare is across the road at the livery," I replied. "I can travel faster by horseback, and return before dark. Would you want me to make up my absence by working on Saturdays?"

"That won't be necessary, at least not until we see how quickly thy father recovers. And this will be a lost week, for it takes that long for the girls to settle back into their study routines."

"I'm most grateful. I promise I won't take advantage of your kindness."

"This is an extraordinary circumstance, Lizzie. The holy Bible says to honor thy father and mother. Who are we to design otherwise? Go to thy class now, and be at peace."

I had no idea what I would teach this morning since I hadn't had much opportunity for planning my lesson. I chuckled to myself as I walked to the classroom that the students weren't the only ones unprepared for study. We'd might as well review prepositions, and work on prepositional phrases.

"Good morning, Miss Mitchell," the children said as one voice, while they rose from their seats.

"Good morning, students. Please be seated. I hope you're all excited to begin our new term."

"Yes, Miss Mitchell." It always struck me as strange that a group reply seemed to have a sing-song cadence of its own.

"Let's begin by reciting the prepositions."

"About, above, across, after, against, among, around, at, before, beside, between, by, down, during, except, for, from, in, into, near, of, off, on, over, through, to, toward, under, up, with."

"That's excellent. Today we'll focus on the object of the preposition using personal pronouns. What's the objective case for the subjective *I*?"

Blank stares met my gaze. I let the silence hang there for a few seconds before having the girls write *I* and *me* on their slates. "I is subjective, me is objective."

We continued through all the subjective and objective pronouns, though I avoided the Quaker *thee* and *thou* because I wasn't sure myself how to use them. By the end of class, we were building prepositional phrases such as *around her* or *beside him*.

"This is easy," one of the students said as we continued our game of identifying the proper object of the preposition.

"Then let's make it more difficult," I said with a chuckle. "Give me two objects of the preposition."

"He came with *her* and *I*," said Sophie, a little sprite of a girl in the second row.

"But you told me that *I* is subjective case, therefore it can't be the *object* of a preposition."

Sophie corrected herself just as the bell rang for the end of class. "He came with *her* and *me*."

"Gold star, Sophie. The assignment for your study session this afternoon is to write 12 prepositional phrases. Five of them must use two objective pronouns. Any questions?"

The students gathered their belongings and chatted with each other as they proceeded to their next class. Susanna and Emmor Kimber were of the mindset that the children should have ample time to communicate with each other. There was no rigorous rule of silence, except during specific times of study. Their curriculum was designed to be a pleasant opportunity to learn in a collaborative environment.

I conducted a similar class with the upper level students, using a method of diagramming sentences for their grammar lesson. My last session of the morning was a story hour with the youngest children. Each of the students was permitted to select a book from the Kimber's library, and I would make a game of choosing which one I would read. Today I picked an illustrated edition of Aesop's Fables, and we delighted in the tale of the *Hare and the Tortoise*.

During lunch, Mrs. Kimber assured me that my services weren't needed for the rest of the school day, and encouraged me to saddle up Bella and visit Pa.

It didn't take any convincing. The moment she uttered the words, I was on my way.

Chapter Thirty-Eight

Ma and Mary were resting on the back porch when I arrived. Julie came sprinting across the yard as soon as she saw me, volunteering to hold the reins while I dismounted, and help me fill a bucket of water for Bella.

"Your pa's sleeping," Ma said when I sat on the stoop. "He had a bowl of Mary's bean soup in the kitchen, but he went back to bed shortly after."

"How is he today?"

"His leg's hurting, and he gets tired real easy. Doc Pyle was here this morning and said he's doing good. Of course, your pa didn't want any tonic for the pain. Stubborn old coot."

"Did Doc say he should stay in bed?"

"Not in so many words. He said your pa can come to the table for his meals, if that's what he wants to do. Doc expects that he'll prefer to sleep a lot, and that's fine."

"I brought a newspaper to read to him later," I said, patting my apron pocket for good measure. "If anything, Ellie will want to see if there are advertisements for fashions."

"You can be sure of it," Ma said with amusement in her voice. "How were your classes today?"

"I struggled as much as the students to stay focused. The children probably have no idea that teachers, too, wrestle with the challenge of picking up where we left off, mentally returning to our tasks. You taught me some fun learning activities, so we had an easy morning."

"I'd like you to be my teacher, Lizzie," Julie said, putting her hand on my arm. "And I'd so love to go to the French Creek Boarding School for Girls."

"Julie's been telling us of her day there," Ma said with a wink. "She made two very special friends. What were their names?"

"Amanda and Susan," Julie said emphatically. "We had a lot of fun together."

"Oh, yes. Amanda and Susan are a delight. They're in my primary level class. In fact, it was Amanda who selected our book to read today."

"You see, Ma? If I went to the school, I'd already know two very nice girls. And Lizzie would watch over me so you wouldn't worry."

"And where will we get the money to pay your tuition?" Ma asked.

"I'll make sweets to sell on Will's truck, like Lizzie did."

We all had to stifle a laugh, knowing that Julie was quite sincere. "Well then, you'd best start saving your pennies," Ma said. "When you get $75, I'll consider it. Now, go see if you can assist Ellie. She's spinning yarn in the den."

When Julie was out of earshot, Ma sighed and said, "That child's been talking about the school since you left yesterday. I don't know what triggered it except she enjoys being with you. In fact, Julie's so much like you, Lizzie, it's like she's your twin. God help us."

Mary and I laughed, but we knew that Ma was correct. And she's wise to give Julie something to aim for, rather than stifle her dreams. Though Julie's 14 years younger than I am, she'd do well at the school. I'd have to think of a way to help fund her aspiration.

"Before you read to your pa, Lizzie, could you go to the springhouse to bring me a jug of milk?" Ma asked as she stood to walk into the kitchen. "Guess I'll make a nice egg custard this afternoon."

I knew that was one of Pa's favorites, and it would be good nourishment for him. It didn't take me long to walk to the springhouse, but the latch on the door gave me some trouble.

Suddenly, I was startled by the heavy crunch of dry leaves behind me, and caught a whiff of disgusting body odor. I knew before I turned that the uncle was back.

"Ain't you a sight for sore eyes," he said, as he put his arm on my shoulder. His breath reeked of alcohol, and his voice was slurred.

I pulled away from him, but he caught my wrist in a stronger grip. "Let go of me," I said with a voice of steel. "I told you before..."

"I like me a feisty woman," the man chortled. "What say you and me have a little fun."

"Don't even *think* about it," I said with a vehemence to disguise my inner fear. "Why'd you set a trap to hurt my pa?"

The revolting old man gave a raspy snicker before coughing up a wad of phlegm and spitting it on the ground. He used his arm to wipe his matted beard, all the while gripping my wrist.

"You mean he ain't dead yet?"

Chapter Thirty-Nine

George Mitchell's words set a fire in my belly, anger to the like I've never experienced. In a flash, I swiveled, using my other hand to reach for his rifle. He reacted quickly, tossing it as far from me as he could without losing his grasp on my arm, then threw me to the ground. I gasped for air before letting out a bloodcurdling scream, even as I tried to scramble away.

The uncle landed on top of me, putting his thick tongue in my mouth. I bit down, drawing blood. He recoiled from pain, giving me time to scream again.

Gathering new strength, he tore at my bodice until my breast was uncovered, while reaching down to unbutton his breeches. I tried to kick and bite him, but that seemed to incite him more. With a practiced swoop, he had pulled aside my petticoats and was between my legs. He spat on his thick fingers, and began to rub the spittle inside of me.

"Please," I cried in pain. "Please don't do that!"

I heard the footsteps before he did, opening my eyes to see Mary standing five paces from us, the uncle's rifle aimed at the center of his back.

"Get off her," she yelled. "Get off her now or I'll shoot."

The revolting scum of a man was indeed startled. He slowly raised to his haunches, then guffawed when he saw his wife prepared to pull the trigger. I tried to roll away from him, but he grabbed my leg, ripping my petticoat.

"It's not loaded," he scoffed.

"Oh, it's loaded," Mary said. "I've made certain of it. Now get moving."

"I told you she was tetched," the uncle said with a snort. "Now she's threatening to kill her husband."

"You ain't my husband. You ain't George Mitchell. I know that for sure."

"You're as crazy as that weak-bellied jackass you was married to. Him thinking we'd be friends out there on that prairie. Telling me all about his family and his homestead. Once them Indians got to you, I knew it'd be easy to come east, and take possession of the Mitchell farm. Now, give me my gun afore someone gets hurt."

"You killed my George Mitchell, just like you tried to kill his brother by setting the trap."

"So what if I did? I ain't no thick-witted ass like either of them Mitchell's. My name's John Mason, and once I get rid of you and the whole Mitchell clan, this here will be my property."

"You belong in a crazy house," Mary said, above the high-pitched chortle of laughter from the demented man. "You and that mangy dog of yours."

"Ain't got Dawg no more. The stupid mutt got what was comin' to him. Like you're gonna get."

"Where's my baby girl?"

"Told you. Them Indians probably took her."

"You didn't go looking for her like you said, did you?"

"Hell, no. I would a killed you back then, too, but figured folks would take kindlier to me if I was toting a sickly woman."

Mary's eyes took on a darkness, as she stepped closer so not to miss her target. The man jumped to his feet, grabbing the barrel of the rifle.

I rolled as far as I could get, noticing Ma and Benjamin standing a short distance away. Mary and the man wrestled with the firearm, he the stronger and larger. I could see Ben wanting to run to help, but Ma held him tightly by the arm.

Suddenly, John Mason reached a leg around Mary's left ankle, pulling it forward and throwing her off balance. She fell backward with him on top of her as the rifle discharged. Ma and I both screamed at the same time, she and Benjamin running to save Mary.

Ben reached down to pull the man off Mary, gagging at what he saw. John Mason no longer had a face, brains and blood splattered over Mary. Ma cried, reaching for Mary. "Dear God in heaven! Don't be dead. Please don't be dead."

Mary gasped for a breath and opened her eyes.

"I'm alive," she wheezed. "Go see about Lizzie."

I had turned to my side and was retching puke, shaking from head to toe. When my stomach was empty, I couldn't move. Ma noticed my bare bosom, and arranged my bodice to cover it. Then she laid on the ground next to me, holding me in her arms, crooning that I'd be all right.

Matt and young George came running, after hearing the gunshot from their fishing spot at the pond. They stopped short, seeing Ma and me lying in the grass, with Ben helping Mary to her feet next to the body of John Mason.

"What's going on?" Matt asked, fear in his voice.

"Get a tarp to cover the uncle," Ma said. "He's dead. Then go check on your Pa. I don't want him trying to get out of bed to see what happened."

"Did Mary kill him?" George asked, edging closer to look at the remains.

"He killed himself, by accident," Ma said. "Now, go do what I told you."

Mary limped over to me, and reached her hand down to mine. "Come child. We'll go to the pond. Just you and me."

My brain could barely register what Mary was saying; her words seemed a jumble. I didn't want to open my eyes to see the activity around me, though I could hear Ma standing to brush the folds of her dress.

The two of them helped me up, leading me from the devastating scene.

Chapter Forty

Taking my hand, Mary led me to the pond. On the bank, we slipped off our shoes, then walked fully dressed into the nippy water. I knew I should be feeling the muck under my feet, and the coolness of the October afternoon, but I sensed nothing but revulsion and defilement.

As the chilly water reached my shoulders, I stepped out of my petticoat, then pulled out the pins holding my braids. Finally, I submerged, holding my breath, and let my hair float freely. I wasn't aware of anything in that moment under water, just the mindless drifting in darkness.

Once I regained my footing, I noticed Ma standing at the water's edge with towels and fresh chemises. She tossed two bars of soap, and Mary and I each washed off all physical traces of our ordeal.

Mary was done long before I was, and I saw her slowly make her way back up the bank and take the towel that Ma handed her. I washed my hair and every inch of my body, and continued scrubbing long after I was clean, as if the lather could eradicate the violation to my spirit.

Finally, I joined them, drying myself with the cloths and donning the clean chemise. Ma embraced me, rocking me in her arms. And then I cried with deep wrenching sobs, releasing the horror I had experienced.

"I'm so sorry, my darling," Ma said with tears in her eyes. "I should have listened to you and your pa. Did the man…?"

"No. Mary saved me just as he was about to… finish his business. Still, what he did was brutal. Like an animal."

"That's when I knew for sure he wasn't George Mitchell," Mary said. "I suddenly remembered out there on them plains when he'd have his way with me. Your uncle was tender and loving, not vicious and cruel. Why I couldn't know for sure that the man wasn't who he said he was is beyond my ken."

"Doc Pyle said your brain was shut down," I muttered. "Now I understand why. What you experienced had to have been unbearable. The fact that you remembered must be a sign that you're recovered."

Mary slowly nodded in agreement. "I just wish I had gone looking for my Bridget. Maybe she just went to hide because she was scared. Maybe the Indians didn't take her."

"Or, maybe she's in heaven with Jonathan, watching over you," Ma said, gathering up the clothing we had scattered on the bank. "No matter making yourself crazy about what you could or couldn't have done. You keep them babies in your heart."

By the time we got to the porch, Pa was setting out there waiting for us. He patted the seat of the rocking chair next to his, indicating that I was to sit there. Pa reached over to take my hand, and squeezed it like he'd do when I was a youngster, telling me how much he loved me.

"We were right," Pa said, looking out over the tree line and watching the remaining ochre leaves fall to the ground. "You and me, Lizzie."

"It was Mary who figured it out," I said. "His name was John Mason. He killed your brother."

"How'd he know about us?"

"He said your brother believed they were friends. Guess they'd talk over the campfire when they went hunting. Don't know whether he killed the uncle before or after the Indians got to Mary. I'm thinking he probably waited in ambush when he noticed no smoke from the cabin chimney."

"Why's that?"

"Your brother always told me to keep the fire burning," Mary interjected. "It was his way of knowing that his family was all right."

"My pa used to say that to my ma when he was fighting in the war. Don't know if he really could see the smoke, but we kept it going."

"Where are the boys?" Ma asked.

"Making a grave. I told them to dig a hole in the woods on the other side of the stream, then throw the man's sorry ass in it. Along with the mangy mutt, if they can find it."

"He killed his dog," I said in a daze. "Just shot him dead like he was going to do with us."

"Oh, William," Ma said with a frown. "Matt will be having nightmares."

"Best he gets used to it. Life and death. That's what we're on this earth for. Can't quite figure out how Mary survived, what with the shotgun going off between the two of them."

"Near as I can say," Mary said, "it's the way he tripped me. When I fell backwards, I still had a finger on the trigger. But with the force of the fall, he had wedged the rifle to his chest. I'm guessing the muzzle was under his chin to have blown off his face."

"You're lucky to be alive," Pa said. "The good Lord must have other designs for you. I'm just grateful you were there for my daughter."

"Me, too, Pa," I said, my eyes meeting Mary's. "Do we need to send for the authorities?"

"Don't see why. The man was a drifter. Just happened to kill himself on our land. That's the way I see it."

"When Ben returns from the grave," Ma said, "I'll send him to the school to tell them you won't be returning. Maybe he can stay with Will at the livery tonight so's he won't have to ride back in the dark."

Pa shook his head in agreement, while I sat wondering if that was my best recourse. Staying here will make me relive every moment of the ordeal. I wasn't ready to handle that.

"I need to be away from the memory of what happened," I said. "Ben can take me back to Kimberton this evening in the buckboard. Once I'm immersed in my schoolwork, I won't have time to think about today."

Ma looked like she was going to argue with me, but Pa understood what I was saying. He quickly settled the matter.

"That might be wise, Lizzie. I know you came here to help me. But I'm on the mend. You've got some healing to do yourself. And we Mitchell's, we need some time to ourselves for that."

This time, I squeezed *Pa's* hand.

Chapter Forty-One

Kimberton, Pennsylvania
June 1825

Despite morning showers, I opened the drapes and pulled up the sashes to chase the stuffiness from my bedroom. Last night's storms had been powerful, with claps of thunder continuously waking me from a fitful sleep, as it did for Emily, Joe, and their three children.

Through the walls, I could hear 6-year-old Becca cry out for her mother, who was likely comforting 4-year-old Rachel. Joe was walking the hall with 2-year-old Joseph, his footsteps padding back and forth past my doorway. My pillows did nothing to mute the commotion through the night, and my mood was dour.

After dressing and straightening the bed covers, I stood at my front window perusing the scene at the crossroads. A steady stream of wagons had been lined up at the grist mill, no doubt filled with baskets of harvested winter wheat. Farmers stayed close by, chatting with neighbors while holding their place in cue. Wives toted umbrellas and avoided the puddles as they lugged their barters across Kimberton Road to the general store. The mercantile is always busy on a Saturday morning.

Calling myself to task, I opened the science book on my desk, trying to wrap my mind around Dalton's *A New System of Chemical Philosophy.* This is the text that my mentor, Walter L. Jones, suggested I read to expand my education. But it's so very boring.

The Kimber's introduced me to Walter last year, when he arrived for a tour of the French Creek Boarding School for Girls. Walter's a graduate of Harvard, and has an interest in science. Still a rather young man, he's principal of the Schuylkill Valley Academy. In that role, he advocates for the establishment of seminaries to provide further education for teachers, including women.

I've spoken to Abby Kimber numerous times about this very topic. That women have limited opportunities to expand our knowledge unless we study under a tutor. Though she supports equal rights for women, Abby's currently a staunch abolitionist.

Don't misunderstand. I agree with her position. I will not condone slavery, and would assist anyone of color who seeks freedom. But my focus is on teaching, and the ability of women to have an education comparable to men. Walter shares that passion, and I'm grateful that he has offered to meet with me monthly to help me expand my knowledge.

"Drat!" I said to myself, closing the textbook. I no more felt like reading chemistry on this dreary day than fly to the moon. Instead, I pulled out the packet of Tom's letters from the desk drawer and untied the ribbon to spread them across the bed.

Though they arrive few and far between, my collection has multiplied over the past four years. Tom decided he didn't want to be a rancher after all. He and his traveling companion parted ways in Evansville, Indiana. James Moore continued his journey to Texas, but Tom was hired by Vincent Bowles, a blacksmith situated on the alley between First and Second Streets.

Tom wrote that the village of Evansville, located on a bluff above the Ohio River, was founded by Hugh McGary, but named for Col. Robert Evans, a hero from the War of 1812. Tom said he does a lot of horseshoeing for John Foster, a circuit attorney for the surrounding counties, and they've become good buddies.

As I read through each of Tom's letters again, I could imagine the deeply rural and provincial location, log cabins surrounded by thick forests. He says that Evansville is growing at a faster rate than Kimberton, but it's not surprising since the village was developed beside the great Ohio River, which is a commercial mecca.

Tom has never mentioned any woman in his letters, except for John Foster's wife who died in childbirth three years ago and the Negro cook whose name is Bella. John has remained single, though he's raising two children, one of his own and one he adopted.

Bella's a freed slave, which Tom says is quite common there, and she's paid for her work. Tom mentioned that he spends a lot of time at John's cabin, even if John is travelling. He enjoys Bella's cooking, playing with the children, and reading John's books.

Although I replied to Tom several weeks ago after I received his last letter, I felt the urge to send another missive today. I don't want him to forget me, and continue to hope that he'll return to Kimberton. To me.

Settling myself at the desk, I wrote that Will and Esther have announced their engagement. Esther's dowry will include a parcel of land from her father, and they'll make their home in

Charlestown, only a few miles from my family farm. Will plans to continue his traveling vendor enterprise, as well as construct a permanent storefront on their land that Esther will oversee.

I added that Ellie and David McClure are expecting their first child near Christmastide, just about a year from when they first married. They're living with his parents until their home is constructed.

Julie now attends the French Creek School, I wrote, so only the younger boys are at home to help Pa run the farm. Except for a slight limp, Pa hasn't slowed down. In fact, he has expanded the herd of dairy cows as there's talk of a train line to run through Kimberton and Yellow Springs, transporting milk to less rural areas.

After letting the ink dry, and re-reading for at least the third time, I made a tri-fold of the paper and sealed it with several drops of hot candle wax. I wrote Tom's address on the front, rummaged for a dollar from my reticule, then took the letter downstairs to the post office.

^^^

"How lovely to see you, Lizzie," Lucretia McClure said as I passed by the millinery department. The bonnet she was eyeing is as ugly as the nose on her face. "You must think I have nothing better to do than gawk at hats."

"Nothing of the sort, Mrs. McClure."

"I'm just making myself useful as I wait for Mr. McClure. Quite honestly, I came with him today because your sister needs crackers from the barrel. Morning sickness, you know."

"Do tell Ellie I'm thinking of her. Julie and I will come for a visit soon."

"I'm sure she'd like that."

Anxious to be on my way, I bid farewell and turned to take my leave. Mrs. McClure took hold of my arm and whispered, "Have you heard the rumors about Emmor Kimber?"

"I don't pay much heed to idle gossip."

"Nor do I, my dear. As you know, I pride myself on being a good Christian woman. However, it has come to my attention that Mr. Kimber must present himself to debtor's court. As I have said many times, the man extends himself into too many sectors."

"You can set your mind at ease, Mrs. McClure. Mr. Kimber is an industrious Quaker. He'll arrange his financial matters to the satisfaction and welfare of all."

"I'm sure he will. I just wouldn't want to see any negative impact on your well-being."

Biting my tongue from giving an angry retort, I thanked the old busy-body for her concern and pulled away. The young man who occasionally clerks at the post office took my money and stamped my letter, saying that it should arrive in Indiana in just a few weeks.

Before I returned upstairs, I checked on Emily's children in the back room. I peeked in to see that their boy was sound asleep, and Becca was playing with her younger sister. Rachel was rocking her baby doll, while Becca pretended to prepare a tea party.

"Would you like a cup of tea, Lizzie?" Becca asked, batting her expressive blue eyes.

"That would be lovely. Do you need any help?"

"No. Everything is ready. I even made some crumpets."

I sat at the table as Becca made a great show of pouring imaginary tea into three cups, one for each of us. Making believe I was taking a large bite of crumpet, I told Becca how delicious it was. Rachel followed my lead, agreeing that our meal was quite good.

"Will other guests be arriving?" I asked.

"Probably they will," Becca replied with her bright smile.

"Then I shall leave a space for them at the table, and go back to my dreary room to study."

"When you return, I'll have made blueberry muffins."

"My favorite!" I exclaimed.

Rachel clapped with glee, her chubby cheeks flushed with enjoyment. "You must tip-toe, so as not to waken my baby."

Feigning a light step, I backed out of the room through the double doors into the store, practically knocking over Henry Harris and his very pregnant wife.

"How nice to see you both," I said with an embarrassed giggle. "I was so busy playing with the children that I didn't watch where I was going."

"You're looking fine, Lizzie," Harry acknowledged before his bride tugged him to the housewares. I had heard that Harry married into a rather wealthy family in Paoli, not the most attractive lot, including the daughter. Nonetheless, I'm pleased that Harry obviously has found affection.

I waved to Emily as I trekked upstairs. She was busily engaged with two women needing fabric, but managed a wan smile back to me. We would all need to hit the sack early tonight.

Once in my room, I opened my chemistry book and spent three hours studying the composition of compounds. I was about to finalize my notes when I was startled by a sharp rap on the door. Emily burst into my room, asking if I had seen Rachel.

"Earlier," I said with a chuckle. "We had a make-believe tea party."

"No. Not then," Emily said, her voice betraying an edge of anxiety. "Now. Becca said Rachel came upstairs to find you."

"She hasn't been here," I said. "Did you look in your room?"

"She's not there. My goodness! Where could she be?"

The two of us ransacked the upstairs, checking every closet and storage room, loudly calling Rachel's name. Emily's face expressed her alarm, and she began to cry.

"Stay calm," I said. "You know Rachel can be a tease. She must be hiding, playing a game with you."

I followed Emily down the steps. The few customers who remained in the store were helping Joe search every cranny of the main floor, but she was not to be found.

Emily took Becca by the shoulders, shaking her. "Where is she?" she yelled in panic. "Where is Rachel?"

Chapter Forty-Two

Becca, too, began to cry. "I don't know, Mama. She was going to find Lizzie, and then I was busy with Joseph and forgot about her."

Joe put his arm around Emily and reached down to pull Becca into their embrace. By that time, the baby was also crying. I picked him up, and rocked him in my arms.

"Rachel couldn't have gone outside, could she?" I asked in as calm a voice as I could muster.

"I don't think so," Emily said, wiping her eyes with the handkerchief in her apron pocket. "Joe or I would certainly have noticed, despite today's steady stream of customers."

A young couple I didn't know, and several old codgers said they'd walk along Kimberton and Hares Hill Roads. Mrs. Emery took the baby from my arms and offered to also watch Becca, while I suggested to Joe and Emily that we check the mill race.

"Rachel would never go near a running stream of water by herself," Emily said, terror in her voice.

"Probably not, but she has seen the girls from school swimming there."

We searched from the crossroads to the top of the hill, but there was no sign of Rachel. Joe, Emily, and I called her name repeatedly, crossing over to the spring house behind the store.

"Dear God. The pond," Emily all but whispered.

We ran forward, all three of us. On the bank was Rachel's doll, lying close to the edge of the water. Emily scooped it up, holding it to her bosom.

"Rachel! Rachel! I know you're nearby! Don't be hiding from me," Emily called, choking back tears.

Joe removed his shoes and shirt, wading into the water until it was chest high. Suddenly he stumbled, giving a blood curdling shriek.

"Damn you, God!" he yelled at the top of his lungs. Then Joe reached down to pull the lifeless body of his little girl from the muddy bottom.

Emily kicked off her shoes and sprinted through the murky waters, screaming all the while until she reached them. I'll never forget the feeling of helplessness, as I stood weeping at the edge of the pond, watching Emily and Joe hold their beloved daughter while they sobbed with despair.

^^^

Emmor Kimber closed the general store for three days following Rachel's death. His wife, Susanna, and I helped Emily bathe and dress the child in preparation for visitation. Joe made a simple pine coffin, placing it on a table next to the hearth on the main floor of the mercantile. For two days, there was a steady stream of friends, family, and customers paying their respect to Joe and Emily, offering their help and prayers.

Surrounded by her mother and sisters, Emily sat by the fire next to the body of dear Rachel. She felt barely able to greet the visitors. Joe acted as if in a daze, thanking those who came to express their sorrow. I cared for little Joseph and Becca in the back room, though Becca often insisted that she stay by her mother's side.

Pa brought Ma and Mary to the wake after Will rode out to the farm to tell them of the tragedy. Mrs. Kimber informed me of their arrival, and I went to greet them.

"I'm so glad you came," I said in a low tone as I gave each a kiss. "Come see Emily."

Ma got down on bended knee to embrace Emily, and she wept with her. Mary, too, had tears streaming down her cheeks. In fact, there wasn't a dry eye in the room.

"Mary and I have both lost children," Ma whispered to Emily. "I know that you feel a grief like nothing else in this life. Your pain will never go away, but your burden will ease over time. I promise you."

Emily nodded, but had no words. All that emitted was a low keening, deep in her chest. Suddenly, she gripped Ma's hands and murmured, "But it's my fault that Rachel's dead. I should have watched her more closely."

"Rachel's death was not of your doing," Ma said gently. "The Lord giveth, and the Lord taketh. So says the Good Book. You're a fine mother, Emily. Lizzie tells me often that she wishes she could be like you. Our babies grow under our guiding hand, but we cannot mind them every moment of the day."

"Do you ever wonder why? Why does an innocent child have to die?"

"I think of it often," Ma said. "And we'll never know the answer to that question. Look around the room. Most of the parents who are visiting today have lost at least one child. We know your grief. We have lived your mourning."

Ma stood up, leaned over the coffin, and kissed Rachel's cold forehead. "You will always carry this little angel in your heart," she said. "And she will forever watch over you. God be with you, Emily."

The next day, Rachel was buried in Emily's family plot in West Chester, next to her father. Emmor Kimber delivered the invocation in the Quaker tradition, even though Emily, Joe, and their kin are not Friends.

I thought Mr. Kimber's words were uplifting, and his tribute was fitting. But I knew that nothing could take away the heartache of my dear friends as Rachel was lowered into the earth.

Chapter Forty-Three

Placing the newly arrived letter from Tom in my pocket, I joined Emily on the front porch of the general store. Becca was practicing numbers on her slate, while Emily held a tired and cranky Joseph. It has been only two weeks since the funeral for Rachel, and Emily just recently returned with the children after spending an initial time of mourning with her mother in West Chester.

"Will's coming for supper tonight," I remarked, sitting on the rocker next to Emily. "He's bringing a rack of pork ribs and will get Joe to help grill them out back."

"That's fine," Emily muttered.

"Mrs. Kimber sent over a crock of beans," I added. "They can warm on the grill as well."

"The Kimber's have been very kind," Emily said, swatting a fly away from Joseph.

"Mama, look at my numerals," Becca said, holding up her slate. "Are they good enough?"

Emily glanced at Becca's work, barely giving her child the attention she was craving. "Your 2's need work. Practice more."

"Let me see," I said. "Ah, you have a very strong hand for the straight lines, Becca. Your 4's and 7's are lovely. But I agree with your mother. Can I show you a trick for the curlicue on the 2?"

Becca nodded as I said, "You hold the chalk, and I'll guide your hand. Let's try it together."

Before long, we were both laughing as we made larger and more elaborate 2's. It even brought a smile to Emily's face, and she mouthed a *thank you* to me.

"I can do it now," Becca said, stealing her slate from my lap. "I shall practice over and over."

"Have you met with your tutor while I was away?" Emily asked as she watched Becca work on the numerals. "What's his name?"

"Yes, I have. His name's Walter Jones. He spent several hours with me at the school last week. Quite an interesting fellow, he is."

"Is he married?"

"I don't believe so. Walter's very focused on his career and professional standing. Do you know that he'll be visiting the Marquis de Lafayette at the Germantown Academy in just two weeks?"

"*The* Marquis? The gentleman from France who was commissioned to serve our nation in the Revolution?"

"Exactly. Lafayette's finishing his tour of America, and will return to Paris at the end of this month. Walter has the honor of meeting him when he's presented to the students and the Board of Trustees at the Germantown Academy. It's by invitation only."

"You seem to have more than a professional interest in your tutor. Perhaps you find him attractive?"

Emily's question gave me pause. I hadn't thought much of Walter Jones in any terms other than academic.

"He's not handsome, by any stretch of the imagination," I said with a chuckle. "But we can talk for hours about the genuine need for teacher preparation. Currently, there are no standard requirements. And, of course, with more women hired to teach, there are few institutions of higher learning that permit women to attend. It doesn't make sense to me, nor to Walter."

"Have you written to Tom about him?"

"Only that I have a tutor. Tom would have no interest in the topic of teacher education, though it captivates my attention. Oh! Speaking of Tom, I received a letter today."

"What does he say?"

"I don't know. I haven't yet opened it."

I reached into my apron pocket to show Emily, then tugged at the seal. I read through quickly, highlighting some of the details.

"Tom says that he, too, has a mentor. He's been studying law under the tutelage of John Foster. That's surprising. I never thought that Tom would be interested in law. John's a circuit attorney who brings his horse to Tom for shoeing. I told you about him."

"Only that they're friends."

"Oh, my," I said as I continued reading. "Tom has quit his job at the blacksmith in Evansville. He's working for John Foster as personal assistant, traveling with him to the courts. He says that his constant companion is Blackstone's *Commentaries*, the text which is required reading in preparation for demonstrating his knowledge to the circuit judge."

"It sounds to me that Tom's becoming a lawyer," Emily said. "Isn't that interesting?"

"Quite so. It's hard to imagine."

"You don't seem very pleased. I thought you had wanted him to be more educated."

"I don't know what I'm feeling," I said as I folded the letter and returned it to my pocket. "I suppose I'm disappointed that Tom has forged a new life for himself. It doesn't seem as if he plans to return."

"We're two peas in a pod, you and me," Emily said. "Both saddened by events beyond our control."

I reached out to take her hand, and we sat in silence as the evening sun faded behind the trees.

Chapter Forty-Four

The following Sunday, I invited Emily to come with me for an afternoon family visit. I planned to bring Julie, and there would still be room for Becca and little Joseph. Joe and Will were busy with bookkeeping, so it didn't take much convincing for Emily to agree.

My buggy's a lightweight phaeton, which requires little maintenance, but gives me flexibility to drive the country roads. It took four years of savings for me to finally afford it, and Pa was generous to give me Bella on my last birthday. The mare seems to enjoy her outings, particularly if it means returning to her former pasture.

During our excursion, Julie served as surrogate big sister for Becca, and took her responsibilities quite seriously. As soon as we arrived at our farmstead, Julie gave Becca a tour of our home, then took her to the chicken coop to look for eggs. Emily insisted that Becca was to keep in sight at every moment, and I assured her that we could sit on the porch to watch the children play.

Always hospitable, Ma embraced Emily and welcomed her warmly. Mary offered each of us a glass of sweet tea, then joined us out back.

"It's good to see you again, Emily," Ma said. "I'm glad Lizzie brought you for a visit."

"Thank you, Mrs. Mitchell. I'm not up for socializing these days, but I feel that you and Missus Mary are kindred spirits."

Ma nodded, reaching out a comforting hand. "You can let your boy play on the stoop," she said. "When Julie was that age, she liked making piles of stones."

"Joseph does like anything to build. And bugs. He can sit for hours playing with ants in the grass."

"Good heavens, I know about that," Ma said with a laugh. "My youngest son was always in the dirt. When the boys return from the fields, George can show Joseph how to find worms."

"Have you seen Ellie lately?" I asked when we finally got comfortable.

"Yes. She and David were here for a visit yesterday. She's looking a little peaked what with her pregnancy, but she's not yet showing."

"I'll bring Julie to visit her one day soon, but I wish she'd soon be in her own home. The thought of spending an afternoon with Mrs. McClure makes my blood run cold."

Ma gave me one of her looks, so I quickly changed the topic of conversation. "You'll never believe what Tom told me in his last letter. He's going to be a lawyer!"

"Good for him," Ma said. "Is he attending school?"

"No. He's apprenticing with an attorney. And he's reading law books. Can you believe it?"

"Don't see much need for a lawyer if folks would just follow the rules in the Good Book."

"I think it's rather fine that Tom's working to improve his lot in life. Of course, maybe there's a need for attorneys in the wilderness. What's it like there, Mary?"

"Can't recall much about it, 'cept the Ohio river. Villages were sprouting up all along that great waterway. Your Uncle

George and me, we'd get off the flatboat when we could, and make a campsite near the river. Get some of that pent-up energy out of little Jonathan."

"Were you scared?" I asked.

"Sometimes. More from wild animals than anything else. Sleeping by a camp fire didn't give much protection from the bears and wolves. Wildcats, too."

"I think you were brave to travel westward," Emily said. "Especially with a youngster. Don't know how you did it."

"And another on the way," Mary said with a chuckle. "Sometimes I'd get off the boat just to puke, then get back on. But you don't think on those things when you're looking for an opportunity to succeed."

"Would you ever want to go back?" I asked.

"Not unless I had reason to. Besides, I got a good home here, and a generous friend." Mary reached over, and put her hand over Ma's.

"What about you, Lizzie?" Ma asked. "You got a hankering to live with Tom out there in Indiana?"

"Don't be silly, Ma. Tom's making himself a new life. And I have my teaching."

"Might be they can use some schools out there."

"Whether it's here or there, women can't be hired as a teacher if they're married."

"Knowing you, you'd figure out a way if you wanted it bad enough."

"A way for what?" I asked. "Being with Tom out west or teaching in the wilderness?"

"Whichever way you want to look at it. Not that I want you traveling to some god-forsaken place. But I'd like to see you back together with Tom."

"My thoughts, exactly," Emily said. "Lizzie needs to figure out what she wants, then make it happen. Can't spend a whole life pining for what might have been."

On that note, I changed the subject and we settled into an easy conversation, sheltered from the afternoon sun. Little Joseph sat at our feet, engrossed with the pebbles he found along the walkway. Julie retrieved her old doll from the den, and the girls played house by the garden.

It was the first time in weeks that Emily was finally able to relax.

Chapter Forty-Five

Walter and I spent the following Saturday afternoon together on the back lawn of the school. After a brief review, he tested my knowledge of various chemical compounds. When I successfully completed the exam, Walter suggested that I begin to focus on chemical elements from the soil. Another boring topic.

"I don't understand how you can be so excited about the study of chemistry," I said. "It's rather tedious."

"It's fascinating, and changing quite rapidly as innovative technology becomes available. Ten years ago, scientists held an entirely different interpretation of chemical matter."

"What use is it to you in your role as principal?"

"As you know, I occasionally teach a class. In time, I hope to return to lecturing. Perhaps even do scientific research."

"Would you stay at the Schuylkill Valley Academy?"

"I'm not sure. The Board is sometimes too involved in our daily activities. What about you? Will you stay at the French Creek School?"

"I don't know," I said, glancing at the windows to see if there were any watchful eyes. "I enjoy my work, yet I crave more autonomy."

"You could start your own school."

"Is it possible?"

"If you have the resources to do so. You'd need finances, of course."

"Then it's only a dream, and a foolish one at that."

Walter took the time to mark the chapters in the text that I was to study, highlighting aspects that he thought would best serve my advancement in science. While he was engrossed, I took stock of Walter's features.

He has curly brown hair, slightly receding, thick brows, and long sideburns. His aquiline nose is somewhat large for his slender face, with no bridge to keep his spectacles from sliding. The cleft in his chin is distracting, as it seems a little too deep to shave cleanly. I wondered if he's often bothered with nicks.

"Will you be staying overnight in Germantown after Lafayette's visit?" I asked.

"I'm not sure. I'm just eager to welcome a man of his stature to the academy. When Lafayette was quite young, he served with General Washington, wintering in Valley Forge. He's familiar with this entire area, you know."

"My grandfather probably knew him. Pappy served in a local regiment of the Continental Army."

"No doubt they were acquainted. Did your grandfather survive the war?"

"Yes. We now own the farm that he and his ancestors leased for several generations. That's how it was in Pikeland."

"Settlers couldn't purchase the land?"

"Ownership was denied; held up in court battles with the powers that be in Britain. Pa told me it wasn't but 30 years or so ago that the farmers were finally permitted to pay the mortgage. Of course, then they argued against having to pay back taxes for all those years."

"Your family's lucky they didn't lose their land. I've heard others weren't so fortunate."

"I think I'd like to study history," I said. "After we finish this next section of science. Is that possible?"

Walter smiled engagingly, small lines at the corners of his eyes. He has very nice teeth, I noticed.

"Perhaps you would find history more interesting than chemistry," he said, with amusement.

"I believe so, though knowledge of all subjects in the curriculum is my goal."

"You're a fascinating woman, Lizzie. I enjoy your zeal for learning. Perhaps you'd be kind enough to permit my return in two weeks, rather than a month?"

I could feel the flush that creeped up my neck, yet I'm not sure why my body was responding in such a way. Tom never elicited such a reaction, at least not to my recollection.

"That would be fine," I said, reminding myself that Walter is my tutor. Nothing else. "I'd be grateful if you'd bring a history text."

"Quite right. Then I shall meet you here in the garden on Saturday, the fortnight, at 2 p.m."

^^^

Throughout supper, I regaled my usual companions with stories of Lafayette, and Schuylkill Valley Academy, and chemical elements. Joe and Emily didn't have much to say, and Will was looking bored. Only Becca gave occasional responses, though they weren't always appropriate.

Realizing that I was monopolizing the conversation, I stopped mid-sentence. No one seemed to pay much heed, all busy buttering their biscuits or downing their stew. Even little Joseph was playing with his peas, rolling them across his plate.

"You're all mighty quiet this evening," I said, reaching for the butter myself.

"We can't get a word in edgewise," Will replied with a chortle. "Besides, guess everyone's as worn out as I am. Between work at the grist mill and my deliveries, I'm rather tuckered."

"We had some disturbing news today," Joe said, glancing at Emily. I noticed her slight nod that Joe could continue.

"Mr. Kimber stopped by this afternoon. Seems he's in a financial predicament."

"I know he has to appear at debtor's court," I said. "He'll make the necessary arrangements to cover his obligations."

"Yes. Well, we're affected by the changes he's making. Mr. Kimber will be offering some of his holdings for rent, including the store, the blacksmith shop, the tannery, and his school."

The knife I dropped made a raucous clang when it hit the pottery plate. "What does that mean?"

"Our services are no longer needed," Emily replied dully.

"That can't be!" I exclaimed. "Where would you go? What will you do?"

"We don't know," Emily said, dabbing her eyes with the napkin. "But the change is imminent. He has already signed a lease agreement on the store with a gentleman from Manavon."

"Why didn't he give *you* the option?"

"Perhaps Mr. Kimber felt he could charge a higher rent with an outsider. It doesn't make sense since he was pleased with Joe's work."

"Does this affect your living arrangements?"

"Of course," Joe said. "And yours, as well, I imagine."

"Oh, my," I said, looking at Will. "I hadn't thought of that."

"You may also be out of a job if the school is rented," Will said with sincere concern.

"How could Mr. Kimber do that? And never even advise me of any of this!" I could feel my anger and frustration rise to the surface. "Once again, women are no more than chattel."

"In his defense," Joe replied, "you were occupied this afternoon. That's when he came by to tell us. But, apparently, only the store is currently leased."

"When do we need to move?" I asked.

"By the end of the month," Joe said. "I imagine we'll go to West Chester and live with Emily's mother until we determine our course of action."

The realization that I'd be losing my best friend hit me like a ton of bricks. I reached for Emily's hand and gave it a squeeze.

"I suppose I could get a room at the inn," I said hesitantly. "Unless that, too, is up for rent."

"That's Kimber's cash cow," Joe said. "And it would cost you a pretty penny to live there."

"I know a widow on Prizer Road who's got a few rooms for rent," Will said. "Nice old lady. Her husband passed a couple of months ago, so she's taking in boarders to make ends meet."

"You going to move there? Might be better than sleeping on hay in the livery."

"I'm thinking on it. Want me to find out the cost when I make her delivery tomorrow?"

"Might as well," I said, recognizing that everything I had become accustomed to is changing. "Maybe there's room for Joe, Emily, and the children, too."

"As much as I'll miss you," Emily said, "I prefer to be near my mother. And my baby girl buried next to my father."

I nodded, aware that Emily would be wanting to sit by Rachel's grave, as Ma did with her two deceased boys. It's a rite of passage, I'm sure.

"I've been meaning to ask you, Lizzie. Are you cognizant of the goings-on at night over there at the school?" Joe asked.

"Like what?"

"I heard horses' hooves outside my window the other night. When I got up to see who was making the racket, I noticed two Negroes being whisked through the side door. Looked to me like Abby let them in."

"Haven't seen anything like that during the day," I said. "Of course, the Kimber's are strongly abolitionist. Do you think they're helping runaway slaves in the dark of night?"

"Don't know. Just wondered if there was any talk of it over there. Of course, most folks around these parts are against slavery. But it's pretty risky to hide runaways."

"All this makes me wonder if I should try to find a new teaching position," I said as I helped carry our dirty dishes to the counter. "It's overwhelming."

"Might as well take it one day at a time," Will said. "Just keep your eyes and ears open."

Chapter Forty-Six

The following morning, Mr. Kimber stopped me on my way to the classroom to say that I would, indeed, need to seek new living arrangements. He seemed quite upset to be the bearer of such unwelcome news, even confiding that his Quaker associates are perturbed that he has overextended his finances.

"When should I plan to vacate my room?" I asked glumly.

"Within two weeks, by the last day of the month. I'm truly sorry, Lizzie. I wish there were some other option I could offer thee."

"Will my salary increase since I'll now need to pay rent for my housing?"

"Unfortunately, no. I don't have the resources to offer any such remuneration."

I'm sure my countenance expressed my distress. Mr. Kimber could offer no solace, so he turned on his heels with a strained "Have a pleasant day."

The rest of the day was a blur as I taught my lessons, wondering all the while where I would live and how I would manage without Emily. At supper, our conversation centered on our plans for packing and moving.

Will offered to drive Joe and Emily's belongings to West Chester as soon as they had cartons ready to go. Then, he would provide the family's transportation to Emily's mother's home on the last day of the month.

Will had visited Mrs. Goetz, the widow offering rooms for rent, during his afternoon deliveries, and she presented a fair charge for room and board. Nonetheless, it was more than half my monthly salary. He suggested that I plan to visit her after school during the week to see if I like the woman, as well as to clarify her arrangements. Regardless, I'd have the evenings to pack.

In some ways, I was envious that Emily had Joe to rely on as we have the rug pulled out from under us. My brother was certainly being helpful to me, but it's not the same as having the support of a loving husband. The entire situation is giving me second thoughts about remaining a spinster.

That evening, I sat at my desk and penned another letter to Tom. I told him of the recent events and shared my anxiety of finding a place to live, as well as having to bid farewell to my dear friend. By the time I finished, I had written two full pages, which would cost double the postage.

Unburdening my spirit to Tom was somewhat cathartic, though I would find a similar benefit just by writing my thoughts in a journal. I mean, it's not like having an ordinary conversation with Tom. By the time the mail arrives in Indiana, I'll have already settled in my new home. And since he now travels the circuit with John Foster, there's no telling when he'll finally receive my letter.

My mood increasingly bleak, I blew out the candle on my desk and undressed in the darkness. Standing at the window in my chemise, I observed the sliver of a moon visible just above the tree-line. Knowing that it would enlarge each evening of the month was a reminder that all things in life change, and I'd best just accept them. Else I'll become a cantankerous old dowager, attractive to no one.

^^^

Will drove me to widow Goetz's home after school the next day. It's a two-story stone house, reminiscent of our own home, though a mite smaller, just a 15-minute walk to the school. We strolled up the front path, surrounded on both sides by fragrant dianthus and hyacinths, and climbed four steps to a cozy covered front porch. That's where we found Mrs. Goetz, gently rocking in one of the four rockers facing the road.

"Look at me, acting like I've got nothing else to do but watch the goings-on," she said with a delightful titter. "It's nice to see you again, William. Is this your sister?"

"Yes," I said. "I'm Lizzie. It's a pleasure to meet you."

"And you may call me Pearl. Like the jewel. Leastways, that's what my dear departed husband always said."

Pearl was wearing her mourning black dress and apron, with a white kerchief and cap. A few gray curls protruded, giving a softness to her wrinkled face. Sparkling blue eyes and a broad smile bestowed the look of a kindly grandmother. I knew already that I liked her.

"William told me of your predicament, my dear. It seems as if we might be able to help each other. Never thought I'd need to be taking in boarders, but the good Lord sometimes has other designs."

"Yes, ma'am. Do you have any children?"

"Eight of 'em. Three dead and five moved away. Truth be told, my youngest girl lives in Paoli with her brood. She's got six young'uns and one on the way. She wanted me to come live with her after her father passed but, God help us, I'd rather stay in my own home."

"How many boarders do you have?"

"If you and your brother sign on, only two. But there's room for two more. I'm not in any big hurry to expand, and I'm going to be very particular about who stays here. A woman can't be too careful, you know."

"Is supper provided in the rent?"

"Of course, my dear. And I'm a pretty good cook, if I might say so myself. All meals are included. Now I suppose you'd like to see the rooms."

Each of the bedrooms was furnished simply, but in good taste, with a bed, wardrobe, and desk. An attractive quilt and fine draperies made the rooms seem cozy and comfortable.

The kitchen has a large hearth, with a long wooden table along the far wall. I could envision spreading out my books to study or spending an evening conversing with this friendly, talkative woman. It wasn't a difficult decision that this would be my new residence.

"What do you think?" Pearl asked as we stood in the kitchen doorway.

"Your home is lovely," I replied with my most engaging smile. "Would you accept me as a boarder?"

"Me, too," Will said.

"Definitely," Pearl said with a chuckle. "To think I'll have my own deliveryman under my roof. And with his lovely sister, a teacher at the French Creek Boarding School. I consider myself blessed."

Will and I made the arrangements before we left, each of us leaving a deposit for the rent. Will told Pearl that he'd be moving in the following day, and I said that I'd start bringing my belongings over the weekend.

"That sounds wonderful," Pearl said with a glowing smile. "We'll have a special supper next Sunday to celebrate."

Chapter Forty-Seven

Emily looked haggard as we prepared supper the next evening. While I peeled the potatoes and carrots, she attempted to make biscuits, but it seemed a lost cause. Joseph was fussy and Becca vied for Emily's attention, neither of them giving their mother any peace.

"I don't know what's the matter with this boy," Emily said in frustration. "He's been like this all day."

"I'll finish here if you want to take the children outside. Perhaps they need fresh air."

Emily nodded, reluctantly leading Joseph and Becca to the front porch. Without their distractions, I quickly completed the preparations, filled the kettles and pans, and got everything onto the banked fire. Once I set the table, I lugged in a bucket of water from the pump, then joined Emily. She was rocking little Joseph and telling Becca a story.

When the tale of Red Riding Hood was finished, Becca climbed up to my lap and arranged herself in a comfortable position. "Are you going to miss me when I go to grandma's house?" she asked.

"More than you can imagine," I said, giving her a squeeze.

"Mama said we'll be leaving very soon. Can you come with us?"

"I wish I could, sweetie. But I must teach my classes at the school."

"Will you visit us?"

"I surely will. Perhaps Julie and I can take a ride to West Chester in a few weeks."

"That would be nice, wouldn't it, Mama?"

"We'll look forward to it," Emily said with a smile, wan as it was. "But remember what I told you, little one. Distance doesn't ruin a friendship, as long as we keep those we love close to our hearts."

"We won't ever forget you, Lizzie," Becca said, looking up at me with her beautiful eyes.

"You'd better not." I said, tickling her funny bone. Becca giggled, then squirmed away.

"Go get your slate," Emily said. "You can practice your numerals while we're waiting for your father to finish today's ledger."

Becca skipped off, giving me an opportunity to chat with Emily. Joseph was asleep in his mother's arms, literally unaware of the upheaval ahead of us. Emily gazed across the road, as if she were identifying details to tuck in her memory.

"I'm leaving sooner than we planned," she said abruptly. "Joe and I talked about it today. He thinks that it would be easier to pack our things and tidy the store if we didn't have to focus our attention on the children."

Emily paused, waiting for my reaction. Finding none, she continued.

"Since your brother is already planning to transport our boxes to West Chester on Saturday afternoon, the children and I will go with him. Joe will finish up here and join us next week.

Our decision was much easier knowing that you've found suitable lodging."

The news was overwhelming, to say the least. Still, it's much like pulling off a bandage stuck to a wound. Might as well do the painful deed quickly and without fanfare. In my head, I knew Emily's course of action was sensible, but my heart said otherwise.

"I understand," I said sadly. "It's practically impossible for you to do what needs to be done with the children underfoot. I'm not much assistance because of my classes during the week, but I can help you on Saturday. And you'll be much happier when you're settled."

Emily nodded, wiping her misty eyes. "Enough of this depressing mood," she said. "We shall enjoy our last few days together. Let's get supper on the table!"

^^^

Will got Prince to pull the wagon as close to the side entrance of the general store as possible. He and Joe first loaded Joseph's small crib and high chair, pushing them as far back as they would go. Then we all lugged cartons.

Young Joseph played with the ants in the grass, paying little attention to the rest of us. Becca did what she could to assist, carrying traveling bags that could be squeezed into small spaces. We tried to convince her to add her doll to the pile of goods, but Becca was adamant that her baby was to stay on her lap.

"I can't believe how much we've accumulated these past years," Emily said, shaking her head. "There's still more to pack, but Joe will finish during the week. Thank goodness, we don't have to worry about the furniture. Except for the baby's bed and chair, the rest belongs to Mr. Kimber."

"I was thinking the same thing," I said with a chuckle. "I have only a few boxes of personal items and school materials. When Will returns from West Chester, we'll take them to Mrs. Goetz's home before dark."

"You've decided to move there tonight?" Emily asked.

"It's only proper. Poor Joe will be all alone."

"What ever will I do?" Joe said dramatically, picking up Becca and twirling her around.

"You'll be very busy, Papa," she replied, quite serious. "The faster you get everything done, the sooner you'll be with us."

We were all laughing when I noticed Mr. and Mrs. Kimber walking across their lawn. Obviously, they were coming to say their farewells to Emily and the children. I was still annoyed with them for causing this upheaval, though I admitted to myself that it was kind of them to pay their respect.

While Emmor Kimber spoke with Joe and Will, Susanna Kimber hugged Emily, wishing her a safe and pleasant journey. "We thank thee, Emily, for all thy work on our behalf. It's a sad day for us."

"For me, as well," Emily said in a firm, but gentle, voice. I wondered if she harbored any anger toward the Kimber's. If she did, it was well concealed. "I wish you and your husband much success for the future."

"Thou art very kind," Susanna said, distracted by Becca pulling on her skirt. She turned and leaned down to kiss Becca's forehead. "Be a good girl, and help thy mother."

"I shall," she promised. "Perhaps someday I'll attend your school. Lizzie's sister is my friend, you know. And she likes it very much."

"We shall welcome thee with open arms," Mrs. Kimber said with a chuckle. "Now, where is thy brother?"

"He's playing with bugs over there. Why he likes them, I'll never know."

"Perhaps he's studying their habits," Mrs. Kimber said, "Shall I give him a kiss, as well?"

"You can try, but he won't want to be interrupted."

"Then thou must give one to him later. From me."

"Yes, ma'am."

Before I knew it, the men finished their conversation, and Will announced that it was time to get on the road. Joe and Emily embraced, unabashedly and publicly demonstrating their deep love. Becca climbed up to the center of the front seat, excited to help Will drive. Joe helped Emily get settled next to Becca, then handed little Joseph up to her.

I stood off to the side, deep emotions welling up within me. Mr. and Mrs. Kimber waved good-bye, then crossed the road to return home. Will jumped up to his seat, grabbed the reins, and urged Prince forward.

Joe watched with me until the wagon had rounded the bend. Shoulders hunched, he walked back into the store to conduct business as usual.

And there I was. All alone. Standing at the crossroads, sobbing like a baby.

Chapter Forty-Eight

It seemed to take forever to fall asleep last night. My new accommodations were comfortable, but my mind traipsed along many diverse paths. By the time I came downstairs for breakfast, Will had already departed to Charlestown for the day. He and Esther planned to work together on his finances, or so he told me last evening when we transported my things to the boarding house.

Later, while unpacking the carton with my desk items, I found myself sidetracked by writing another letter to Tom. In it, I described my new abode and recounted Emily's departure from Kimberton. I shared with him my deep sadness, though I tried to keep my emotions at bay. No use having him think of me as a histrionic or melodramatic woman.

After arranging my clothing in the wardrobe, it was time for study. Walter would be testing me in a week, and I hadn't yet finished reading the material he outlined, let alone memorize it. Once again, without a doubt, I knew that chemical principles did not capture my interest.

By early afternoon, a steady rain was falling, reinforcing my dismal spirits. My room was stuffy, and I was in dire need of a cup of tea and some companionship. Textbook in hand, I went looking for Pearl.

"Are you quite settled now?" Pearl asked, hands covered with the dough she was kneading.

"I suppose I am. I've also been studying, and my brain is calling for a respite."

"Then do keep me company. There's a fresh pot of tea on the trivet."

I poured myself a mug, and refilled Pearl's cup, before joining her at the table. In no time at all, her loaf was ready to proof and she was cleaning her board and bowl.

"I'll be lucky if my bread rises on a day like this," she said, taking a sip of her brew. "I should know better, but don't have much choice with two guests in the house."

"You mustn't go to any trouble for me or my brother. We're used to fending for ourselves."

"Quite honestly, I enjoy baking. At least I won't have to worry about the bread going moldy. I can remember a time when I'd need to make several loaves a day. Now I'm relegated to feeding the birds if there's too much."

"I suppose this large house seems so empty, now that your husband and children are no longer here."

Once I said the words, I realized that Pearl and I have something in common. There can be all sorts of reasons why someone is alone, and we all need to find ways to fill the void.

"Ah, but I have memories, and good ones at that. I miss my Karl dreadfully, but we had 46 happy years together. That's saying something."

"Did you always live here in Kimberton?"

"No. My parents came from Germany when I was a young girl. We settled in Vincent township. Karl's family was also of German descent. They had a farm over near the clover mill in Pikeland, and we lived there after our wedding. Unfortunately, the Goetz's lost their land because the man who took their rent all those years absconded with their money and turned traitor. Karl's father died from the stress of it, then his mother passed shortly after. Karl and I rented acreage from Mr. Prizer here in Kimberton, until we could afford to buy it outright. It was a struggle at times, but Karl was an industrious, hard-working man."

"Our farmstead isn't too far past Clover Mill Road, over on Yellow Springs Road."

"Your family go to St. Peter's? The Lutheran church up on the hill, not far from the mill."

"No. We're Presbyterian. Closest place of worship is in Paoli."

"I wondered why you didn't go to church today. Thought maybe you were a member of the Friends, being that you teach at a Quaker school. But you don't talk like one, with all their thee's and thou's."

"We're not church goers in my family," I said, pouring another cup of tea. "Of course, we were raised with the Bible. Pa says we can pray on our knees at home, just as much as we can in church."

"Guess that's true. Still, a Sunday doesn't feel much like keeping the sabbath holy unless you go to church. Karl drove me and the children every time the preacher was there for services. I'm thinking I'd like to start going again. If you could take me."

I wasn't sure what to say in response. I know what Ma would tell me to do out of kindness, but it was disconcerting to think about entering a Lutheran church. Perhaps it's even sinful. Regardless, benevolence should be my guiding principle.

"It would be an honor," I said. "We can have Will stop by the parsonage to learn when the next service will be offered."

"You're such a blessing, my dear. Why is it that no man has yet determined your worth as a potential wife?"

"I plan to be a spinster and continue my teaching."

"Glory be, child! That's ridiculous. Why would you even consider such a path?"

"I cannot marry. I'm sullied. Tarnished." On that note, I put my mug in the dishpan and went out to the porch,

^^^

Pearl followed me out and sat on the rocker next to me. The rain was falling heavily, puddling in every rut and pothole of the road. Occasionally, I heard a rumble of thunder in the distance, but I was surprisingly tranquil.

I'm not sure why I made such a statement to Pearl. Only Ma and Mary know the full extent of what had happened to me four years ago. Not Emily. Not Will. And certainly not Tom. Yet the memory is always with me.

Pearl and I sat in silence for a good 10 minutes, until she finally said, "You've been with a man?"

"Not by choice."

"Do you want to talk about it?"

"No. Suffice it to say that no upright gentleman will want damaged goods. My chastity would always be questioned."

"That's not true," Pearl said, gazing above the tree line. "A man of wisdom and understanding... a man like my Karl..."

I looked at Pearl, wanting her to continue, sensing again that we're kindred spirits.

"You must promise that this conversation is between only the two of us," Pearl said, almost in a whisper. "I'm sure you understand."

I nodded my agreement, urging Pearl to share her own experience. She took a deep breath, then looked deep into my eyes.

"When I was but 12 years old, I was raped by a neighbor's boy. Repeatedly. He was old enough to know better, almost a man. I was afraid to tell anyone. He said he'd shoot me dead, and then kill my parents."

I wanted to retch, thinking back to that horrendous experience of being trapped, violated. I felt my eyes moisten, my body shudder from the memory.

"How long did you endure the torment?"

"Three years. Then I became pregnant. Still, I told no one. Finally, my secret could no longer be hidden. My parents blamed me for the indiscretion, and sent me to live with German friends in Pikeland until my child was born. That's when I met Karl."

"He knew you had a child?"

"His mother helped my delivery. Unfortunately, the baby died just a few days after birth. He was very small and couldn't survive."

"Did Karl believe you when you told him it wasn't your fault?"

"He did. As did his parents. Within a few months, I knew I loved him, but I was frightened about being with him. In a wedded way."

"I fear the same thing."

"There's no need to worry if you choose the right man. Karl was patient with me. We courted two years before I began to shed my anxiety, before I literally could feel passion."

"Making love became enjoyable?"

"More than you can imagine," Pearl said with a chuckle. "I suppose that was an insensitive statement, and rather crass, but you might as well know. Do you have an interest in any local gents?"

"Not really. My best friend besides Emily was Tom, but he moved to Evansville, in Indiana, a few years back. He asked me to marry twice, but I turned him down because I wanted to teach. And then he left..., and then I was molested. He doesn't know about that."

"Perhaps he'll be back for you."

"We communicate by mail, but I feel certain he's forging his own life now. I haven't heard from him in several weeks. There's also my tutor, Walter Jones. We'll meet next Saturday for my studies."

"Are you attracted to him?"

"Perhaps, a little. But the relationship is totally different. I don't often think about Walter, but Tom is frequently a specter of my dreams."

With that, a sudden bolt of lightning and very loud clap of thunder sent us scurrying indoors. "Might be that's a sign," Pearl said with amusement as she closed the front door.

"A sign of what?"

"I have no idea. It's whatever you make of it."

Chapter Forty-Nine

The girls were swimming in the mill race when I arrived at the school on Saturday afternoon for my review session with Walter. Julie sprinted across the grass in her bathing costume when she saw me, giving me a soggy welcome. It's hard to believe that my smart and independent younger sister will soon be 11 years old, but her maturing frame assures me it's so.

"I told my friends that I'll stay with you until your tutor arrives," Julie said. "Will you be studying in the garden? It's such a lovely day."

"It's probably less distracting if Mr. Jones and I work in a classroom today," I replied with a chuckle. "But I'll be happy for some company while I wait."

"Do you like your new abode? I can't imagine what it would be like to live in a boarding house."

"It's no different from you living at the school, just more like living at home. You'll like Mrs. Goetz when you meet her. Perhaps we can get permission for you to have supper with us tomorrow. Just you, Will, me, and Pearl. I'll ask Mrs. Kimber later."

That seemed to satisfy Julie, and I thought it would be comforting for her to realize that I'm still close by. Of course, we see each other daily, but Julie knows that I can't demonstrate any favoritism at school. We're literally like two ships passing in the night.

Within minutes, I spotted Walter driving down the hill on Kimberton Road in his phaeton, intent on avoiding the potholes and gullies, barely noticing any of the residents he passed. It made me ponder about how single-minded he is. I suppose that's how a recent graduate of Harvard could already have achieved a position of authority at a reputable private school.

"Here he comes now," I said. "I'll introduce you to Walter, then you can return to swim with your friends."

"He looks quite serious," Julie said as she squinted in the sunlight. "Very bookish."

"I suppose so. But he's quite nice."

Walter carefully hooked his reins over the hitching post before acknowledging my wave to him. Then he retrieved his book and cautiously walked across the lawn, as if he would encounter a horse plop here or there.

"I thought you might like to meet my sister, Julie," I said when he finally reached us. "She attends the French Creek School."

Julie did a little curtsy, saying, "Pleased to meet you."

"Likewise," Walter said with a genteel bow and a smile that highlighted his splendid teeth. "There is definitely a family resemblance. I believe you'll be as fine-looking as your sister in a few years."

If Julie took offense at the back-handed compliment, she didn't express it. Rather, she interrogated Walter about his educational background and his current role as principal of the Schuylkill Valley Academy.

"Mr. Jones recently met the illustrious General Lafayette when he visited the Germantown Academy," I said to distract Julie from her cross-examination. "How was that, Walter?"

"Quite impressive. I was honored to shake Lafayette's hand. You know he was a great friend and supporter of our distinguished George Washington."

"I know he served with him and wintered with General Washington and the troops in Valley Forge."

"Yes. He told me that he was amazed at the growth of this whole area in the past 50 years. During the Revolution, he often forded the Schuylkill River, and recollected the dismal outcome of the Battle of Germantown."

"I'd have thought he'd be dead by now," Julie said. "I mean, General Washington is long gone, but Lafayette still lives."

"Lafayette was quite young during the Revolutionary War," Walter replied. "Perhaps only in his early twenties. He's now an old man, still agile despite his injury during the Battle of Brandywine, but slowing down. It was his long-awaited dream to tour America, and the Germantown Academy was one of the last stops on his journey."

"I suppose he'll be remembered in history," Julie said politely, though I could see she was losing interest.

"Without a doubt," I said. "Now hurry back to your friends before your swim time is done."

Julie gave another curtsy, somewhat awkward, before taking her leave. "Don't forget to ask about tomorrow."

"I won't," I said with a chuckle. "I promise."

"She's a lovely child," Walter said when Julie was out of earshot. "How nice that you see her every day at school."

"The French Creek School has been good for Julie. At home, she's the baby of the family. Here she can demonstrate her strengths. I do believe that she may one day follow in my footsteps."

"I'm sure you're very proud of her. I've brought a history text to begin after your chemistry examination. Where shall we work today?"

^^^

It was all but a miracle that I successfully completed the science regimen. Between my lack of focus and my increasing distaste of chemistry, I forced myself to memorize only the sections that Walter had marked. Luckily, those were the topics that he tested.

Walter suggested that we begin our study of American history with the pilgrims at Plymouth. While that's somewhat elementary, he brought the characters sailing on the Mayflower to life. Their journey must have been so very difficult. It made me think about Ma as a young girl, losing her entire family at sea.

We became so immersed in the stories of the brave men and women who labored to forge a settlement in this new world that we lost all track of time. It wasn't until the students began to assemble in the hallway that I suggested we'd best continue elsewhere. Walter looked at his pocket watch, bemoaning that he needed to be on his way.

Walter and I strolled to his phaeton, he with the textbook I had returned, both of us conversing easily. We made plans to meet again in two weeks before he bid farewell. It was obvious that he wanted to see me more often than had been our original arrangement.

Flicking the reins to begin his journey, Walter turned to wave to me. That slight distraction brought the front wheel of his carriage into a deep rut that literally threw him to the ground. His horse became startled, straining to pull forward, sending the phaeton into the air.

Dashing across the lawn, I ran to assist Walter who was sprawled on the packed dirt trying to locate his spectacles. Two patrons waiting at the grist mill rushed across the road, one getting hold of the mare and the other checking on Walter's injuries.

"I'm fine," Walter said in embarrassment. "Nothing more than a bruised ego. Can you help me raise the trap?"

The men heaved the vehicle aright, but it listed far to the left. "You've got considerable damage to the front wheel," one of them said.

"Damnation!" Walter exclaimed with a rather unpleasant expression. "These roads are atrocious!"

The other two men chortled before one said, "You have to watch where you're driving. Don't think you'll be getting on the road any time soon."

I set off to find Will at the grist mill, hoping he might be of some assistance. Walter was cussing up a storm, using words like the uncle's imposter, a trait that unsettled me. By the time I returned with Will, the other men were on the ground under the phaeton, with Walter demanding that they hurry to solve the problem.

Will unhitched the mare as I introduced him to Walter, who was in no mood to be social. "Your horse needs water," Will said, trying to be helpful. "Do you want to follow me to the stream behind the mill?"

"You can take her," Walter replied brusquely. "I need to know what's wrong with the wheel."

"Looks like a damaged suspension," one of the men said, extricating himself from under the vehicle. "You might want to see if the blacksmith has time to look at it today."

"How long will that take? I need to be on the road to Valley Forge before dark."

"I'll take you to find him," I said, wishing it were Tom I was locating, not his replacement.

"Just go get him," Walter said curtly. "I don't have time to be traipsing all around Kimberton."

Walter's foul mood upset me. It took all my control not to give a snide remark. Who is he to speak to me as if I'm a servant? Even then, there's no cause to wield power with crassness.

I was still talking to myself when I met up with Will, walking Walter's mare back to the scene, and the blacksmith who Will had persuaded to come check out the buggy. The other two men, along with Will and the blacksmith, worked together to repair the buggy, while Walter sat on the side of the road, muttering under his breath.

"No use being perturbed," I said to him. "Accidents happen. Luckily, you didn't get hurt."

"Small talk is not necessary, Lizzie," Walter muttered, his top lip curled in disdain. "I don't need you, or anyone else, to tell me to keep my chin up."

"Then, I shall be on my way. May you have a safe trip home."

Chapter Fifty

Julie, Will, and I were seated at Pearl's large kitchen table, abiding by her insistence that no one should get in her way while she was finishing the preparation for our meal. She placed a platter of steaming roasted chicken and vegetables at the center of the table, then a bowl of fluffy mashed potatoes. When she finally joined us, Pearl told Julie that she could say the blessing.

Julie looked at me with such a quizzical expression that Will and I began to laugh. "You don't know how to say grace?" Pearl asked. "Are you a bunch of heathens?"

"Guess we're not in the habit," I said. "Bless this food, and Pearl who prepared it."

"I suppose that'll do," Pearl said, shaking her head as if to wonder about our upbringing. "Take what food you want, and pass it around. I thought you'd be spending this fine day with your fiancé, Will. Are you in the doghouse?"

Will was already gnawing on a succulent leg bone, but he put it on his plate to politely respond that he wanted to spend time with Julie. "I'll take a ride to Esther's place after supper."

"Don't know why you're waiting to get hitched," Pearl said, scooping a large spoonful of potatoes to her plate. "You wait too long, and she might get second thoughts."

"I need to make sure I make a decent living to provide for a wife and family,"

"Hogwash! If a girl's ready to wed, she's ready."

I could see the flush begin at Will's collar, while his brows furrowed like he was trying to think of an intelligent response. Perhaps he figured one wasn't necessary because he shrugged and took another bite of chicken.

"Yeah, Will," Julie said, agreeing with Pearl. "Even Ma says she doesn't know what you're waiting for. You should have the wedding in August, when Lizzie and I are on school break."

"Can't. Winter weddings are the norm in Esther's family."

"That's because they're farmers," Pearl said, reaching for several more roasted carrots. "It's always been a customary practice to tie the knot when there's no more harvesting to be done. But you're a merchant. Seems to me, the sooner you get wed, the sooner you can build your store. That'll make your income grow."

"Hadn't really thought about it like that," Will said. "I'll talk to Esther and see what she wants to do. You trying to get rid of me?"

"Of course not," Pearl said, then gasped. "Mercy, me! How will I ever have a successful enterprise if I don't retain my customers? You're right, Will. It's best that you take your time to marry."

We all laughed, though I did think that Pearl gave good advice. And, despite the playfulness, it appeared that Will listens to Pearl's counsel. Julie seemed to be enjoying the banter, and added her two cents. "Lizzie also has a beau, you know."

"You're aware of something I don't know?" I teased, putting down my fork. I had a notion of what she was surmising, and I certainly didn't want a conversation about Walter. Then again, she might have been referring to Tom.

"Your tutor, Lizzie. I think he's sweet on you."

"Not anymore," Will said with amusement. "Guess you didn't see the commotion on Kimberton Road yesterday."

"What happened?" Pearl asked. "I didn't hear a thing."

"Walter Jones wasn't watching where he was driving. Got himself into a ditch, and was none too happy about it. Guess he and Lizzie had words. She left him standing there, one arm longer than the other."

Pearl and Julie were both gazing at me, but Pearl's look held a thousand words. "Do tell, my dear," she said.

Just the memory of Walter's behavior infuriated me, a slow burning anger that had been fueled by my thoughts all through last night.

"It's not worthy of discussion," I said. "Suffice it to say, a person's true colors become apparent when adversity occurs."

"You weren't attracted to that boorish brute, were you?" Will asked.

"I believe she was," Pearl said. "After all, she has no other suitors clamoring for her affection."

"He wasn't *that* bad," Julie argued. "I met him yesterday and we had an interesting conversation. He *is* boorish, though."

"The man was angry that his wheel was damaged," Will explained. "Besides cussing like a vagabond, he was rude to all who tried to help. Do you know, he didn't even offer to pay for the blacksmith's services?"

"You had words with him, Lizzie?" Pearl asked.

"Not really. After the way he spoke to me, I wouldn't give him the time of day. I just walked away."

"Do you plan to continue your studies with him?" Julie asked. "I know you want to further your education."

"I have no idea what to do. I tossed and turned all night."

"You'd best end his services," Will said emphatically. "He may be a two-sided character. And he's got a temper. No telling what he'd do and say in anger."

"I agree with your brother," Pearl said. "You should send him a letter tomorrow.

I nodded my agreement, yet feeling distress about losing another friend. Or, at least, a possible suitor. It seems that I'm destined to be alone.

"And don't be sitting there feeling sorry for yourself," Pearl admonished. "You can bring over the peach cobbler I made this morning. We'll show your sister what she's missing at the Goetz boarding house."

^^^

Pearl and I enjoyed the evening air on her front porch after I returned from walking Julie back to the school. Her hydrangeas were particularly fragrant, and the bountiful blue blossoms decidedly beautiful. The sweet-scented breezes had a relaxing effect, and I felt myself letting go of the negative notions that had taken captive of my spirit.

"Did Julie have a pleasant afternoon?" Pearl asked. "She's such a sweet girl."

"She loved every moment. In fact, Julie feels that you are like the grandmother she never knew. Mammy passed before she was born."

"That's a lovely compliment. We must include her when she's permitted to visit."

"She'd like that. And you must join us the next time we take a drive to our home. Ma would be happy to meet you."

"I'd enjoy making your mother's acquaintance, as well. We'd have a lot to talk about. Nonetheless, I hope your mother and father don't consider me usurping their parental rights."

"Why would you think that?"

"Who am I to suggest that your brother marry sooner rather than later? Or that you should terminate the employment of your tutor? It's not right for me to meddle in your business."

"No offense was taken by me or Will. In fact, Ma and Pa would probably agree with you."

"But I hurt your feelings."

"Not at all. Walter did that of his own accord. It saddened me that he's not the man I thought he was. Even as a young girl, I was determined to consider marriage only to someone who would treat me as an equal partner. I will not be subservient to anyone."

"Tom always treated you with respect?"

"Very much so. In fact, you probably knew him. He apprenticed here at the blacksmith shop."

Pearl scrunched up her nose and pursed her lips as she tweaked her memory. In a second, her face lit up in recognition. "That handsome young man? Oh, yes. I do recall him. Seems to me, he carried my parcels from the mercantile several times."

I nodded, thinking back to the first time I met Tom at the general store. From the moment I saw him, I was smitten.

"Why ever did you let him go?" Pearl asked.

"I was young and headstrong, determined to make my own way in life."

Pearl seemed amused, probably thinking I'm no different than I was in my youth. Still, I tried to explain that I didn't expect him to have the wanderlust, nor the desire to further his own education.

"Are you upset that he's studying to be a lawyer?"

"Of course not. I find it an attractive trait. No doubt, some woman will swoop him up—if he's not already taken."

"You could be his wife, if you hadn't been so stubborn."

"Why would you think me obstinate? I write to Tom often. Then wait for the longest time for his letters."

"Do you tell Tom that you miss him? That you're longing for his return?"

I shook my head vehemently. "No. It wouldn't be proper."

Pearl pondered my response. No doubt she was trying to find the words that would help me understand my faulty thinking.

"Karl often reminded me that women are different from men. In fact, he'd say we cause them consternation when they can't read our minds. Whenever I got myself in a dither, Karl would tell me to speak up or get over it."

"It's strange that I can be frank about so many things. But not this. I refuse to beg for someone's affection. Either Tom wants to be with me or he doesn't. It's as simple as that."

"Would you consider living in Indiana if Tom asked you to journey there?"

"Ma once told me that she loves Pa so much, it wouldn't matter where he wanted to make his home. She'd be happy just to be with him. I suppose I now understand her perspective. Yes. I'd travel to Indiana to be with Tom."

Quite honestly, I surprised myself with my response. I had always wondered how Mary had the gumption to up and move farther west when her Ohio farm failed. Of course, I always related that question in tandem with the belief that the disgusting creature who called himself George Mitchell was her husband. Now I realize that she wanted to be with the man she came to love—the real uncle—and she'd have gone anywhere with him.

"Seems to me, you've got some thinking to do," Pearl said with an extended yawn. "And I need some sleep. I'll light the lantern in the parlor window so Will can find his way to the front door."

"I'll wait here for his return," I said with a smile. "The crickets are singing a lovely tune."

"Their chatter could wake the dead. Good night, child. I'm so glad you're here with me."

Chapter Fifty - One

Each afternoon after school, I stopped at the post office to see if a letter from Tom had arrived. It had been more than a month since I last heard from him, though I had written to Tom each week.

Despite my disappointment about that, I was comforted to receive mail from Emily, who wrote that she's now settled and the children are doing well. Joe has been helping Emily's mother expand her baked goods business, which may turn out to be a highly profitable enterprise.

Pearl has accepted two new boarders. An older gent, Howard, who is newly arrived in Kimberton from Pottstown, and a widow lady, Ruth, from Manavon. Both bring a stimulating dimension to our evening conversations, and Pearl's enjoying the additional company.

Preparations for our August break from classes had me scurrying to complete grading of the students' assignments and end-of-term examinations. Julie was excited about having two weeks at home, and I promised to accompany her. I knew Ma and Mary would be grateful for help with canning and pickling.

Will and Esther decided that they'll plan their wedding date to occur at the end of harvest, probably coinciding with our

October school holiday. In the meantime, Will has been working overtime at the mill and doubling his delivery of farm goods. He says the extra income will go directly towards the construction of his storefront.

It was a decidedly humid morning when I picked up Julie at the school for our drive to the farmstead. Huge, billowy white clouds and a dark western sky suggested that it would be a day of storms, so I quickly loaded Julie's valises into the back of the phaeton. She, on the other hand, was saying farewell to the other girls waiting for their rides. While I'm happy she's developed such pleasant friendships, I was anxious to get on our way.

Finally ready to depart, I helped Julie up to the front seat, then took the reins. A chorus of "Good-bye, Miss Mitchell. Bye, Julie," could be heard until we rounded the bend on Hare's Hill Road.

"Oh, no!" Julie exclaimed. "I forgot the picture I painted for Ma."

"We're not going back, Julie. We'll be lucky if we get home before the storm."

"I suppose I can make another, but we don't have water colors at home. I *did* learn in botany class about plants that release dye when wet. Perhaps I can experiment."

"That's a great idea. Ma will be quite impressed."

I glanced at Julie, and noticed that she was beaming with pride. In addition to her stellar final grades, Julie has matured greatly this year. I, too, am so proud of her accomplishments.

We took the more straightforward route to our farm, and I could hear distant rumbles of thunder as we made our way up our driveway from Yellow Springs Road. Pa and the boys were in the barn thrashing the wheat when we arrived.

Julie jumped to the ground and sprinted to Pa's embrace while I unhitched Bella and brought her a bucket of water. "It's good to have my girls home," he said, a grin lighting up his face.

"Ben and Matt, help Lizzie get her buggy under the eaves. George can lead the mare to a stall."

I gave Pa a kiss on his cheek just as large drops of rain began to pelt the dusty ground. "Make a run for it," Pa said with a chuckle. "Your ma's working in the kitchen."

Grabbing Julie's hand, we raced across the yard, reaching the back porch as the heavens opened. A bright flash of lightning lit the sky, followed by a loud boom that startled the two of us. We made it home none too soon.

^^^

Julie entertained us with her stories about school during supper. Apparently, she and her two dearest friends have experienced more escapades than I was aware, often under the guise of studying botany or astronomy. Her roommates, Amanda and Susan, were allies in this delinquency, although all three of them exuded virtue in the public arena.

The Kimber's are strong proponents of personal freedom and curiosity, often encouraging students to explore the flora and fauna of the surrounding streams and wooded lands. It's doubtful, however, that they were ever aware that Julie and her two companions had built a fort in the copse of trees behind the school.

On occasion, the girls would furtively sneak out at night in their chemises, lying on their backs in the grass to watch the stars. We laughed when Julie told us that they've now curtailed their nocturnal sojourns because of a pesky skunk that likes to visit.

"Did you get skunked?" George asked with a snicker.

"Almost. We ran like the dickens, the stink following us 'til we got back in the house. Lucky for us, though, the skunk's spray didn't get us. We just tip-toed up the back steps, grateful we wouldn't have to explain that one."

"I got skunked once," George said. "Seems to me it was Matthew's fault."

"You were the one teasing the blasted animal," Matt said. "Guess you learned your lesson."

"I remember it well," Ma said amusedly. "Near about had to wash the skin right off your bones to get rid of the smell."

"At least I now know just about all the constellations in the night sky," Julie said, reaching for a biscuit to sop her gravy. In fact, all three of us got 100% on the examination."

"I'm glad to know that the money I spend on your tuition is being put to good use," Pa said dryly. "Best you be sleeping snug in your bed instead of traipsing around the countryside."

"Yes, Pa," Julie said demurely as she cleared the plates from those who were done. "Anyone want a piece of blueberry pie? Mary made it, and I whipped some cream for the topping."

"It'll be nice when our summer kitchen gets built," Mary added. "It's going to have a real baking oven built in."

"Might be when pigs can fly," I said with a chuckle.

"Foundation's already laid," Pa said with a wink to Ma. "Should be done in less than a month."

"Really? Where's it going to be?"

"Between the water pump and the spring house," Ma said, smiling from ear to ear. "It'll be large enough to have a work table and sideboard, even two windows."

"Would've been done by now, but Jacob Moser's been busy as all git out," Pa said as he took a forkful of his slice of pie, making sure it was covered with whipped cream. "It's going to be 120 feet by 180, made of stone to match the house."

"Plenty of room for cooking and washing clothes, all at the same time," Ma said. "Even a pantry near the hearth and a wood shed under the eaves."

"Clothesline's on the other side of the house," I reminded Ma. "You'll have a long way to carry the wash."

"Your pa's going to string a couple lines from the new kitchen to the spring house. He'll get me a nice barrel to collect rainwater so's we won't need to lug so much from the pump. When all's said and done, we'll have everything right there."

"Sounds great," I said. "Guess it'll be ready for operation by the time Will and Esther get hitched."

"No doubt, it will. Mary and I are already planning what we need to make our kitchen modern and functional. We'll make use of it for all kinds of celebrations. By the way, they'll be here tomorrow, as will Ellie and David."

Julie was about to question why, when Pa announced that the party will be in her honor. "For my birthday?" she asked, her voice quivering with excitement.

"Quite sure," Pa said with a hearty laugh. "We'll have the whole family back together. Your ma's going to be in her glory."

Chapter Fifty-Two

The air had cleared overnight once all the storms passed through. Though the morning sun was already drying the dew that covered the grass, the humidity was low and there was a northerly breeze. It was a fine day for a family get-together.

After breakfast, Julie and I were on the porch shucking a couple dozen ears of corn. Ma told Julie to stay out of the kitchen while she and Mary made her birthday cake, which was to be a surprise. Later she could help pluck the chickens, a task that no one relishes, though gutting the innards is nastier.

"One thing I was wondering," I said as I tugged on the silk strands of my corn cob, "is whether you ever saw Negroes being brought into the school when you snuck out at night."

Julie hesitated, then said, "Guess we did. But don't tell anyone about it."

"You weren't involved, were you?"

"No. And no one knows we saw anything. Not that there's any secret that Miss Abby's on a mission to free slaves. She says that it's sinful to hold people in bondage."

"I agree," I said. "But I don't know anyone around these parts who would consider owning another person. Of course, there's indenture, but that's different.

"Miss Abby says slavery is rampant in the South. Every plantation has a slew of Negroes who are forced to work the fields. Many are mistreated, or their children taken from them, and there's no way out of the situation. She says we need to help them to freedom."

"But some say that abetting them could be construed as stealing another person's property. Of course, the basic premise is wrong in the first place, but those who assist the slaves could be punished."

Julie paused, as if thinking through her own assertions. Not that she needed to convince me of the need for abolition of slavery, but I wondered about the wisdom of hiding runaways within the confines of a boarding school. Would there be any danger to the students? Could the girls inadvertently mention the nocturnal goings-on and alert authorities?

"One night, when Amanda, Susan, and I were watching the stars, we saw Miss Abby open the door for a Negro family. The *whole* family, Lizzie. There must have been six children, and the mother was carrying a tiny baby. Those young'uns looked scared, the whites of their eyes glowing like celestial bodies in the darkness. It made me so sad."

"Did you see them the next day?"

"Didn't see hide nor hair of them. Didn't hear them either, not even the little ones."

"The Kimber's must have a secure hiding place," I said. "Perhaps they feed the runaways, and give them a place to sleep, then whisk them off the next night on their journey to freedom."

"That's what I think, too."

"Just be careful, Julie. Don't be talking about what you observed when you're with Amanda and Susan. The slightest inkling could jeopardize anyone involved. Even that family you saw. And don't be sneaking out at night. You could get into a lot of trouble."

Julie nodded in agreement, standing to shake the silken threads and husks from her apron, letting them blow into the garden. "We're done just in time, Lizzie. Here come Ellie and David!"

^^^

David joined the boys in the barn after lunch, while Ellie and Julie combed and carded wool on the back porch. Mary and I peeled potatoes and carrots, as Ma finished kneading her dough. Mary told me to peek under the clean towel to see the cake that was cooling on the counter, a vanilla butter loaf that wafted a heavenly scent. I offered to make a sweet glaze for the top, knowing Julie would be delighted.

"I'm looking forward to Esther's visit," I said as I rinsed the potatoes and put them in a kettle of fresh water. "It's been weeks since I've seen her, what with Will always going over to her homestead lately."

"You have a soft spot for that girl," Ma replied. "And I can see why. Will was lucky to fall prey to her charms."

"I always thought Esther would become a teacher. She did well in her classes, and was offered a tutoring position at our school, but she turned it down."

"Guess she didn't want to be prevented from marrying," Ma said with a wink to Mary. "Wonder what became of her friend. The diplomat's daughter."

"Last I heard, Anna's in Britain. Betrothed to some Lord or something. I believe that Ellie corresponds with her."

"The two of them did get along nicely," Ma said. "Perhaps Ellie will someday achieve her dream of traveling to the fashion houses in Europe. Wouldn't that be something?"

"Won't be anytime soon, with a baby on the way," I said. "But at least she might be able to visit Philadelphia the next time Anna returns."

Mary was about to add to the conversation when Julie called out that Will had arrived with Esther. "And he brought someone else," she added.

"Best be peeling another potato," Ma said to me. "Wonder who that could be."

Walking to the pantry to get another spud, I looked out the window to observe Will helping Esther down from the buckboard, and another gent with a wide-brimmed leather hat limping around the back of the wagon.

The stranger has a thick beard, somewhat straggly, reminding me somewhat of the time Will and I brought home the uncle's imposter. While he was portly, this man's a mite too thin to be healthy.

"Perhaps it's one of Esther's brothers," I said. "Can't see his face, but it's definitely not the one I met awhile back."

"We'll find out soon enough," Ma said, returning to her task. "I'm just glad that Will feels comfortable about bringing another guest."

Esther entered the kitchen with a large bowl of fresh salad and placed it on the counter. She had a strange expression that I attributed to embarrassment, but I wasn't sure the cause.

"Will's bringing the garden tomatoes," she said. "I'll cut them for the salad later."

"That's fine," Ma said, wiping her hands to give Esther a hug. "We're glad you could be with us today."

When Will joined us, he gave Ma the basket of tomatoes, then turned to introduce the stranger. It surprised me that the man didn't remove his hat, as it seemed rather rude, and he kept his head low. Like he was ashamed of something.

Will gazed at me intently, seeming to send me a message with his eyes. Finally, the gent looked up and I gasped.

It's Tom!

Tom has come back to me!

Chapter Fifty-Three

Bounding across the room, I threw myself into Tom's arms, nearly knocking him over as I did the first time we met. This time, however, he winced and pulled away as if my touch caused him pain.

Quickly gaining composure, Tom gave a faint smile and caressed my face with his right hand. "You're a sight for sore eyes, Lizzie," he said softly.

"Tom arrived in Kimberton this morning," Will said. "A little worse for wear if you ask me. Luckily, he found me hitching Prince to the wagon before I left to get Esther, and I convinced him to spend the day with us."

"Take a seat, Tom," Ma said. "Looks like you could use a cup of coffee."

"Yes, ma'am. I'd surely be grateful."

I watched Tom tenuously lower himself into Pa's chair, while Mary set a steaming mug in front of him. I sat to the right of him, barely able to contain my deep happiness that Tom has returned. Will and Esther joined us at the table, while Ma and Mary bustled about, brewing a fresh pot of coffee and plating biscuits with jam.

"Did you get injured on your way home?" I asked Tom as he took a swig of his coffee.

He nodded, setting his mug back on the table. "I was accosted somewhere in western Pennsylvania. About two days ride from here. The two ruffians stole my saddlebag and took my shotgun. Almost got away with my horse, but she escaped them and came back for me."

Tom took off his hat and placed it on the table. His left eye was nearly swollen closed, purple and red skin surrounding it. Ma quickly went to the pump with a clean rag, then handed the soggy compress to Tom.

"Put this on your face," she said. "I'll make a poultice while that's soaking."

"I got bruises from head to toe," Tom said. "Think maybe I busted my shoulder, and sprained my ankle, too."

"I'm just glad you didn't get killed. You're safe now," I said gently. "And here."

"I missed you, Lizzie. You have no idea. All that time out there, I thought about you. Dreamed about you."

"Well, you sure didn't write much."

"That's another story. But I enjoyed your letters. Fact is, I figured out when to expect them. I'd wait at the boat dock for the bag of mail to be unloaded, then follow the carrier to the post office and wait while the letters were sorted."

"What made you decide to come back?"

"Will's letter," Tom said with a nod to his friend. "He told me you were getting sweet on your tutor."

My eyes grew wide with astonishment, incensed that Will would interfere in my business. "Don't get your bloomers in a knot, Lizzie," Will said. "Esther put me up to it. And Pearl."

Before I knew it, Ma and Mary were bent over laughing. Their amusement was infectious, and we all joined in, even me.

"What's so funny," Pa asked as he entered the kitchen, having finished his work for the day. That set off a new round of giggles, with Ma trying to explain.

Pa glanced at the table, barely recognizing Tom. Mostly because of the weight he'd lost and the rag he still held to his eye.

"It's Tom," I exclaimed with glee.

Pa took one long look at him, then shook his head. "Good to see you back, boy. But by the look of things, you were front and center to a right hook. Who beat you up?"

"A couple of thugs up to no good."

"Best call in Doc Pyle. Will, tell Ben to saddle up and go get the doctor."

"Don't want to be any trouble," Tom muttered.

"Can't have you moaning and groaning all through Julie's birthday celebration. If anyone can fix you up, Doc can."

^^^

It took another two days for the swelling to recede from Tom's face. Pa insisted that he stay with us, making his bed in the loft over the kitchen. Doc had given Tom a salve for his eyes, wrapped his ankle, which turned out to be a mild sprain, and recommended exercises for his left shoulder. In the meantime, Tom's been resting with his leg elevated and enjoying Ma's meals, sleeping more often than a possum with her babies.

Esther had invited Julie to her home for a couple of days, thinking she might enjoy the companionship of her numerous nieces and nephews, and I promised to drive her there today. Tom said he felt up to an excursion in the buggy, wanting to revisit some of the places familiar to him.

We planned to ride to Manavon once Julie was settled, perhaps having a picnic by the Schuylkill River. Mary packed a basket of delectable treats, and we were on our way as soon as morning chores were finished.

Esther and her mother were expectantly waiting for us, warmly welcoming Julie upon our arrival. Mrs. Kingsly has a stocky frame, soft graying curls under her cap, and laugh lines at the corners of her eyes. I can see where Esther acquired her positive nature.

"It's nice to see you again, Miss Mitchell," she said as she reached for Julie's satchel.

Realizing that she still knew me more as Esther's teacher than future in-law, I said with a smile, "Please call me Lizzie. We'll all be family soon enough."

"That we will," she chuckled. "And this must be Tom. Esther's been talking up a storm about him coming back east."

Tom touched the brim of his hat and gave a nod. "Happy to meet you, ma'am."

"I'd invite you all in, but Esther said Tom had a bit of an accident. Hope you're feeling better."

"Yes, ma'am. Getting stronger every day."

"That's fine," Mrs. Kingsly said as Julie scampered off with Esther. "We have lots of activities planned for Julie, so don't come for her at least until Saturday."

"Remind her to mind her manners," I said, flicking the reins to be on our way.

Turning left from the Kingsly farm, we took Charlestown Road into Manavon. From here I wasn't sure which direction I should take, but Tom suggested a route that led through the heart of the village to the banks of the river. He pointed out the Phoenix Iron Works that's providing numerous jobs in the nail-making operation, as well as other start-up businesses typical of a growing settlement. We finally found a nice spot, not far from the convergence of French Creek and the Schuylkill River.

I parked the phaeton near a copse of trees that would provide shade for Bella, then spread a blanket nearby where we could enjoy the serene river view.

It still felt like a dream that Tom was sitting next to me, not quite the man I remembered, but delightful all the same.

Chapter Fifty-Four

Tom seems different to me. Not only in appearance, but with a more serious, intense expression. Don't get me wrong. Tom is still a tease, and he makes me laugh. But there's a depth in his eyes that indicates he's troubled in some way.

No doubt, Tom's journeys have influenced the changes I perceive, yet I know so little about what it was like for him to travel to unsettled territory. My inquisitiveness was getting the better of me.

"Tell me about your friend, John Foster," I said, handing him a hunk of bread from our basket.

"He's a good man. I'll always be beholding to him."

"For helping you become a lawyer?"

"That, and more."

Obviously, Tom's not feeling very talkative. Whenever Pa gets in a quiet mood, Ma just lets him be. Same with me, I guess. He'll talk when he wants to.

Tom looked out across the river, watching a couple of gents load a wagon. "I always thought the Schuylkill was a large river," he mused. "Until I saw the Ohio River. Impossible to compare."

"Would Manavon remind you of Evansville?"

"I don't know that we could liken the two. I suppose in some respects, they're similar. In the sense that they're both growing settlements. Perhaps the iron works here has brought more industry, and people follow job opportunities."

"But we still have our surrounding farm land."

"Farming's a mainstay in Indiana, as well. It's a source of livelihood for most settlers. But it's still a wilderness out there in the far western counties. Homes are rustic log cabins, set here and there in the woods. Heck, you still have to keep watch for bears and Indians."

"But you love it there?"

"In some ways, I do. In some, I don't."

I foraged in our basket for something to drink. Finding the decanter, I took a swig and passed it to Tom.

"I got something to tell you, Lizzie," he said after he about guzzled all our water. "And I'm not sure how to say it."

"You got a woman and passel of kids back in Indiana?"

For the first time in days, Tom laughed. A deep roaring hoot from the base of his belly. Suddenly, he pulled me close and put his mouth over mine in a prolonged kiss.

I pulled back in a panic, remembering the degradation of the vulgar molestation four years ago. I regretted my reaction immediately, but it's as if my body had a mind of its own.

"I'm sorry," Tom said contritely. "I don't know what came over me, except you looked so fetching. And I love you so much."

Hearing those words triggered an emotion so great that I began to weep. Perhaps I was crying more because of my great fear of intimacy with a man I love dearly, than merely hearing terms of endearment. Nonetheless, Tom was distraught that he had caused my distress, and he begged me to forgive him.

"It's not you," I wailed. "It's me. Something happened to me."

"Well, aren't we a sorry pair," Tom said bemusedly. "I was going to tell you that I'd been injured, and you must have experienced something bad as well."

"You were injured?"

"And I lied to you."

That stopped the waterworks and got my dander up. Dabbing my eyes with the corner of my apron, I stood tall and straight, my right hand on my hip. "There's nothing worse than speaking untruths, Thomas Hawks. I cannot abide a liar."

Tom grabbed me by the hand and pulled me down to the blanket. "Settle down and hear me out."

"I'm listening."

"I told you I worked for a blacksmith in Evansville. And that's the truth. That's how I met John Foster. But the sequence of events that I wrote in my letters was not true."

"Meaning?"

"Meaning I didn't forsake blacksmithing to become a lawyer. I studied law while I recuperated from a catastrophic accident. John Foster took me in, let me read his law books, and suggested that I might want to apprentice under him."

"What happened to cause your injury?"

"A fire. The owner of the blacksmith shop was working with molten iron. I was out back, shoeing a horse, when I heard his screams. By the time I could get to him, the whole place was aflame, like a box of matches totally engulfed."

Tom shuddered with the memory, then unbuttoned his shirt. His entire chest was a wrinkled mesh of lumpy scar tissue.

"Dear God," I exclaimed, embracing him. Then I pulled his head down and kissed him fully on the lips. "You could have been killed."

"Almost was. The boss didn't make it. If I hadn't had on thick gloves when I was working with that horse, I would've lost my hands."

"And the rest of you?"

"I have some scars on my legs. But for wearing a leather apron, it could have been much worse

"How long was your recovery?"

"Three years. Spent the last year on the circuit with John. Once the Judge signed off on my knowledge of law, and gave me the attorney certificate, I had to decide what to do. John knew I was pining for you. Told me I should just come on back here and show you what I was afraid to tell you about. If you rejected me, then I'd know my decision."

"Oh, Tom. If only you had told me. I'd have gone to be with you, no matter how long or difficult the journey."

"Guess we can't regret water over the dam," Tom said, as he held me in a gut-wrenching embrace that I didn't even try to wriggle from. "I'm just glad I listened to John. We're together now."

Chapter Fifty-Five

Tom and I sat cross-legged on the river bank for quite a while, his right arm around my shoulder, watching the water lap along the edge, the sun casting shimmers on the ripples. I felt an amazing sense of peace and contentment, an awareness that there's a greater power in the universe that places us in the right location, at the right time.

We both needed to stretch at the same time, a signal that it was time to gather our things and return home. As we carried our basket and blanket to the buggy, Tom remembered that I, too, had something that needed to be told.

"What did you mean when you said something happened to you?" Tom asked, giving me a boost up to the driver's seat.

"I don't know how to tell you, but it's what made me recoil when you first kissed me."

"Did your tutor take advantage of you?"

"No. Walter was a gentleman in that respect. It was the uncle. Or, rather, the uncle's imposter."

"I don't understand."

"Come sit by me, and I'll tell you about it as we drive."

I finished my story by the time we got to Yellow Springs Road. Tom suggested I pull over to the side, under the shade of the trees. Right there, he took me in his arms and kissed me once again. A deep passionate kiss that nearly took my breath away. There was no denying that I perceived a strange feeling deep within me, one that awoke a fiery hunger and insatiable desire.

"I love you with all my heart," Tom whispered. He kissed my eyes, my forehead, my neck, finally returning to my lips. "What you experienced was reviling, and if the man hadn't killed himself, I'd have hunted him down. You were not at fault, Lizzie."

Tom's words brought tears to my eyes and unbelievable relief from the haunting memories that couldn't be squelched. Finally, I believed that I could let them go, sending them off as a flock of menacing crows taking flight from my soul.

"I don't know why I doubted your love," I said softly, returning his kiss.

"Then marry me."

"Yes, my darling. Oh, yes."

^^^

Tom and I sat close together in the buggy as we slowly traversed our hilly drive. He stole another kiss just before we came in sight of the house and, though I wanted more, I told him to behave lest we be seen.

"It's no matter," Tom said, laughing at my expression. "We'll be telling everyone that we'll soon be wed. We should marry tomorrow."

"That would be lovely. But not possible."

"Why not?"

I let Bella take the lead, knowing she'd head straight to her stall. Then I said, "Because of my teaching. I'll need to give notice so that another instructor can be located."

"How long will that take?"

"I don't know. But, surely, a few weeks."

Now I was the one who laughed at Tom's crestfallen face. When the buggy came to a complete stop, I handed him the reins and jumped to the ground. It took Tom a bit longer to climb out of the phaeton with his sore shoulder and ankle, but he soon managed to help me unhitch Bella.

"There's also something else to consider," I said, teasing as I retrieved the bucket for Bella's water.

"What's that?"

"Your beard."

"What's wrong with it."

"I don't like it."

"It's pretty typical in Indiana."

"Is that where we're going to live?"

"I don't know. What do you want to do?"

"Don't you see? We have so much to talk about. So much to decide," I said, filling the bucket from the pump.

Tom took the pail from me with his good arm and we walked back to the barn. Once I got Bella settled, we sat on a bale of hay to continue our conversation.

"Maybe we should stay here in Pennsylvania for a while," Tom replied. "I can investigate what it would take for me to hang out my own shingle, to serve as an attorney in the county."

"That's fine with me. Though, for your information, Tom Hawks, I'll go wherever you go. You're not getting away from me this time!"

We both laughed, and kissed again. I tugged on his beard for good measure.

"I suppose it's time for a shave," he said, shaking his head. "What I won't do for you."

"I know where Pa keeps his shave kit. And I might be able to help. Let's do it now, while we still have some privacy. And we can talk about when we'll marry and where we want to live.

^^^

During supper, everyone teased Tom about his clean-shaven appearance. He did look funny with his tanned forehead, black eye, and pale cheeks. Guess he felt a little embarrassed, but he laughed when young George said his face looked like a baby's behind.

By the time everyone had a plate full of food, I couldn't contain our announcement any longer. I told the family that Tom and I plan to marry at the end of the school term in October, perhaps having a double wedding with Will and Esther.

"I'll inform Emmor and Susanna Kimber when I return from our holiday so they can find a replacement before the start of the next academic year," I said, feeling a touch of irony that belied my overwhelming happiness.

"It's about time!" Pa exclaimed with a hearty bellow. "I gave Tom my permission more than six years ago, if my memory serves me right."

Ma practically lunged across the table to hug me, her smile lighting the room. "Congratulations to the both of you," she said, adding an enthusiastic pat on the back for Tom. "I have no doubt that you'll be happy together."

Mary gleefully added her good wishes, while the boys giggled and made funny faces. It was plain to see that Tom would be a fine addition to our family.

"You heading back to Indiana?" Pa queried, his eyes expressing a semblance of worry.

"No," Tom said. "At least not anytime soon. Lizzie and I have been discussing our future plans. We think we might want to build a house along the banks of the Schuylkill, near Manavon. We found a nice spot today. I can set up a law practice there, and maybe we'll start a school."

I nodded my agreement. "And we'll work together to make higher education a priority for women. They'll have equal opportunity to attend college."

"Now that I think about it," Tom said with a gleam in his eyes, "perhaps that's what we should do. Start a college for girls."

"How would we do that?"

"I have no idea," Tom said, causing all of us to laugh. "But, without a doubt, we can do anything we set our minds to. And we have our whole future to accomplish it."

Author's Note

The inspiration for *A Specter of Truth* came from a visit to the Kimberton post office. As I gazed at the stonework of the old building, I thought that it must have been constructed about the same time as the Kimberton Inn on the opposite corner. Its signage indicates that it dates back to 1796. Directly across from the post office parking lot is another large and stately dwelling, Kimber Hall. The structure on the fourth corner seemed old, but different in style. I wasn't sure that any of them were connected by time or ownership.

Curious about their historical significance, I conducted a google search upon my return home, and learned that the crossroad of Kimberton Road and Hares Hill Road was steeped in antiquity. The buildings on each corner were erected before Emmor Kimber purchased 200 acres of rural farmland, but his entrepreneurial endeavors made them the start of what is now the village of Kimberton, Pennsylvania.

Kimberton is located along the French Creek, just 3 miles from Phoenixville, earlier called Manavon, in Chester County. Of course, the entire area is lush with history of the Revolutionary War. The powder mill at Rapp's Dam that George Washington and his troops tried to protect is only minutes away, the spa and hospital at Chester Springs, formerly Yellow Springs, that were restorative for the soldiers is just a few miles south, and the army's place of encampment during the dismal winter at Valley Forge is right on the other side of Phoenixville.

I chose not to focus on the Revolutionary War era, about which so much has been written. Rather, I wanted my story to center on the crossroads in Kimberton beginning in 1818, for it was then that Emmor Kimber, a Quaker, started the boarding school for girls in his home.

Though I often reminded myself that I was writing a novel, not a history book, I sought to retain accuracy about the period between 1817-1825 in and about Kimberton. Let me share with you what is fact, to my best knowledge, versus what is fiction.

Kimber Hall became the home of Emmor and Susanna Kimber and their children in 1817. It soon also housed the French Creek Boarding School for Girls, a progressive school of the Quaker tradition.

What is currently the Kimberton post office had been Chrisman's grist mill, but then came under Kimber's ownership. The Old Bear Tavern on the opposite corner was converted to a general store and post office by Mr. Kimber, and a tenement across the street became a hotel of sorts for the parents of students and out-of-town guests. Visitors would arrive by stagecoach from Philadelphia, which stopped there several days a week.

I tried to remain true to the history of all the known facts, particularly about Mr. Kimber and his family, though I used creative license for a few elements of my story. For example, it was said that Emmor Kimber hired single men with no family to run his businesses, yet I made Joe Price with his wife Emily in charge of the general store. Whether anyone lived on the second floor of the store is not known, but it made sense to me because of the architecture of the building.

Prior to purchasing the land in Pikeland, Emmor Kimber had been a math teacher at the Westtown Quaker School and wrote an arithmetic textbook. Although his wife, Susanna, initially taught at their new boarding school, she eventually managed the curriculum and allowed her daughters to teach. It was Abby who carried on her father's legacy, running the school until it closed in 1849. Abby was also a staunch abolitionist and the school served as a stop on the Underground Railroad.

Emmor Kimber was an industrious Quaker, establishing thriving businesses within the structures that were located at the crossroads. But he apparently overextended his resources and was taken to debtors' court at least once, in 1825. To cover his losses, he did plan to rent some of his operations, including the school, though I couldn't find reference that it had actually been leased. Abby sold the building in 1852, after her father's death.

Letters from former students indicated that Mr. Kimber could be long-winded when he was preaching, and would rant on about many topics at their weekly Meetings. Susanna, on the other hand, was said to be kind and thoughtful. A genealogical search showed that she was older than he.

The cost of attending the boarding school was said to be $75, in two installments, very expensive in that time period. The girls were permitted to swim in the mill race, a stream that flowed down the side of their property to the grist mill. The mill race is no longer there, though a rock culvert is still visible from the current post office. And there is a pond on the other side of the spring house behind the general store.

I have no knowledge of a boarding house on Prizer Road, though there is a large old residence still standing there. Perhaps a kindly woman like Pearl once took in boarders to make ends meet.

Maps of the surrounding farms gave me the names of landowners at the time of my story. I used common surnames, but did not include factual information specific to their families. My imagination crafted their first names and their children's names. Any other similarity is purely coincidental.

My main character, Lizzie, her family, and the Mitchell farm, are also completely fictional. Yellow Springs Road is not.

My parents' ten acres, high on the hill across from Pine Creek, served as the inspiration for the Mitchell farmstead. I learned, however, that our land had been a quarry during the time-frame of my story.

There was also a grist mill in operation on Pine Creek, much closer than Kimber's mill. It would have been logical for the imaginary Mitchell family to use the mill right down the road, but I wanted the connection with Kimberton for Lizzie to attend the French Creek Boarding School. Still, it *was* true that Kimber had the cheapest toll rates of any of the local mills. As such, it wouldn't have been out of the question for Pa to tell Will to take the grain there.

My research about teacher education in the early 19th century provided the foundation of my story that centered on the school. At that time, there were no professional standards for teachers. It was not until 1837 that Horace Mann became an outspoken advocate of public education for children and normal schools for teacher training.

In earlier years, men were primarily hired as instructors, but the salaries were low and other career opportunities were becoming available to them. Many young men were drawn to the adventure of traveling westward, leaving no other option but to hire women to teach. Unmarried women only.

Typically, a young woman might be offered a teaching position if she attended a sectarian school and excelled in the courses; advancement within the ranks, so to say. Very few non-sectarian schools, however, permitted attendance for girls. The Quakers were very proactive in that regard.

On the other hand, colleges that admitted women at that time were few and far between, if any. I found references of five academies or seminaries for girls in the United States prior to 1821, but none operated distinctly as a college. Some eventually became chartered. To further her education, a woman needed a tutor, a man with a college degree.

I sought numerous sources to find such a mentor for Lizzie, and discovered Walter R. Johnson. He was a graduate of Harvard, and principal of the Germantown Academy, located within a reasonable distance from Kimberton. He wrote many articles about the importance of establishing teaching standards and higher education for all, including women. He also gave a speech to welcome Lafayette to his school in 1825.

Walter Johnson might have worked if I were writing a history, but I needed to fictionalize his character. Thus, I created Walter L. Jones, who bears only a veneer of likeness to the real Walter. I made my Walter principal of the imaginary Schuylkill Valley Academy. Other than that, any similarity of the fictional Walter to the real Walter is purely coincidental.

I can't begin to acknowledge all of the fabulous historical resources within the local community. The Chester County and Phoenixville Historical Societies offer a wealth of information, as do the East and West Pikeland, Phoenixville, and Charlestown websites. Estelle Cremers' book, *10,000 Acres*, was a valuable reference, and I'm grateful to her family for lending me a copy. A local storyteller, Susannah Brody, was kind enough to serve as a beta reader for my book and point out any historic inconsistencies.

And, lest I forget, John Peirce's painting that hangs in the Kimberton Inn depicts life at the crossroads as he imagined it was 200 years ago. Likewise, the tiny village of Kimberton captured my fancy, and I added my own spin by crafting Lizzie's story. I hope you enjoyed it.

ABOUT THE AUTHOR

Kathleen is an educator, an author, and a registered dietitian. During her professional career, she taught and mentored students of all ages, through grade school, high school, and college. She also served as a university administrator at three colleges.

Kathleen's writing genre of women's fiction is meant to be uplifting, with a focus on women of all ages who are strong, generous, compassionate, and capable. Her characters and settings are drawn from memories of people she has met, and places she has experienced. *A Spector of Truth* is Kathleen's first historical novel.

Kathleen currently lives in Southeast Pennsylvania, near the French Creek that is steeped in American history. It is here that she was captivated with the early beginnings of the village of Kimberton and the French Creek Boarding School for Girls.

89224877R00163

Made in the USA
Columbia, SC
19 February 2018